THE NAIRA WORSHIPPERS

OGED OREKYEH

ISBN: 0692635300
ISBN-13: 9780692635308

THE NAIRA WORSHIPPERS

A FICTION NOVEL.

AUTHOR'S NOTE

All characters in this novel (with the exception of a few who are obviously historical) incidents, situations, industrial companies and localities mentioned are fictitious. They do not relate to any persons living or dead, and any possible coincidences are accidental and unintentional.

THE NAIRA WORSHIPPERS

OGED OREKYEH

The Naira Worshippers details the lifestyle of high-class society. A group comprised of privileged Nigerians, whose philosophy is: "That one must earn fast money by any means necessary and that a person only lives to enjoy opulence forever".

This novel is more or less a case study of a generation of Third World "greed-is-good" entrepreneurs. They dream of international renown. This is cut short by IMF imposed Structural Adjustment Program (SAP). They are victims of the Third World Debt Crisis.

The Naira Worshippers portrays a class whose definition of success in life is material acquisition. They lust after the fleeting enjoyment of wanton wealth. The more they acquired, the more they wanted and the less satisfied they became with what they had.

Pedro da Souza, denied of political office abandons his ambition. He chooses self-exile in Switzerland. A study of his history is the experience of many generations of gifted Africans. They experience the repercussion of their political ambitions. Pedro's failure becomes the basis of our collective confusion. His determination for benevolence restitution is the bedrock for our better future. Abba Abdulmalik, favored with great fortune could blame neither his heredity nor his environment for his wanton recklessness. He misuses unprecedented economic opportunities. He is remembered primarily for opening the door for all his tragedy. The Naira Worshippers shows that the only way to acquire true freedom is to gain wisdom from past mistakes. The reality is that history repeats itself without the active intervention of God. Those who do not learn from their past suffer repeated tragic consequences. Therefore, God is the only Hope for mankind. MARANATHA.

AUTHOR'S NOTE:

HAIL MARANATHA!!!

GOD is personified in His compassion. He commands that love be shown even to those who hate us. Thus, we can overcome rejection through forgiveness. The Church as His voice exists to wire the globe with chains of Jesus' love. Godly grace can only be impacted to the world through Jesus' good works. It is through Amazing Grace that human beings can run the global rat race in the spirit of true love.

Ted Hunter, came to Lagos as editor of Metropolitan Newspapers in 1956. His noble quest in a lawless world made him become a generous giver to The Society of African's Missionaries. He had contributed to the missionary schools built by this Irish Christian establishment in Nigeria. Their social development programs encouraged the local nationalists. These grass root activists labored tirelessly to force the colonial masters out of Lagos. Their confrontations with the British authorities were abetted by the Irish clergy and the foreign editors of Fleet Street. Hunter's interaction with the Lagos political activists deepened his wisdom. He gained insight into the lawlessness of political manipulators.

All students of power learn early to acquire the trait of ruthlessness. This was a global norm. Those who must build empires either have it or they don't. The politicians' endpoint is 'kill or be killed'. Political ruthlessness that results in 'kill them all and stand up alone', may work for a season. However, those with such myopic mindsets, forget this ancient wisdom. That God is angry with the wicked every day. Therefore, the end of every power drunk ruler is determined by the sovereign God. He works behind the scene, overturning the devilish human ambitions to enthrone His divine order. Many are blind of His fiat. He alone, promotes authentic order in our lawless world. Only a few remnants know this reality.

"So Christ was once offered to bear the sins of many; and unto them that look for him shall he appear the second time without sin unto salvation." Hebrews 9:28. KJV Ted Hunter observed this reality. It is the longsuffering grace of God that allows puny man to play out their grandiose folly in global politics. The Sovereign Creator of the universe permits political jackals and foxes to hijack power for a limited season. Therefore, all political power brokers are expendable. The tragedy is that humans refuse to acknowledge this. The spirit of Machiavellianism and self-aggrandizement makes the world's powerful elites blind like Julius Caesar.

The ascendancy to power stature begins very early. To succeed in the power game of governance or corporate business empires one must master the act of ruthlessness. Some have this gene inherently. Others don't. Many learn to acquire it. Those who have it need little pressure to bring out their innate beastly trait. They can hurt or kill if they have to. The majority who lack this trait are considered cowards. They are too afraid to try to win.

The masters of this quest for power are many and lurk in every aspects of society. They include ruthless politicians and erudite lawyers. The fraudulent businessmen and even down to over-ambitious athletes who use drugs. They all shun fair play to win but leave a bad odor and a nasty aftermath. Those who shed blood beget blood. Ruthlessness breeds further lawlessness. Yet the world loves the ruthless winner. The winner takes all. The heroes are honored without noting their falsehood and craftiness.

Top Nigerian politicians copied the British elites 'Old Boys Network' idealism and mannerism. This English snobbishness started when Great Britain Empire dominated world affairs. The English public school system of the 1900's was designed to groom boys into the role model as world conquerors. They were trained to acquire statesman diplomatic skills necessary for running the British Empire. Their European contemporary, the Germans mastered technical knowledge and birth forth the German Machine promoting global industrial operations. Global dominance was a vital part of the English curriculum. Their inherent method of 'Divine and Rule' was exported to Nigeria. Every civilization flourishes by educating its citizenry into civilized role models. Those trained in the role as empire builder and technocrats often excel in arts of Machiavellianism. Many educated Britons mastered the 'Divide and Rule" tactics that promotes global governance. This learned role playing model ruled their hearts of British technocrats. It propelled them to seek and gain power at the least minimum cost.

Among those who received such training at a young age were some Nigerians. Their education in the English schools gave them early elevation into vocation to acquire political power at all cost. This prompted their ambition to rule their nation. History records that, this dark ambition for power was played out in the Nigerian Civil War and the Biafran secession. Today this innate rebelliousness still rules many young ambitious men. This curse of impatience and ruthlessness to cut corners still propels most Nigerians.

The truth is this. Every human is involved in a battle to win the laurels of life. All harbor greed and lust for power. The problem of the political pharaoh and god player is multiplied. This increases because, he lacks the courage to deal in godly wisdom. They lack the self-control to audit their actions. They stubbornly hold on to power in self-conceit. Most political tyrants cannot discontinue their lust for power after there is any justification for such obstinacy. The truth is every gifted professional plays god to some certain degree. Those who spend years building own fantasy path to attain self-glory and grandiose are cunning. They readily kill to attain power. They develop a paranoid mind that begins with the destruction of their innate common sense. The power grabber and egocentric person compares to one with deep cancer.

Ted Hunter also discovered that, the displacement of God as the center of our soul leaves the egoistic self in charge. This is the basic sin of most gifted intellectuals. To seek to bring God back to His original position will be seen in the mind of the gifted person as an outrageous indignity. The chief problem with the power seeking god-player is that he is blind. He lacks the spiritual power to redeem or deliver himself from satanic bondage.

Many powerful politicians trade their God fearing status for a delusion of divinity. Many top politicians assume a messianic thinking mentality. They promote personal half-truths, falsehoods and vanity. They enhance their impersonation of God. It is this human factor in the gifted professional that will one day birth forth the anti-Christ. Nothing will come out right for the person who either consciously or subconsciously makes the universe revolve around their carnal self.

The political tyrants who play god will fight to preserve their convictions of always being righteous. Others are always wrong. There is this stubbornness and rigidity that goes with the conviction of infallibility. It often results in childish indecision and the display of obstinate strong-headedness. Those committed to the glorification of the ego will work hard to preserve their delusion of always being right. Those with this mindset forget that truth out of balance becomes error.

The world as it exists today displays the power dynamics of the jungle. Most playing the power game live by hunting and killing others to achieve own selfish ends. Many people have developed the character traits of serpents, foxes, vultures and wolves. They all live off hunting others. The global communities are victims of corporate serpents who steal billions from innocent customers.

Yet, it is obvious that the world cannot do without religion. Humanity having been made in God's image has an inbuilt desire to worship. Either man worships the true God or they fix their worship on something else. Man worships money, idols, rules and rituals but forsakes truth. Thus, it is great when God gives one the gift of discernment and wisdom. Then one is able to distinguish the wolves from the lambs. That one can tell the foxes from the dogs and the eagles from the vultures.

Life in these times becomes a real chess game scenario. The game of chess contains the concentrated essence of life. To win in this game you must be patient. You must have knowledge of vital strategies and must be foreseeing. One must learn to be proactive and to act when the time is right.

The game of chess is built on patterns and whole sequences of moves that have been played before. At any fresh game, it is the same sequence that will be replayed with different variations and alterations.

To win you must deeply analyze the patterns your opponent is playing. If you analyze correctly, then you are able to foresee your opponent moves. As you study to know and predict his moves, – you must also at the same time concentrate to hide your own pattern of play. You must allow your opponent nothing predictable to base or formulate his own strategy. Once you block his ability to detect or plan his formidable game plan, you have a great advantage with which to win. Next you must master your emotion but yet maintain the ability to get others to react defensively to your moves. Today's world as a global village has human who display varied carnal traits. Some of them are loud and intrusive in your face. They bully others with their arrogance. Many exhibit the mark of jungle beasts which makes them very dangerous. From the vast types of jungle beasts, there are a few types with distinctions worth noting.

The Arrogant: This group are oversensitive and disguises their pride as they hunt their prey. They are politically correct, greedy and very aggressive.

The Insecure: This group have fragile ego that is very insecure. When they feel threatened, they bites like rats. They can nibble as a rat does, and it may take time before one notice their viciousness.

The Suspicious: This group sees the worst in others. They are afraid that others are after them or simply out to get them. One remains friends with them by siding with their suspicions at all times. When the suspicion is turned on a friend, it is best that the friend avoids them.

The Serpent: This group consists of individuals having a long memory. This type is as sleek like the snake. They do not show their venom on the surface, but will calculate and wait for the opportune moment to strike at their enemies. They are cunning and cold and have no love for anyone.

The Plain Unintelligent Man: This group are the blunt type. They go about life assuming that God will do what He says He will do. Yet this type will not make the effort to obtain or develop faith.

The Church Goer: This group bears a Christian name, but lacks the power of the Holy Spirit. They know that God has blessed them, but will not surrender to Jesus.

We know from the Lawlessness of our Age, that Marantha is our Hope. The Coming of Lord JESUS is man's true hope in this World. When He becomes our most valuable treasure, then we will see the superficiality and vanity that reigns in life. He is the only one who can give true peace, wisdom, joy and love in this decaying world.

Our hope does not rest in the affairs of this world. Yet it is true that without stable financial support, our dreams to live out a godly life shall be impossible. Therefore, we need faith in God. Faith is His gift. It increases our vision of seeing God renewing the earth. By faith, our five senses are overruled. Faith is the spiritual version of all the five senses and includes everything represented by them. By faith, our survival and drive for human excellence is activated.

Faith is the medium of exchange by which we receive life's true perspective. Faith empowers the God-chasing person to win life's laurels. Faith that feeds on the pledge and promise of God is true faith. It is perfected by the finished works of Calvary. It is sealed by the Blood of Jesus. By this costly faith, Christians run the race unto Christ's likeness. They pay the high cost of renunciation of earthly privileges. They deny self and reign in Christ. By faith, the true believers will love the unlovables on their pathways.

To achieve this utopia, God sent prophets. They exist to proclaim God's due divine order. They present the presence and reality of God. They demand that God rule and reign in human hearts. Prophets purge our imaginations of carnal and cultural assumptions. They preach that humans should walk in obedience to the oath of simple faith and trust in the triune God. True faith defies all that the world admires and rewards. God's chosen few the remnants like Daniels are to be the earth's king makers. Therefore, we shout, Hail Maranatha. Amen.

THE NAIRA WORSHIPPERS

The gulf between how one should live and how one does live is so wide that a man who neglects what is actually done for what should be done learns the way to self-destruction rather than self-preservation."
--Niccolo Machiavelli, 1469-1527
The Prince

THE NAIRA WORSHIPPERS

The New York Times, Monday, August 9, 1983

NIGERIAN WOMAN IS SHOT IN ELECTION VIOLENCE

Lagos, Nigeria, Aug. 9 (AP) – A woman was shot and critically wounded and more than 58 people were arrested in incidents connected with Nigeria's presidential election on Saturday, published reports said today. The shooting took place in eastern Nigeria in an attempt to steal a voter's list on Saturday, the News Agency of Nigeria reported.

The New York Times, Thursday, August 11, 1983

OIL GLUT LEADS TO FISH GLUT

Tromson, Norway, Aug. 11 – The rest of the world is awash in oil these days, and there's an awful lot of dried fish here to prove it. The 16,000 or so metric tons of dried fish are out of view, stored in hundreds of warehouses up and down the rugged coastline. But no one here has any trouble seeing their line with the oil glut.
It is a link that connects Norway with, of all places, Nigeria. By the end of last year, the combination of the recession, the demand for energy efficiency and the high levels of oil production has heightened the industrial world's appetite for the high priced crude oil of Nigeria and other members of the Organization of Petroleum Exporting Countries...

The New York Times, Friday, August 5, 1985

REPORTS DIFFER ON LOAN FOR NIGERIA
Lagos, Aug. 5 (Reuters) – Nigeria and the International Monetary Fund have reached agreement on a new credit to help the country out of severe recession caused by a drop in oil sales, Transport Minister Umaru Dikko said today.

He told reporters he could not say how much Nigeria would draw under the agreement. However, the Fund had waived its usual requirement of devaluation as part of an austerity program. That meant more money will be available for foreign payments. The brutal snag was that domestic spending must be drasically cut back...

THE AGE OF LAWLESSNESS

Only GOD can turn today's global mess into a Miracle. Only He can renew the mind of World Leaders. Those who misinterpret the past are already condemned. They bungle the present and on the wings of human error-history repeat itself.

At the turn of the 1900 century, Western diplomats adopted the adage:

"Falsehood ceases to be falsehood, when it is understood on all fronts that the truth is not expected to be spoken"

This axiom continues to play out in global politics to this very day. Thus, history repeats itself on many fronts. That is the norm without the active intervention of Omnipotent God. This is a faithful saying.

CHAPTER ONE

British Protectorate of Lagos – 1950's

"Who is able to defeat the Lawless Ones! The world rulers must seek righteousness. Without which a nation cannot be exalted " thundered Father Murphy.

The gathering was a fellowship for Christian diplomats who served in Lagos. The majority of those in attendance were Irish and Italian. The tiny hall was dimly lit with by flames emitting from many candles.

Ted Hunter sat glued to his seat. He could not distinguish the difference between Father Murphy's thunderous sermons and those he had been used to in Northern Ireland. The fiery preaching was the same. Those who condemn the wrongs dealt to the common folks have the same crusader tone. They pontificated on God's ancient wisdom.

Father Murphy continued, "The Bible states in Second Timothy Chapter 3, verses 1-5…"

Even though Hunter was desirous to worship, he wasn't really listening. His was in the escapades he experienced in his native town of Northern Ireland.

"Why bother, this isn't Belfast?" resounded in the stillness of his mind.

He absent mindedly picked up his Bible and wondered at the same time why he felt a sudden sense of dread. He pinched himself again to remind himself that this was Lagos. The city started as a slave outpost when the Spanish and Brazilian slave masters traded humans on the coast. The legacies of their culture still colored the city. The streets had many buildings with Brazilian grandiose architectures.

"...In the last days, perilous times shall come. For men shall be lovers of their own selves, covetous, boasters, proud, blasphemers, disobedient to parents, unthankful, unholy...having a form of godliness, but denying the power thereof..."

The Father's words echoed on through the recesses of Hunter's mind, building upon nostalgic memories of his past. He straightened his shoulders as increased apprehension flooded his heart.

He recollected the numerous times those same Bible passages had bothered him. The local Sunday school teacher had impressed upon him that God's blessings had no sorrow. He had taken that as "gospel truth". As a child, Hunter wanted no sadness attached to his childhood.

Father Murphy's sermon had spotlighted his rain chase for godliness in a lawless age. The Belfast city of Hunter's youth was stricken with religious violence. He lost many relations in sectarian brawls.

He thought of a Sunday service he attended when he was ten years old in Belfast. The sermon theme from the pulpit was harsh but radiant, like the sunlight. The padre forcefully proclaimed: "Only God can turn human lawlessness into Miracles." The word impacted Hunter powerfully and furnished him with hope for his future. That was the first time he remembered dreaming of greatness. At the end of the service, the Reverend Father had spoken kindly to him.

"Young lad," he bellowed in Irish slang, "Ye must always give your best for Christ's uttermost. Pray to become a light and salt in this world. Live your life for the truth and cry out daily for Maranatha."

Hunter full of apprehension had smiled and thanked the Reverend Father. Later on as he walked home, the statement plagued his young mind. He questioned whether or not Maranatha was one of the commandments of the Bible. What is Maranatha? What language is it? What promise did Maranatha have as the solution to a lawless age? These questions raced through his mind. He mentally resolved within himself to find the mystery of

Maranatha. When he reached the poor structure of a brick building he called home, he commenced his search.

He still remembered the joy of discovering the meaning of Maranatha – even now, "Come LORD JESUS." Joy flooded his heart to overflowing. That was twenty years ago. He continued to reminisce in his childhood memory until an usher gently woke him from his daydream. The usher had the poise of a religious zealot. He was a man totally punctual to sinecure service. He stretched out the offering bag, as though motioning for Ted to put an offering into the bag. Ted obliged, reached into his coat pocket and placed a sizable sum into the bag. The usher bowed and smiled with exulting gratitude at Hunter's generous offering.

Hunter smiled back. He had always believed that giving was better than receiving. That people ought to do what was noble and charitable. He had learnt as an altar boy that only ten percent of church congregation gave to its welfare. The rest of were free loaders. It was incomprehensible to him that many church folks have not figured out this logic. That God loves a generous and cheerful giver. This common sense was not always common. He had studied journalism in his quest to be a world changer. His vocation had taken him to many capitals of the world. Three months has passed since he became editor for a British newspaper in Lagos.

Experience had taught him many lessons. Most significantly, that the connections between logic and reason are not made by instinct. And that reason and the mind do not work automatically. In fact, he learned that logic and reason were not everything. He had surmised that faith in God was the principal thing. Therefore, the quest to mature in faith to change the world had been his hidden agenda since he could remember.

The church service afforded him the comfort to renew his quest for Maranatha. The one hour helped to revive his faith. When the session ended, Hunter strolled into the sunlit street. The sunlight ray like fire burned his skin. He walked with long strides and in twenty minutes, he was within sight of his office building. Many construction sites worked frantically at raising masterpiece structures in preparation for the nation's independence. The commotion of heavy machinery equipment and clashing metals filled the streets. The loud joviality of the army of laborers complemented the boisterous environment.

Hunter turned the corner and walked proudly into the stately Metropolitan Building. He felt secured. The building was the hub of journalists in the city. News mercenaries competed for their livelihood in the marble hallways. The place had been the nest of local nationalists and foreign journalists. They were both united towards the common goal – to overthrow British Imperialism. One could feel the aurora of power that emanated from the solid structures. The quest for freedom united the building occupants. Working relentlessly, they gladly gave flesh and blood for the utopian ideal of gaining national independence.

Hunter walked the stairway into the busy corridor. The typing pool room seated rows of news reporters. They typed at top speed. The clicking keys emitted sounds of speeding train wheels. The pounding of power words echoed an axiom: "The pen is mightier than the gun." History, records that every passionate pen professional rebels at lawlessness. They wince at injustice. The battle for justice against empire builders and global looters was a noble quest.

Hunter tactfully studied the scenery. Here was a team of crusaders: people who did their best to expose polished falsehood. They lived to open up cans of worms. Although inspired by his surroundings, his thought was glued to the Maranatha resolve. With a burdened heart, he walked through the spotless halls into the office of Sam Thompson.

Sam sat rigidly at his oak desk. His posture revealed his restlessness. Sam Thompson had started as a printer boy in London Fleet Street. He had worked his way up the ranks. As the top dog of Metropolitan Newspapers in Africa, he had relocated from Cairo to Lagos. However, to accomplish this feat had cost him. The industrial "grapevine" had rumored that Sam Thompson was on his way out. The gossip indicated that he was not qualified to be the chief editor. This made him even more defensive. He was envious of Hunter's aristocratic poise. His square face and fearless blue eyes intimidated Sam.

Sam looked fifty but was only forty. His bald forehead with thin graying hair made him look wiser than his worth. His mouth looked obstinate and petulant. His tall slender frame seemed drained and restless. Resentment colored his face and flared from paled eyes.

He seemed surprised at the sound of the door opening and

lifted up his head in irritation.

"Don't bother me! I have a deadline to complete. Don't bother me; I hope to be free in the next three hours," protested Sam.

Hunter marched toward the desk fearlessly ignoring Sam's rantings.

"This is most vital, Sam," he said, slightly raising his voice.

"All right, all right, what is it that can't wait?"

Hunter reached into his pocket and took out the telegram that came through London that morning.

He stared intently at Sam and said, "It is the Suez Crisis." He noticed Sam's alarm in his shifting posture.

"Gamal Abdel Nasser has nationalized the Suez Canal, "

Hunter announced.

"Nationalization of the Canal? That is not possible. It is crazy!"

Hunter continued as though Sam had not spoken and said, "Britain had been unanimous in condemning Nasser and comparisons have been made to Hitler and Mussolini in the 1930s."

"There must be some mix up. The Egyptian army cannot withstand the British Force. There must be some mistake," Sam muttered.

Hunter was shocked and silently analyzed the dullness of Sam retorts. His face showed disdain. He stared straight into Sam's eyes with his own blue eyes wide and questioning. He opened his mouth in puzzled wonder.

"What do you want me to do?" snapped Sam. "You know I have enough trouble keeping sane with the vile Lagos nationalists."

"I think that you can try and go to the city of Alexandria. It is under your cover. Either that, or you can raise the resources for me to go" Hunter suggested.

Sam's bald head heaved. He was visibly shaken. His heavy eyelids widened, yet he continued to stare. Like a pent up boiling kettle, he gasped for air. He continued to stare as he carefully chose his words.

"There's never been any question of me abdicating my headship to you. I resent your thinking such. I resent it very much. You are not a patient vulture," Sam said. He fumbled irritably with his coat collar, buttoning it as he spoke. His reddened face visibly showing.

"It is advisable to be cautious," Hunter parried coldly.

"Cautious. What!" Sam returned, throwing caution to the wind.

"What right have you got to lecture me on diplomacy. I have been in this business for years. I know it as the back of my hand. I resent your smooth operator antics, you will not deceive me. I know your type. You try to reap where you did not sow"

"Come on, old boy, watch your tongue. You have no right to accuse me of being a leech. I have contributed my own quota. I have a meritorious track record. So please swallow your pride. Get a grip on your ego" Hunter shot back. His Irish temper flaring.

Sam recoiled. He had seemingly lost control of his tongue. He regretted having spoken so harshly. He knew he had blown it. Silently he muttered a prayer and cursed at the same time. As he did this, his sharp brain came to his rescue. He labored to change the topic. He refocused back to reasoning.

The realization of knowing that he had met a formidable opponent in Hunter sobered him up. Paradoxically Sam was satisfied to have begun the conflict. It presented a way to release his pent up emotions. It was also a way of escape from the drudgery of the office.

Sam suddenly came alive. His creative genius booted, working out an escape for him.

"So you tell me. What is your game plan for this difficult undertaking complete with dangers and complications? Do you know how much is at stake?" Sam concluded.

Hunter stood up fuming. He held his head as one who faced a challenge and found joy in his capacity to meet it. As he turned to leave, Sam called out "Ted! Did you know that the New World Globalization quest started on this maxim:-

"Falsehood ceases to be falsehood when it is understood on all fronts that the truth is not expected to be spoken." The Cold War political jingoism rested on the strategy of, "Talk, Talk, Talk and More Talk with no Action." And as, George Santayana insisted:--"those who misinterpret the past are condemned to bungle the present." Sam cheerfully explained.

Caught off-guard by this rhetoric, a puzzled Hunter stared back at Sam.

"No, I didn't". He replied.

"You might want to look into it, Ted. This is the basis by which political decisions are made. It is the key factor strategy to the enigma of the Suez Canal" Sam added.

Hunter left the meeting with Sam resolved to write a thriller over the unfolding of the Suez Crisis. History, he knew always repeated itself. He had recently determined that having a desk job as editor was not his forte. He knew he wanted to write a best seller. And so, the next day, he drafted an application to Sam requesting leave of absence from Lagos.

The following week he took off to London on the first phase of his dream and vision to write a bestseller on Maranatha. He spent four weeks in Fleet Street, the center of the London media industry. His research provided him much insight into the crisis. He discovered that the Suez Canal Nationalization was pivotal to a new era in global power. The politics of Europe, the Middle East, America and Africa interplayed in the Suez diplomatic row to heighten cold war era. The diplomatic row also promoted Pan-Arab Nationalism. It completed the transformation of the Israeli-Palestinian dispute into an Israeli-Arab one. The venture escalated diplomatic falsehoods, intrigues and lawlessness in high places.

In 1956, European politicians had ruled the vassal nations in Africa. The might of the British imperialists was resented in Egypt and Nassar's nationalism quest emboldened other post-colonial leaders. The hidden lesson exposed how global lust for ephemeral power corrupts the world.

Hunter spent four weeks tracing the intrigues of the Suez Canal Crisis. His investigations uncovered many lapses in Europe foreign policy. The Suez Canal was Britain's Imperial lifeline for oil. It was the lifeline through which ship tankers supplied Arabian oil to England.

France had a financial stake in the Paris-based company that ran the Suez Canal. The President of Egypt, Gamal Abdul Nasser, had overthrown the monarchy in 1952. To consolidate his government, he planned the building of the Aswan Dam on the River Nile. This was basic to Egypt's economic survival. He therefore reasoned that the seizure and nationalization of the canal was strategic. It would help source the funds to complete his ambition to modernize Egypt. The revenue from the canal would replace the foreign loans promised by Britain and America.

Nasser had a blueprint of his conquest. He worked on it for a long period. In 1956, he boldly took over in a coup to the amazement of the Europeans. To counter his move, Britain and France planned for military invasion. A re-occupation of the canal by force was in order. The battle line was drawn. They planned clandestinely to move against Egypt in the summer of 1956.

The cold disinterest by America under the "Peace President" cut off the steam of the proposed Anglo-French military action. The Americans were motivated by deep-rooted anti-imperialism attitudes. They remembered their hard earned freedom from the British Empire. This made them refuse to take sides. American diplomats argued that the military action against Egypt would start a cold war. They looked at the big picture. Angered by Nasser's arrogance, the Europeans refused to see as the Americans. The Americans were right. The alienation of the Arabs drove Africans and Asians into rapid Nationalization. Some became allies of the Russian Communist. The U.S political masterstroke propelled Anglo-French politicians in fruitless rounds of talks and conferences.

Talk and more talks convinced the Europeans that they were on shaky ground for their military invasion. The Americans refused to partner in a foreign imbroglio. They knew it could cost the incumbent president the White House. So they kept sponsoring the diplomatic talk conferences, which bought time. The result was that the Anglo-France momentum for military action began to cool off. The diplomatic merry-go-round continued as it seemed forever.

This made the quest for regime change to eliminate Nasser take on another dimension. The invasion of the Canal Zone and the quest to topple Nasser started in secrecy. The Europeans launched out without America's knowledge. When the news of the invasion leaked, President Eisenhower moved with speed. He threatened to cut off IMF loans meant to bail Britain's shaky economy.

Forced with this ruthless reality that their funding would be jeopardized, the British backed off. This forced the French troops to disengage. The French took this let down as reason to initiate the European Economic Community. History gained from the Suez Canal crisis. Colonial states pushed ahead for their Independence from the British Empire. Lagos Nigeria was one of such.

The Suez Canal Crisis motivated the nationalists in Lagos. Four years later, the momentum cumulated in Nigeria's independence. In October 1960, the Union Jack - the symbol of British Imperialism, was lowered for the last time in Lagos.

CHAPTER TWO

Geneva, Switzerland

Four Doberman pinschers romped and barked as humming birds darted about the trees. The barking of the dogs was in anticipation of their afternoon meal. There was also the soft murmurs' hum of bees. The crispy silken rustle of fallen leaves contributed to the sound in the mellow but whining scenery. The serene atmosphere was interrupted by the whimsical noise from a powerful automobile engine. A chauffeured Silver-Spur Rolls-Royce came to a stop near the entrance of the main hall of the mansion.

The massive San Marino country estate was positioned on the eastern section of the lower banks of the Rhone River in Geneva, Switzerland. It housed an extraordinary financial baron, the mystical Pedro da Souza. The sprawling exquisite mansion presented a sight so beautiful, nobly displaying a lifestyle of the 'rich and famous'. The architectural masterpiece speckled with sun glint strands in a girdle of secure trees. The estate revealed gracious dignity and divine comfort. The scenery stirred memories of solid English homes in Windsor. Long gentle slopes adorned the walkway as one approached the house.

The only occupant in the vehicle, a man in his late forties, alighted into the hot sunlight of the spring afternoon. He expertly surveyed the impressive dogs with mixed feeling. His mind raced through the sharp contrast between this beautiful palace and the wild streets of Lagos where he lived and worked. A place of homeless beggars, where armed burglars, carjackers and muggers proliferated the streets. Each person busily sought his own haven. Lagos city was a place of paradoxes. Within the city, the contrast of riches and poverty endured. The raw energies of the waifs conflicted with the endless enjoyment of the affluent. The wonder of it all is the placidity that rules the seemingly overcharged atmosphere. Everyone seems to wait on mother fate to prosper their destiny. 'Chop and let's chop' was the moto of the dwellers.

San Marino was uniquely palatial. The dogs of San Marino stopped their barking as the man whistled to them. He snapped his fingers and looked in the bright brown eyes of the dog nearest to the car. It refused to approach him, concealing its lust for battle. There was something sinister in its steady, yet uneasy look and silence. Its fringed tail, uplifted and gay, dropped suddenly. The man read distrust in its eyes. He thought best to get into the house as soon as possible. He therefore hastened towards the massive door.

"Damn these dogs," he quivered. He had never liked dogs. His gambler's instinct informed him that the dogs had been selectively bred for fighting. They had become accustomed to love, gentleness and indulgence. He knew they would not attack him. So he had taken the risk to see if they would respond to his wooing. They did not and this hurt his gambler's vanity.

The manservant ushered him into the great square hall. It was polished, dim and cool. The sunlight filtered through white Venetian blinds onto the rich Persian rugs, which covered the floor like dark mirrors. The guest quickly took in with appreciation the contemporary Italian tables. He noted the crystal lamps, the silver candlesticks on the white marble mantle-piece and the delicate rosewood furniture. He looked with frank pleasure at the black walnut Ormolu clock ticking daintily in the peaceful silence.

"Aha!" he thought to himself. Here was all he had ever wanted. Everything he had worked hard to achieve. A picture began to form in his mind. Abruptly he saw himself in such a similar home in Lagos. He daydreamed that he would someday, perhaps within five years, be lord and master of such a manor. The man became absorbed in the study of the oil portrait in heavy gold frame that hung on the ivory-colored wall. He was lost in thought when the manservant returned with the secretary. The secretary was there to screen him before he would be permitted to see the boss. The secretary looked polite enough, but the visitor could detect some uneasiness in the secretary. The secretary disdained him.

"Are you Mr. Bulus Musa, the lawyer from Lagos?" the secretary asked.

Barrister Bulus nodded and the secretary continued, "I'm to bring you along to the master's personal aide. Your appointment will be in the next hour. But first, the master understands that you must be hungry. He instructed that a special lunch be prepared for your enjoyment. He, however, regrets his inability to join you. He wants you to feel completely at home."

Bulus grinned and responded, "I suppose lunch will be just fine for me. I've been living on junk food since I've been on this trip. I'm sure your menu will be to my utmost delight." He yawned in anticipation of the food.

"Yes, sir," replied the secretary, smiling. "I'm aware that lunch consists of Coquille Saint Jacques, Oysters, Chateaubriand. A Bibb lettuce salad, Brie and Cappuccino. Dessert will be soft Swiss cheese."

After the sumptuous lunch, the male secretary conducted the lawyer through the delicate white spiral staircase. They walked along the spiral stairway and through the door. It opened into the office of the personal assistant and chief of staff. Andy Lincoln promptly brought the visitor to the host and master of the manor. Presenting the visitor, the personal assistant saluted smartly and retired.

"I'm greatly impressed by your enormous generosity. The meal was exquisite. Whoever would have thought there was such cooking in the entire world. Most importantly, the music of Cecil Taylor's spell-binding piano with its arpeggios and rippling glissandi that accompanied the food. I've come across numerous men of wealth, but your style is very extraordinary." The lawyer spoke with great heave of exultation. He knew he was slightly intoxicated. But something colossal moved him to lose his composure in the presence of the legend called "The Old Fox."

Pedro da Souza greeted the young man with pleasure and courtesy. "The Old Fox" smiled and said, "Of course my chief of staff takes the necessary pain to measure up to my high profile standards. My main worry is that I shall not be around as long as I'd wish to. The doctors inform me I've less than two years to live. A case of pulmonary emboli blood clots in the lung."

"I'm indeed sorry, though two years is still a long, long time," replied Bulus with sympathy in his eyes.

"Ha! I do not mind the end coming as it must. I've done alright for myself. I've transitioned from a small lad who grew up in the slums of the Lagos metropolis, to the enviable owner of the Old Masters." He pointed to a fine Rembrandt hanging on the wall, radiating in passionate blazing jewel-points. The curved frame of fine gold and brown shadow enhanced the mystic of the masterpiece. Over the fireplace with its ruddy flames was his favorite, a Rubens-worldly acclaimed. A unique luxury sought after by members of the "Forbes Four Hundred" mighty rich clan. His San Marino palace was indeed an art gallery.

Pedro da Souza continued his stately walk around the huge room. He expatiated on his obsession for beauty and the unique art forms that he had spent his business trips world-wide buying to enlarge his private gallery. He stood his full six-foot-three. He was an immense man with a matching frame. He was seventy years old and bald. His eyebrow was so bushy it compensated for the patchy hair on his head. His gigantic oblong head was proportionately set upon his broad shoulders like a yacht hunkered on the sea, and he was tremendously paunch in proportion. His eyes were deep-brown, very much alive, humorous and piercing. His nose was short, very broad with equally large nostrils. They were belligerent and resting on a light broad mouth, which was savage in repose. What came out of the mouth impressed upon others the innate intelligence in the massive creature. When he smiled, he revealed a set of perfectly formed strong, white teeth. His smile radiated confident nonchalance.

Abruptly, he stopped pacing and returned to his chair. It seemed a warning had gone into his head that he was showing too much of himself. His composure assumed stricter control on his behavior. His next question brought the lawyer away from his dream of how he could duplicate the great man's material treasures in his Lagos mansion.

"So tell me, what brings one of Lagos' top attorneys to my home? The dossier on you does not have exact details about your family background. It says something about your brilliance to organize non-existent fund laundering companies in either Lagos or Liverpool with the inherent skill of a master craftsman. Your client's profile includes top captains of industry and politicians. Your Law firm is basically one man operation dedicated to manipulating big deals ... shall I go on ... ?" Da Souza asked genially.

"Eh?" Bulus turned to the old man, stung. Suspicion and irrefutable sadness colored his face. "Yes? No, you need not. I suppose you're very thorough. Impressive! You've acquired the best information money can buy. One must not underestimate the Old Fox."

Da Souza laughed out loud. "Of course, I have to be. I'm afraid of assassination! One must always, in the business of life, think and plan ahead. I would not be here today if I was not thorough. You must know it pays for one to do his homework well in advance. Businessmen, like lawyers, must have their contingent plans."

Bulus slowly sipped his brandy. His pretence of enjoyment of the gentleman's drink was very visible. His mind, however, concentrated on how best to win the argument with the man sitting in front of him. He was a hero of his world; feared and admired. His name, his connections, his former position, his business experiences commanded the respect of his class. Bulus rummaged in his mind the best way to tell his story. It was part of his English legal training not to think too fast and too much. The best strategy for victory he knew was to tap into the brain of the opponent as the argument unfolded. A plan to focus on only what may be of practical use at the moment of need began to form on his tested mind. He weighed the options. Caution, red light flashed incessantly in his brain.

Barrister Bulus would have searched for the other's weak points, the skeleton in the cupboard, precariously concealed. But the Old Fox's secrets were open and had been for over three decades.

Sensing that he had formulated a fool proof mental game plan, Bulus adjusted his poise. He looked straight at the energetic old man and spoke with wisdom as best as he could. He pointedly requested that no question be asked until he finished and the old man nodded in acquiescence.

"I'm here to represent clients whose names will not be

revealed, at least not for the time being. I represent men who have the greatest respect for your person. They would do everything in their power to be in good relationship with you no matter the outcome of this meeting. Should your response be unfavorable, then we should understand this meeting never took place." He spoke in a deep voice of hope borne of fear.

Bulus continued on his story for the next thirty minutes. As he spoke, the old man took the time to carefully scrutinize the face and emotion revealed by the learned gentleman.

Barrister Bulus was lean, withered, brownish-black, and nervously alert. He seemed more like an Indian native from Bombay. His cheeks were sunken and heavily furrowed. His forehead was bony, and his small bright eyes were agile as a monkey's. His thick lips splayed and tightened, making his nose rather big with small nostrils. He had a very small skull with black-grey hair.

He was about forty-eight, but appeared ageless. He had the air of one who possessed impeccable discipline. His gait revealed a measure of integrity that was not without its malicious legal cunning. There was no doubting his brilliant intellect. It showed itself in the discolored crease in his face as he pontificated on facts. He mentally labored very hard to make his story more interesting. He appeared not to sympathize with aspirations of his clients. He did, however, work hard at the moment to give such false illusion. This deception impacted the shining gauntness of his sweating forehead. There was no loyalty in his devotion. Greed for fast profit fueled his egotism. His law practice was the only trade he knew how to exploit. He also dreamt for wealth and capital gains to be rich like the Old Fox. He sought for money not taxed by any government. This was his driving ambition.

Bulus carefully presented his case. He spoke for thirty-five minutes, paused to breathe in fresh air and then proceeded to conclude his long entreaty.

"To summarize, we urgently, I mean my clients and associates, greatly need your help. Should you favor our philosophy we will then schedule another meeting in order to plan our course of action. If you're not in favor, then we shall both assume that this meeting never took place. And nobody is ever to know the nature of my discourse of this day. Is that agreeable to you?"

Bulus had been informed that the old man had a reputation

for brusqueness. However, this knowledge did not prepare him for the 'Old Fox' melancholy rhetoric that followed his parting minutes before his departure from San Marino.

"Pompous incompetents!" bellowed Da Souza with the contempt borne out of old money. "You come here to evoke memories of those distant days. You remind me of when everything was so fresh, so surprising, so adventuresome and so interesting. You provoke me to review of the unfulfilled dream of a young man in a nation. I recollect the innate ambition that was so huge, young, rich and full of uncertainties. Nigeria was then a newborn nation. She needed guidance and had such able bodied men to give her the godly leadership. But somewhere along the line comes this curse of futility upon our characters. Then came chivalry, materialism, high sounding sentiments, a supine morality and sullen acquiescence in every form of corruption. We begot a country for our independence, only to become the passive prey of a democratic parody, helpless victims of scoundrels and cutthroats. Our institutions grew to fluster as a mockery, our laws a farce. We matured as a tragic comedy in an epic classical story plot with the major characters devoted to the extreme of strong-headedness into which all and one are destroyed. Our leaders promote self-destructive madness. Two and a half decades ago, I was one of the main actors. God knows I was forced to change into what I have become today.

I now function out of the conviction of practical necessity. My current status is stronger than any abstract political doctrine. The ignominy of my self-exile situation not -withstanding. I have used available opportunity to acquire the practical soul of bold buccaneer. As a tested pragmatist, I know there are no political reasons, but political passions. Each and every one of us has own innate convictions. This in itself is only a particular view of own personal advantage whether practical or delusive. No one is a complete patriot, at least not for nothing. The capitalist calls it the profit motive. I don't have to go into exhaustive details about the motives of the men you represent. I'm not sure if they can fully understand their own ulterior and hidden motives for scheming as they do. History however, tells me I'm right in my assessment of them. Finally, inform your associates that Pedro da Souza cannot afford to be allied with political comets. They shall in a matter of time, burn themselves out.

Tell them that wars and revolutions are the business of fools. They come and go, but the economic power of the Old Fox remains. Old objectives as well as new ones cannot be attained by way of old methods. God has a unique purpose for Nigeria and Nigerians. He will manifest this in the fullness of His own time. We are all to yield to His Lordship. We must learn to become His tools and pawns. Believe this by faith. And finally note this from a tested sage. Remember Biafra was no solution".

Bulus remained silent for minutes. The old man's sporadic outburst was unexpected but he remained thoughtful and silent. He searched for the logic with which he might still, turn the argument his way. Ah! FAB's. He remembered. Futures! Advantages! Benefits! Power! To a man like da Souza, the only thing that could mean anything at his present stage of huge accomplishments was ... power. Power was a term the old man could identify with. He had sufficient money, but not the power to settle the private grudge he had against the feudal lords who had robbed him of his political ambition. Could the candle of hatred be rekindled? Maybe, and maybe not, but it was worth a try.

"I had to include some historical allusion to show erudition, though I tell the truth concerning the nature of the current events affecting the fortunes of the people I represent. They understand your extreme delicate position and would guarantee you some amount of power should you decide favorably."

Liars, thought da Souza without visible contempt and rage.

"How remarkable for these incompetents to offer the only commodity they may never have in life! But are they not aware of the long lasting hell of cramped frustration that becomes the portion of whoever sits in that power post? Why should a man make such sacrifices on behalf of a malevolent people? Why bother with the peoples' multifaceted ethnic grudges that always increases and is hell-bent on destroying anybody occupying that power post? I would rather not be a party to your seemingly innocent proposition. Of course, this meeting did not ever take place."

The facial grimace of da Souza moved in the convulsion that was his smile. Momentarily, he stood up and rang for his aide, motioning to Bulus the meeting had come to a close.

The personal aide promptly appeared with Bulus's silken hat and thick fur lined coat. Bulus picked up his gloves and together they left the drawing room. They headed towards the hall where the driver waited with instructions to take the lawyer back to his suite at the Sheraton.

Bulus left San Marino with the knowledge that he had ignited a spark in the Old Fox's soul. He could bet his last card that before very long, da Souza would make his move, against his Lagos adversaries and contemporaries. Bulus was so sure of his prediction that he felt competent to gamble. His instinct trusted on the next ten months as a possible time frame for the Old Fox's plan to be executed. His gambler's instinct assured him that he had scored a big jackpot.

Time seemed to stand still at San Marino after the departure of Barrister Bulus. Time sped as Pedro da Souza remained motionless. His face looked flushed and angry. He seemed lost in thoughts and in deep mental anxiety. His doctors insisted that such anxieties were not good for a man his age. It led to a host of ailments from coronary diseases, to skin rashes and impotence. da Souza worried more about impotence. His strict adherence to the seafood and vegetable diets imposed on him by Dr. Hans Vanderick of Montbeliard Health Farm, enabled him to enjoy good health. He had companionship of female starlets readily available for monetary considerations. His pro bono charity work acted as anti-depressant, and was very therapeutic. He cherished hard work. Inactivity, on the other hand, reinforces the part of the man wanting to retreat into depression. It was the first sequel to a deteriorating mental state and avoidance of real responsibilities. A man must never allow such undisciplined spirit to bar him from his life objectives.

Pedro da Souza, never a man to run away from his duties promptly rose. He walked towards the ominous black enameled door and opened it.

"Andy, please get me the memorandum from the editor of the Nigerian Newsletter. Bring also the dossier on the Lagos fat cats and any other current information on the subject matter. Do also kindly fix an appointment for the editor, Ted Hunter, to see me at noon next Friday."

"Anything more?" was the brisk reply from Andy as he quickly set about accomplishing the task demanded.

"That will do for now," retorted da Souza, thoughtfully marveling at Andy's established competence. He reasoned Andy was now a man of huge resources. He had however, continued to serve with all his heart. Someday he would set up shop and make more fortune by marketing crude petroleum world-wide. For the present, Andy was content with his chief of staff status at Zeus Incorporated.

Andy was born by an alcoholic African-American father and a Caucasian mother in the Pasadena area of metropolitan Houston, Texas. He grew up with the name of Abraham Lincoln. When the kids at school taunted him at the imitation of the great Abe Lincoln, the name Andy came in as substitute. He had since then retained his new name.

Pedro da Souza had met Andy Lincoln in 1971 during a business stopover in Houston. He flew in to negotiate with the Greenspot Oil Company's chief executive officer, Danny McGovern. The meeting had carried on for a week, and Pedro da Souza had stayed at the Lamar Hotel where Andy worked as a receptionist. He worked full-time and studied computer engineering in the evenings at the Houston Community college. Eleven years had passed since he stayed in that unfriendly hotel. Andy had been over friendly as he sensed the uneasiness of the only black guest in wholly white dominated hotel. He worked hard to make da Souza comfortable during his stay at the Lamar.

A friendship ensued, reaching its peak two years later when Andy graduated from Houston. He had given Andy the money to pay for his tuition at the New York Institute of Finance. Andy studied there to graduate as an investment analyst. Pedro da Souza came to his graduation and offered him a job in Zeus Industries, Incorporated. da Souza explained, his dedication was crucial to co-ordinate the growing activities of Zeus, Inc. and its subsidiaries. Three years later, Andy moved to Switzerland to closely monitor the strategies of the OPEC cartel. Zeus was a major marketer in the worldwide business of importing and exporting crude petroleum.

After ten years at Zeus, Andy had worked his way up the corporate ladder to become the chairman's trusted aide. He had drummed up strings of money-making ideas that made da Souza and his business associates, including Andy, immeasurably rich. In 1973, Andy started the strategy of transporting crude oil in huge storage super tankers called crude carriers into the port of Rotterdam. By disposing it to the highest bidder Zeus generated huge fortunes for six months until the competition caught on. The compounded return of the Wall Street Corporate Stock shares

Andy bought with his own commission on the deal was great. He invested in technologically innovative shares on the New York Stock Exchange. This meant that his compounded annual return rose above six figures before tax.

Andy expertly checked through the huge filing cabinet. Opening the N section, he searched along until he sighted the large dossiers labeled in bold italics alphabets: F cats. He retrieved these and some other files that seemed related to the subject matter. He hauled the extensive paper collection onto his desk. He picked up the phone and called the downtown office of Ted Hunter. He had evolved to become the editor of an indefatigable think-tank on Nigeria, the oil rich West African nation whose national hegemonic symbol of black power was once a model of third world success story. The nation was fast approaching financial bankruptcy laden with corrupt bureaucracy. The civilian technocrats were without the disciplined strategy or political integrity to turn around its financial woes.

Nigeria with its rich oil wells and an epoch of the endless ethnic rifts was desperate for economic modernization. There was an urgent demand to unify its cultural and religious diversity.

Nigeria was a sole cartographic creation of the European colonialists. She was still displaying the inability to harness its unique resourcefulness. She yet wallowed in ethnocentric and religious rivalry. A legacy of morbid colonialism.

Ted Hunter was reputed to be a man of deep knowledge about Nigeria. He had painstakingly researched its history and her process of rapid transformation as a Nation state. His many publications on Nigerian economy and politics made him a modern political prophet. He was gifted with accurate factual insights into the past, present and future governments in Lagos. It is common gossip among his peers, that Ted Hunter knew Lagos like the back of his hand.

CHAPTER THREE

Heathrow Airport London

A closer inspection of the lady and four men, all standing and locked up in earnest conversation would have revealed the fearful tension in their individual profiles. This meeting at the London Heathrow VIP lounge signaled unfolding ominous consequences. The postures of the jet-set members of this "Man pass Man" club was revealing. They seemed agitated. Commonly called the "Naira Nouveax Riche" club, the members consisted mostly of importers and exporters businessmen. These Nigerian builders, contractors, bankers, and real estate barons, were dedicated to transforming their financial equivalence in the naira currency to the British pounds sterling at all cost. These members were mainly from a very poor background and had used political leverage to become rich. They were a smart bunch with too much money. Mother luck had helped them be in the right place at the right time. They had benefited when there was no such thing as oil glut or burst. Lacking economic wisdom they became victim of the world's boom and bust Reality.

These international urban jet setters were all decked in colorful over-flowing attires. This made them visibly provocative .The men displayed vulgarism as they shouted in loud haughty voices. They wore their African arrogance like treasured masks. Their hawkish mannerism, painted them as pretenders unschooled in English grace. Their lack of intricate economics and knowledge of global market operations compounded their foolish exuberance. Their greed for illicit monetary gains and abhorrence of customs due process helped them build up mountains of hot money. Their conspicuous ostentation was preposterous.

"How in the devil's name can one explain this special power given to the president by the Senate, enabling him to automatically put a stop to all my International Letters of Credit?" spat out Binta Lilah. She was the first lady of the club and in her recently acquired crisp English accent. She wore dark sun glasses to avoid eye contact with ordinary people.

Aged thirty-four, Binta was twenty years younger than the average age of her peer group. She had been accepted into their exclusive circle due to her considerable charm. Her gold-rimmed spectacles promoted her tough businesswoman countenance .Her attire accentuated the fabulous body that blossomed below her equally determined chin. Binta's no-nonsense manner and unflappable nature made her unimpressed by false flattery. She resented the acts of aggressive machismo of her male counterparts. She could be very feminine, depending on the business at hand. Six years back, Binta had been a lady in twisted circumstances. She had been worsted after the breakup of her marriage to a drunkard Air Force pilot.

Before any reply could be offered to her rhetorical question, she continued in an alarming tone her tales of woe. "My business agent sent a telex to me yesterday, stating that all my corporate letters of credit opened in Citicorp Bank in New York have been cancelled. The no-credit transfer advice was telexed from First Bank of Nigeria. Citicorp has therefore foreclosed on all my credit until the funds come through from Lagos. Just this morning I called my lawyer in Lagos and was informed that all the import licenses under which my bank's letters of Credit were raised have been recalled. That being true, it means Binta Lilah and Company Nigeria Limited, will lose all the money expended in obtaining the licenses. This is certainly the beginning of the end for Binta Lilah and Company Nigeria. 'But, tell me, Dr. Richard! How would you explain such economic madness? It is suicidal for me as all my planned investments would in time perish unless an immediate solution can be found?" she summed up.

Dr. Richard Kemidare was presumably the most educated

member present in the group. Dr. Richard, however, got his honorary doctor of philosophy degree in humanities from an obscure downtown university in Little Rock, Arkansas. He delighted in the habit of demanding that everybody respectfully address him as "Doctor." Many uneasy scenes had he caused by not responding to contemporaries who refused to acknowledge him as "Doctor Richard."

Any occasion to display his intellectual acumen was always welcomed by Dr. Richard. But on this sad confusion-filled atmosphere, he thought it was wise to say as little as possible. His mind had, since the previous night, been devoted to getting logical economic interpretation from the red light emanating from Lagos. There was an urgent need to generate strategic alternatives and economic shelter. He had been unable to calculate the cost that the unfolding avalanche would bring. He needed time to further evaluate the consequences. Fear of the effects of the President's austerity measures had paralyzed his jolliness. The forum was, therefore, not a day to wantonly exhibit his expansive knowledge. Perhaps the less he said the better.

"Haba, Hadjia Binta! Whatever reason there is for the president's action would be made clearer to us all as soon as the plane touches down in Lagos. I'm, therefore, not speculating on the logic motivating such horrendous decisions. That is until I get to my home base and discuss with influential friends in government circles. Though I can add that our economics do not as a rule, make logical readings to the rational minds in the world finance markets. If you'd care to call my Victoria Island residence this time tomorrow, I may be in a more suitable position to explain in detail. For now, as they say, I reserve my comment and judgment."

Standing considerably shorter in the group was Chief I.K. Madu. He had graying templates and tortoise-shell Gucci glasses. He carried his rugged peasant gaiety with pride. There was a certain magnetic force in his Stride. He radiated an immense power and bullied people with his words. The grape vine stated that to look directly into his eyes was to know fear. The chief's extraordinary force of personality and presence showed in his every gesture. He looked younger than his fifty-five years and was impeccably dressed in colorfully designed traditional robe. His neck was decked with enough solid carat gold jewelry to sink a miniature boat. The chief moved around the world capitals sealing business deals. His multifaceted import business empire was built and operated on cut throat ruthlessness. His speech was filled with the jargon of combative war. His popular adage was" money and treachery will overcome all customs controls."

From his coastal base in Port Harcourt, he controlled a vast network system of smugglers of contraband goods. His import and export concern had grown to include a whole range of textile industries. His company also produced various types of fast moving consumer goods. The chief's huge industrial investments guaranteed that, come what may, his personal assets would continue to increase. By the next year, Chief Madu would be ready to celebrate his fortune reaching the fifty million naira mark during the Christmas festivities.

Expressing a conspiratorial grin to reveal confidence in his ability to overcome government imposed limitations, the chief cleared his throat. He let loose his scruffy voice as his own barely intelligible contribution to the short meeting.

"Na so de man wey de hurry too much de meet delay and stand still. Children of nowadays dem wan waka before them fit crawl. Look me, I can afford luxurious articles today. But I begin to trade more that forty years ago. I learned from my papa brother when I be just ten years. Na for fourteen years I serve my master before he allow me start my own business. But young men of today no de wan work at all. Na so, how e go get rich quick and become millionaire overnight. Dem wan big government contract to steal government dry. Anyway! This austerity wey government bring is correct. It means say money no plenty for government to award over inflated contracts. The ban for importation of leisure good go continue, only say the customs boys go de demand more naira. But the season will soon stop ... and I ..."

"Enough of your loudmouthed bullshit," blasted Dumba. He did not allow the chief to complete his vain - glorious preaching. Dumba's anger was seething. He had never liked Chief Madu whose extreme confidence in his naira power overwhelmed all the other members of the group. The chief's major fault was his arrogance and pride. He often boasted and eulogized his illegal smuggling achievements. A self-made robber baron, he learned early the jungle knowledge of pain and the ecstasy of struggle. He was a man with a barbaric and ferocious determination to win.

In the eyes of the club members, the chief was not considered the richest or the most influential. At least, the members believed Alhaji Abba Abdulmalik was more powerful with his high level contacts in the Lagos civilian administration. "De Alhaji," as Abba Abdulmalik was popularly called in the London business circle, had the means, it was generally believed, to manipulate his domestic and foreign financial worth to massive annual increases.

"We're all very much aware of how profitable your smuggling business is and that you have more naira than social sense. We are not here to be lectured, certainly not by a person who considers his store room more secure than the banks. We are gathered here to consider the drastic consequences that the policy of the men in government will have on our collective business empires."

Chief Madu felt the full blast from the sharp stab of the insult. He began to shake and vibrate for seconds bracing his brain to physically mow down Dumba. His massive body heaved rapidly up, showing great anger. He lost control of his senses, as he prepared to charge and pounce on Dumba. This was averted by the timely intervention of Dr. Richard.

"Please, Oga Chief..., Remember that we are not in Lagos but in London. We can't fight like cats. Be civil and kindly take it easy!

Dumba is only expressing the sentiments of us all. Most of us are caught in this economic crossfire called government austerity measure. This would mean a lot of personal disasters in the long term."

Just then, a vivacious voice came on air, announcing the immediate boarding of the Nigeria Airways flight WT801 to Lagos. This timely announcement hastened the dispersal of the group members. They were grateful to God that he had intervened in the total anarchy that would have ensued. The fight was thus put off.

The smuggler baron had to swallow his pride as each made haste to grab a vantage seat in the plane's first class section. However, in true African tradition, he swore a vendetta on Dumba that must be perfected with time. He cursed as he moved slowly toward the boarding gate.

Alhaji Abba Abdulmalik, Chairman of AAA International Limited, was quintessential and aristocratic. He waited calmly for the final call to board the plane before walking onto the departure gate. He had the gait of a prince of infinite promise and too much money. Abba was perfectly built like an Afro Hollywood star. His dazzling handsomeness mesmerized ladies of sophisticated glamour and high society. He walked tall with a trim athletic build. He was charcoal black. His traditional three piece attire "baba riga" matched his princely poise. His magnetic personality enveloped the opposite sex when he inches closer to toast them. His big ebony features complemented the pencil-thin moustache styled to grace his unique elegance. He was every inch a man at the pinnacle of his might and power. He was a great collector of classy cars and beautiful blondes in many capital cities of Europe.

Beneath his smooth exterior lay the active calculating and ruthless brainpower. This innate trait catapulted him from his nothingness as a peasant boy in Kano, to a position of affluence. He is the envy of all his contemporaries. Mother fate helped the AAA International group win multi- billion naira contracts from the 1980 national development plans. The gain from the government contracts enabled Abba to become rich. His fame spread to many of the world's business communities. He had connections to the 'High and Mighty' in Lagos, New York, Zurich, London, Hong Kong, Tokyo and Brussels to name just a few. He worked tirelessly to promote the popularity he enjoyed in these economic capital cities. He spent eight months in the year jet-setting the globe. His past time was spent with women and when not doing deals, he cooled off philandering. This also cost him considerable fortune.

Abba used his political influence to acquire creditable reputation in world capital cities as a leverage to increase his dollar worth. In three years, he spent over a hundred thousand dollars entertaining and buying acceptable credibility in New York and London. He sowed recklessly to gain authentic influence with foreign diplomats in the hope for million dollar returns. A consummate hometown booster, he used his Lagos power brokers' connections to advance his international business objectives. In the summer of 1983, he orchestrated a fool proof game plan to rule his world. The business empire vision was now beginning to shape into perfection. He was therefore dazed by the telex he received the previous night.

The telex message he read in his Sheraton suite in Brussels was straight to the point. His head ached as he read. He was shocked at the content. The unexpected seems to be unfolding. Something was amiss.

" Zero funds left in AAA's corporate bank accounts. Payment

to the suppliers of building materials had been insufficient. The payment voucher submitted to the junior minister for works could not be paid. There are no more funds to continue the projects for the new capital. It appeared the government was undergoing some sort of financial crisis. The daily unskilled workers on the project site had downed their tools in frustration. Considering alternative source of funds to continue with the Abuja projects".

Abba re-read the telex message and fumed. He cursed the childish impetus of the top politicians in the Lagos civilian administration.

A feeling of misery and fear came over him. He had been wary and terrified by the power drunk and incompetent politicians. They lusted and greedily wanted every penny for themselves. That is, regardless of whom they bled on their drive to self-gratification. This callousness would, in time backfire. They would dig everyone's financial graves. Throwing the telex sheet on the table, he mentally reasoned over the content. A trip to Lagos was in order. This will be executed when the business at hand was over and done with. He had great hope in the outcome of the business meeting at the European Economic Community headquarters in Brussels.

"Ratata, Ratata"   The tap on the door signified that his blonde companion, Maggie Lee had returned from her midnight movie in the hotel conference hall. She would labor hard to make him fully relaxed. Then he would enjoy a good night's sleep. Tomorrow, he prayed, would bring better luck. Life had always brought him luck. This season was not the time that fate should disappoint him. Yet, he struggled to rid his mind of the deepening fear. Some innate fore brooding made him fearful.

Mix expectation swelled his heart as he moved to open the door to the suite. Before turning the doorknob, he switched off the lights plunging the room into complete darkness.

"Hello, have you been missing me like I missed you? Come, come, I've been waiting all day and I intend for you to fill me up," Maggie's voice echoed.

Time meant nothing now as their lustful desires swelled up. They exploded in a passionate quiver that left them spent. They both relaxed in a profound sleep, leaving their worries several miles behind.

The next morning, Abba went to the meeting at the EEC

headquarters, feeling lucky. He prayed believing that if he could get a favorable financial commitment from the Europeans, all will be well. The initial capital expenditure outlay will give his company the needed foreign exchange to pay off short term debts. The Lloyd's Bank in London will restore his overdraft facility.

At the previous meeting in Brussels, the European partners had expressed optimism that all was alright. They trusted that there would be no further problems. The required sum of thirty million Dutch marks had been pooled from the various partners. This will be remitted to Abba's corporate account in Lloyd's Bank in Cheapside, London at the end of the meeting.

The meeting commenced with good expectations. He relaxed in hopeful anticipation of a favorable outcome.

Alas, this was not to be, from midway through the long conference, the German financier, Karl Schmidt, excused himself to make a long distance call. He returned minutes later physically shaken, his face displaying violent reddish coloring.

He took his time to regain his composure. He starred widely at the negotiating table. As if stung, the huge German threw up his big hands crying out in a guttural voice. "It is all hopeless. I've just received a call from an associate in the Dutchsland Embassy in Lagos. All import licenses issued to various companies have been cancelled. I tell you Nigeria is right now the worst place in the whole wide world for us to invest a dollar. I should have known better than think the economic boom would last forever!" he cried out. His face flashed with rage. He felt bitterly disappointed and betrayed.

At the outburst, confusion enveloped the other European partners. They all looked shocked, suddenly realizing their immense losses. The deal would have tripled the export earnings of their respective communities. Their plan for a brewing industry in Kaduna depended on the barley that would have come from their farm districts.

"Import licenses! Is this obtained easily? Yes or no?" asked the placid Frenchman, Henri Segel. His voice was cold and weak. He was annoyed in his ignorance of the issue.

"No," replied Karl Schmidt. He looked around the conference table, noting that the other members wanted further explanation.

"An import license basically is a permit issued by the Federal Ministry of Commerce in Lagos enabling the recipient to bring into

Nigerian Ports an allocated amount of foreign commodity or product. This enables local bank to open an irrevocable letter of credit authorized by the Central Bank of Nigeria for payments to the foreign exporting partners. An import license is, therefore, a normal instrument for the restriction of imports used by most sovereign nations to check dwindling foreign exchange resources. In a country without the manufacturing capacity to produce essential consumer goods, an import license becomes the quickest route to breed millionaires. Unscrupulous businessmen and corrupt officials use the import license allocation as a means of capital flight to buy up real estate in foreign nations. The control measure backfires when governmental checks and balances turn the system into a bureaucratic bondage for patriotic industrialists importing basic raw materials."

Furious at the disorderly manner in which Karl had disrupted the meeting, Abba blared in his baritone voice.

Karl was very nervous. He seemed overburdened with the weight on his mind. He took in a deep fresh breath and proceeded to explain his erratic behavior.

"There has been an extraordinary power given to the President in Lagos by the senators and honorable members of the House. The President has   used this power to impose austerity measures. This is to check Nigeria's dwindling foreign exchange reserves. The President's austerity measure has commenced in full force. Therefore, all unused valid import licenses issued have been recalled and cancelled. Ours, I suppose, is also included. This means we cannot carry out our commitments as earlier agreed".

He took a deep breath and continued. "With these austerity measures, I further assume that Nigeria cannot meet its foreign trade bills. A period of between twelve to fifteen months must pass before the foreign reserves can be restored to a healthy position. This will depend on how much fiscal prudence the government can maintain on the nation. I speak as a German. I lived through economic ravages in the years immediately after the Second World War. Thus, I can assure you that Nigeria is bound to go through economic hell. I mean the citizens of the country must undergo woeful suffering in the coming months. The sad truth is, I am not so sure if the present civilian administration can survive the next two months. We hope we will all live to see what happens".

In concluding, his long speech, Karl stood up in mournful

gesture. "Concerning our meeting of this day, it's best, that we let things lie for now. Of course, Alhaji Abba will keep in touch. We will monitor the situation from our various posts. When things improve, we shall schedule another meeting in Brussels. We pray that this may occur before the end of the year. However, I doubt the feasibility very much."

Karl's long speech was the saddest, Alhaji Abba has ever heard. It seemed that Karl had uncannily prophesized his unfolding woeful fate.

After this, the meeting came to an end. The Europeans wished him the best of luck. Each shook his hand and marched out. It was like they were sending their favorite manservant to answer a deadly intruder. They would await the outcome in their comfort. These tycoons were immune from the financial pitfalls slated for Abba.

Abba hurriedly returned to his hotel suite, furious. He was engulfed in a passion of shamed indignation and resentment. With a twitching lip, he thought on his need to return to London. From there, he would go back to Lagos. He decided to let Maggie stay two more days in Brussels. To suppress her grief and anguish, he wrote out a check for ten thousand pounds sterling. He did this and prayed that his bank manager would be kind enough to honor it.

In his hurry to depart, he left behind a fully signed check booklet. This was a fatal mistake. It would translate to financial suicide and be his greatest undoing.

Five hours after leaving Maggie, Abba finally disembarked from the Aer Lingus plane at the Heathrow Airport. He took a cursory glance at his wristwatch. He found he had barely two hours to board the 10 o'clock night flight to Lagos. He reckoned it was enough time to make a brief stop at his Knightsbridge apartment before racing back to Heathrow airport.

Tonight, he had planned not to arrive early as usual at the check-in counter. He wanted to avoid the other members of the 'Naira Club'. He did not want to mingle or converse with the aggressive members of the group. They would have gotten hint of the economic pitfalls ahead. He figured correctly they would all be locked in their own personal woes. That in their nervousness, each would be most intolerant of the need of others. All were selfish to the bone except Dumba. He respected and would likely discuss some plans of action with him. The man has always fascinated him.

This man had lived in London for over twenty years. He had arrived in London during the Nigerian/Biafran civil war which lasted for twenty months. Dumba had done very well for himself. He made his millions as a real estate developer in East London.

Five years ago, Dumba's bank associates in the city of London had helped Abba in exchanging at very competitive rates the bundle of naira notes he had smuggled into London from Kano. The associates had further reassured him that they were always willing to participate in future deals that other reputable bankers would have considered as unscrupulous and would not touch. The rigid British banking regulations helped bond them together. Over the years, the British bankers became lifesavers to various members of the Naira Club. They helped them in their various dubious trafficking of the naira for exchange into the British currency. Gradually, they had become good friends.

Abba continued his march towards Boarding Gate No. 36. He made a mental note to schedule an appointment with Dumba before he got off at the Kano International Airport.

CHAPTER FOUR

"Alhaji Abba, welcome on board flight WT801 to Lagos. Hope you'll have a very pleasant trip," chanted the hostess as he strolled into the first class cabin making directly for his allocated seat.

As he fastened his seat belt, he noticed the beautifully dressed lady occupant of the nearest seat. She smiled nervously reciprocating his wide grin.

At her smile, his melancholy seemed to evaporate. His body ached in gluttonous anticipation for the female flesh. The lusting for this regal lady became paramount on his mind. She was bedecked with gold jewelry, the cost of which seemed considerable. Their worth in pounds sterling was staggering. He looked further across to catch a glimpse of her face but she was staring out through the window.

"De Alhaji! How are you?" rang out a shrill voice from the front seat on his extreme left. Turning, he noticed Binta sitting next to the party pirate chief.

"Hello Oga Sir! Where've you been? 1 looked you up in New York and left word hoping to have heard from you."

"Hello, Hadjia Binta. I flew in from Brussels in the last two hours. 1 had intended to call you in New York, but nothing ever works out as planned. Business problems crop up to carry one away from friends."

"You've been neglecting me since our last picnic at the Kano Holiday Resort," continued Binta. She stood upright in order to adjust her silk skirt.

"I wonder why you seem to be running away from me."

"Sorry, my dear. I'll make up for the neglect once I've extinguished the fire that is currently burning. You know tyrannies of the urgent."

"I see, Abba! I know, you're not seriously affected. At least not someone as mighty as you. But I presume I'll be in real mess on account of these austerity measures. I'm thinking of coming over to your Katchia residence next Saturday. Would you be free to see me? I'm rather anxious."

"I suppose I can make out time to see you, but it's not a promise. The truth is the austerity blitz has certainly disorganized my schedule."

"Well, I can understand, but you must not worry too much. After all, you have very important connections. I know that you are also very close to the political party in government."

"Yeah, everybody keeps telling me that. Only I'm not sure myself. At least, I'm not so sure these days. Whatever happens, we shall meet either in Kaduna or Lagos. Let us hope for the best and take good care of yourself."

"Oh! Thanks. You know I always take ample care of myself, body and soul. Bye for now."

Soon they were airborne. The seat belt signal flashed on. Within fifty seconds the normal champagne for the first class cabin was prepared by the hostesses to be served to the expectant passengers. As the stewardess reached Abba's seat, he turned to the lady beside him.

"May I order something extra to go with the wine?" He genially jived, showing affectionate amusement.

A momentary wink seemed to escape her. "I think I'll wait until I've eaten. You see, I'm not used to alcohol."

"Perhaps some milder drink will help soothe your spirit," he cheerfully recommended. The lady slightly nodded in passive agreement.

She glanced at the window and buried her attention, on a current issue of the Time Magazine, spread open to conceal her countenance. A gut feeling shot through him but he held himself in check. Give the lady time, he reasoned. All good things need time in which to grow. Besides, he had learned to play skillfully on the emotions of beautiful women. He had mastered the craft of soliciting female companionship in his four years of globe-trotting.

The trick was to open a line of communication on an interesting subject matter with the quarry as soon as the plane takes off. Then keep the pressure on until the aircraft landed at its destination.

As usual, his chauffeur would be on hand to receive him at the airport in one of his vintage care. Of course, he will help the lady through the tedious customs and immigration section. She will be immensely pleased, thereby bestowing her loving affection.

The trick always worked, but this time he doubted if he would have the time to spare. No harm in being friendly, he reasoned at least for now. Lifting his glass of the clear sparkling wine, he toasted to the lady for a safe landing.

She nodded, and a dimple lighted her left cheek, "I pray for an uneventful trip. I'm always afraid of flying."

Time tickled away while he savored his wine. He thought of what to say. "Will you be stopping over in Kano, or are you heading straight to Lagos?" he mumbled. Excited by the inviting smile of the lady, he proceeded to introduce himself by saying, "My name is Alhaji Abba Abdulmalik. I'm an international businessman. That is, I make my home and offices in the various capitals of the world: Rio de Janerio; Amsterdam; Paris; New York; Geneva; and, most important of all, London."

The lady laughed softly out loud, revealing an even set of strong white teeth. "You Alhaji's are always too much and come on ever too strong. My name is Lola Backays. I'm studying Law at Oxford, England."

The name 'Backays' struck a familiar chord in his ears. Time stood still as he spent time in deep thought. He could dimly recognize the resemblance Lola had with the famous Liberian-born, Lagos-based shipping magnate, now a naturalized Nigerian. He recalled Lateef Isaq's tale of the aged frugal financier in the Lagos colony in the early forties. That was forty years ago.

Abba distinctly recalled the three times he had met with the old man. Papa Backays would soon reach his centenary anniversary, as the newspapers reported.

He had met with the frugal old man, Backays, in 1980, while negotiating to buy four ships for AAA International and his Canadian business partners. The deal began with the old man's attorney, Bulus Musa, hinted on an early handover once the sales price was mutually agreed upon. Trouble started when the Canadian associates flew down to Lagos with the professional crew to inspect the ships. It was then discovered, to their horror, that the ships lacked every form of the standard navigational equipment required by international maritime law for Trans-Atlantic container ships. The Canadian team was further angered by the attorney. He cleverly negotiated and overstated the agreed price for the ships. If they had signed in a hurry, the deal would have become a monumental rip-off. The Canadian partners promptly withdrew, making it impossible for AAA International to raise the needed funds in order to pursue the plan of establishing a freight line. Later on, Bulus had called Abba to express sympathy on the old man's behalf. "Business is Business, and the profit motive dominates," Bulus lectured and quoted. Abba, of course, was quick to agree with the logic. At the end of the meeting, he retained Bulus's services when it suited his corporate ambitions. Bulus, the wizard lawyer always delivered. He lived a lifestyle of the rich and famous. His corporate clients like jackals preyed on their unsuspecting customers stealing millions. Bulus with guile and avarice stalk these corporate money bags. 'The love of money is the root of all evil,' Abba whistled and concluded his long flashback.

"Lola Backays," he spelled out in amusement. "Well, Lola, here is my card. Should you ever get bored anytime, anyplace, and need a change of scenery. Then call me at any of these numbers. Usually, I've the right idea on cheering up gloomy souls. I've been known to arrange weekend parties for significant friends at such faraway places as Tokyo at a moments' notice. You see, I've this personal philosophy of enjoying life here knowing that someday death would come to take me away to God knows where. If ever you have the need, either you or your friends, for momentary fantasies, I shall be more than happy to avail you to a little of my hospitalities. All expenses shall be borne by AAA International Limited. And, of course, there is no catch at all. Just that you and other fun -loving people get together to enjoy mutual relaxations."

Eyes aglow, Lola replied, "You Alhajis are forever too boastful. Only Allah knows how you come by your money. My grandfather says maybe you all have oil wells in your gardens."

"That is a secret I can't wait to share with you. Just give me a ring, preferably when next you come to London. I maintain a posh apartment in Knightsbridge. It is a two minute walk from the famous Harrods."

"Thanks for the wonderful offer. My Iranian friends at

Oxford believe only Arabian Sheiks could make such lavish offers. I shall, of course, think seriously about it and will keep your card handy for the proverbial rainy day," Lola enthused.

"Be my guest any day, any time. I shall be most honored," exclaimed Abba, happily aware that the ball has been set rolling. It is only a question of time, and Lola would be counted as one of his girls. He therefore took time to think about the task at hand.

Over the white wine, delicious vegetable and steak dish, he slipped back to his sorrows. He forced his thought to withdraw from Lola. His mind shifted back to Triple A's present predicament.

He knew he had only himself to blame. It was not as if he was not warned. His investment banker, Tim Gallaway, at the Manufacturers Hanover Trust, Wall Street branch office, had informed him of the impending economic disaster almost fourteen months earlier. Thinking back to the never-too-happy memory, he could recollect the force of his own argument. He had reasoned that the civilian administration in Lagos consisting of many men from his own ethnic group would enable him to hear first-hand the news of any impending dangers. They were ten powerful office holders. They had all grown together in Kano. Their loyalty to each other had remained over the years. A sort of old boy's network. All for one, and one for all. They could never betray him so he thought, being fully aware of the massive risk he took on their behalf. They owed it to him to inform him of any anticipated change in economic policy. This was because, he had lavishly funded their political campaigns.

Abba recollected calling from his Central Park apartment in New York to Alhaji Dogon Talata, the junior Minister for Industrial Development. They grew up together and were almost like blood cousins. In 1950, he went to Lagos to learn textile trade, Talata moved to Zaria to further his education up to the University level. He majored in Islamic law and secured a job in Kano after graduation. Mother luck smiled on him, promoting him to a powerful position as a confidant to the political rulers of the realm in Lagos.

He had asked Talata if the Federal Government was having trouble paying its outstanding foreign trade credit. The junior minister had sworn that he was being fed with rumors and that there was absolutely no basis for such thoughts.

"There is absolutely nothing to be afraid of. The country's

relationship with its OPEC members is cordial enough, and the price for crude petroleum is still at an all-time high. Furthermore, many foreign multi-national corporations were lobbying to open up shops in Lagos. The future is very rosy indeed," Talata concluded. Time had lapsed. His false calm in his ignorance of the macroeconomic force at work against his nation was tragic. It was a very expensive error.

Abba hung up. He became convinced that all was fine. Talata's strong pronouncement encouraged him. Coming from a highly placed and trusted friend, he allayed his fears. The next day, he had walked into Tim Gallaway's office on Wall Street, raining abuses on the tiny banker. He further accused Gallaway of spreading malicious C.I.A lies about his cherished Nigeria. So angry was he that he requested Tim to sell off his-not-so inconsiderable investment portfolio consisting of blue chipped corporate shares and municipal bonds. The proceeds he requested should be forwarded to his Lloyd Bank account in London.

Gallaway had meekly taken the insults from the infuriated Abba, with the usual calmness of cool-headed banker. He implored him to at least leave two hundred thousand dollars behind. Such nest eggs could increase with time. It would at the same time, help spread the risk of Abba's portfolio.

He had agreed with the sensible suggestion and left the bank ordering Gallaway to withdraw from passing damaging C.I.A. information about Nigeria, the giant of Africa.

Gallaway bade him good-bye, and told him to feel free to call on him when the bubble burst, as surely it must. Less than ten months, and the bubble did burst beyond all expectations. Of course, Gallaway was right. Talata was terribly inaccurate. A fatal mistake had been made. The end result might well ruin Abba's life plans. His corporate schemes and fantasy.

Tracing his life history, he reasoned that he had grown to become over pampered, too soft. Whatever happened to the courageous young boy of six with the jungle sense of survival and the determination to keep his body fed? He flashed back mentally. The young Abba had clawed for food. He begged as one of the local orphans in the ancient city of Kano.

Cloud of sad heaviness enveloped him, as he shuffled through the memory lane of his "rag to riches" history.

He sat still lost in a painful remembrance of his past as an

"Almajiri" orphan boy roaming about the streets, gathering just enough to keep alive until the next day. It seemed like ages ago but it was true. He had crossed many rivers in his life and had become a legend in his own community. Time brought everything, he surmised. The time pendulum seemed to be reversing its trend. It was as if an invisible hand was pulling him back into a shameful end.

Just as he was lapsing deeper into the dream of his youth, the captain's voice broke the sorrowful silence. He announced the plane would land at Kano airport within thirty minutes. The seat belts were to be fastened and the no smoking sign to be obeyed.

As the plane taxied toward the disembarking ramp, Abba looked at his Rolex President wristwatch to check the time.

"I noticed today is the 13th,"he whispered to Lola Backays who looked up startled. "Do you believe in superstitions as most females do"? He asked.

"Well," Lola started, "I have not exactly given it real thought. But my grandfather, the shipping magnate, never launches new ships on the 13th.His high-rise corporate headquarters doesn't have a 13th floor. He said the number brings bad omen. And as long as he's around, his wishes on such issues would be honored. The fear of the number 13 is called triskaidekaphobia. Some research is being conducted to prove the phobia as an irrelevant superstition. For now, nobody is sure of the facts."

"Yes, when the scientific facts are fully documented, we will then be in a position to know, "concluded Abba.

At this time, the plane had come to a complete standstill. He excused himself from Lola and wished he had no pressing problems. He would have wanted to go down to Lagos to entertain her in his L 'Hotel Eko Meridian suite. "Tough luck," he muttered to himself and promised to make further contact with Lola when next he visited Oxford. By then, he hoped his financial problems would have been straightened out.

Before getting down from the plane, he walked over to Dumba's seat and after the initial salutation, requested that they meet at the Hotel Eko Le Meriden before the end of the month.

The hot blast of desert air reminded him that he was indeed in Kano city. Kano is the ancient cosmopolitan terminal on the trans-Saharan trade route in the medieval days when King William the Conqueror ruled England. Its mid-day temperature ranged between

75-120 degrees, the months of March through July were the hottest in Kano. The extreme cold periods are the months of December and January. Five years ago, it was reported that Kano recorded a lower temperature than London on Christmas day. Kano, with its modern airport, had become an economic nerve center. The city is described in superlatives and its economic future mattered to the outside world.

At the disembarkation ramp stood Haruna, his chauffeur. He anxiously awaited the return of his master. Next to the chauffeur was the senior customs official, Mr. James Abbot. He panted emotionally, full of expectation. It was Abbot's duty to ensure that Abba's luggage was exempted from the normal search conducted by the customs. Abbot would shield his baggage from the hungry eyes of his customs colleagues.

"Good morning, sir, it's a good thing I was still in the office when your messenger brought the news that you were returning to Kano today," exclaimed Mr. Abbot, excitedly. "Hope you had a profitable trip," he continued.

"Ran kai dede, Alhaji," saluted Haruna, the driver, as his rich master approached.

"Yaa ya, Haruna, I hope everybody is fine," replied Abba.

Turning to Mr. Abbot, he handed over the ticket slips with an instruction that his suitcases be delivered to his residence. Abbot and the rest of the men would be adequately compensated.

"Yes, sir. It will be there in about two hours," replied Abbot in a subservient tone.

It often amazed Abba, the way the mind of the customs officials on duty worked. Give any officer some large sum of naira and his eyes would be shut to whatever amount of contraband you imported. It does not even matter how high in rank the officer is, and there seems to be an ongoing competition between the customs hierarchy to accumulate illegal payoff. This entrenched attitude has resulted in the likes of Chief I.K. Madu who boasts of his ability to smuggle any contraband into Nigeria. The fact that the chief had recently been licensed to operate commercial jetties where foreign ships could discharge its container only helped to make Madu's activities more criminally rewarding.

It seemed the chief's profitable trade would always continue to flourish for as long as he greased the palm of the customs officials. And so much for the corrupt public servants, the very office that had given them the platform to serve their nation loyally was now being used as an avenue to acquire their own naira power. The corruption brought an incalculable loss to the taxpayers.

Someday with the use of the almighty silicon chips and advanced computers, it may become possible for the government to calculate to the last naira how much revenue is lost due to the activities of the likes of James Abbot. But until that day, Abba reckoned, it was a wise decision to enjoy the available services received from Abbot and his colleagues.

Thanks all the more to Mr. Abbot, the delay at the Kano airport was minimal. He reached his comfortable Lamido Crescent home within thirty minutes of stepping off the plane from London.

The design and building of the twin bungalow had been accomplished by an Italian construction firm based in Kano. The furnishing and other interior decorations from the famous Giovanni collection had been flown in from Milan.

The most remarkable architectural design displayed in the vast compound was the special arcade unit that housed the remarkable world class automobiles that Abba had acquired over the years.

Cars and women were the marked symbol of his machismo. Notable among his women folk were his dozen blondes. They were specially chosen from different capital cities in Europe and the American continents. The blondes were usually present at his parties for highly influential friends with political clout. He used them as a bait to achieve business objectives.

His collection of cars included a 1965 Jaguar E type model, a Porsche929, a 500SEL Mercedes coupe, a 1982 model of Lotus Excel and the king of them all, the latest model of the Silver Spirit Rolls Royce. His collection was the most envied fleet owned by one individual in the city of Kano

Not displayed in the arcade was the Mercedes-Benz 450SE Aerodynamic 1982 model. It was currently in use. The other superbly engineered Japanese cars were parked at his Industrial Estate. He was therefore extremely popular in Kano as a successful international playboy. As a man of huge resources and extremely blessed by Allah, his popularity was such that, should he decide to run for political office, his victory would be certain.

The sky was pale, like polished silver as he walked around the arcade, happy at the evidence of old successes. He wondered what Mother Fate had in store for his future. When he was alone again, the sorrow of the trouble that lay ahead enveloped him. Suddenly, the pleasure he got viewing the parked vehicles evaporated. He became aware of the subtle invading symptoms of the malaria fever. He was accustomed to being attacked by the sickness intermittently whenever he was in the city of Kano.

His valet opened the white paneled door revealing Imam Dan Fulani, the astrologer and spiritual guru. The white-haired old man had deep clefts in his cheeks where dimples once had been. He came into the hall and greeted Abba with a grief stricken face. He tried to hide the agitation in his spirit.

"We've been waiting for you," he said frigidly in Hausa dialect, muttering prayers in Arabic undertones.

"This bad omen I have been telling you about is just about to have its physical manifestation. You're to be very careful. Those weird women must be dropped before they cause your downfall."

"Yes, I understand. I have never doubted your wisdom, although Allah's will shall prevail," Abba concurred.

"You must pray and fast. I've since gathered ten other imams together. We must pray and fast earnestly for all your intentions. We shall continue to do this until the omens cease and go away. I am very much afraid," the old man prophesized. His tone suggestive of concealed anger.

Apprehensive about the revelations of the guru, he opened his briefcase and gave out a bundle of ten naira notes to the sage.

"You must book a flight to Mecca. Take ten imams with you. You're to do all in your power to ensure we don't perish with the bad wind. In the afternoon, I'll set out for Kaduna, and I'll want some good-luck talisman. Can you let me have them before I leave?" he implored with voice trembling.

"I know," responded the Imam. "In fact, I've prepared all necessary amulets with which to fight the evil spirits and the tough time ahead. You will have them before you leave."

"Thank you Imam. I'll leave word with my wife to give you more money when you need it. Just so long as you keep praying for me,"

"Have hope still that Allah, the merciful, will never forget the faithful in difficult times," prayed Imam Fulani in a brighter tone.

With a strange wave of confidence, Abba began to feel better. He made a vow to at least pray five times daily until the trouble was over.

Leaving the Imam in contemplation and praying stance, he strolled over to the guest chalet, whereas instructed, John Chibuko, the accountant, was waiting. From him, he would learn of new developments. He would map out his strategies and move on to Kaduna to commence the battle for AAA's corporate survival.

CHAPTER FIVE

Chibuko's eyes were sunken, with lines cut deeply into his puffy face. He stood up with his shoulder stooped as his boss entered the guest chalet. Although the two men were the same age, the comparison between them stopped short at that. While Abba was elegant in presence, Chibuko was too plain and modest. He did not participate in the glamorous erotic fantasy of the starlets that Abba chased round the world.

The only star quality possessed by Chibuko was his honest disposition. He was AAA's corporate accountant and meticulously guarded Abba's money as though they were his own. Chibuko was not just a qualified accountant as he was designated. He had been Abba's co-worker at the United African Company's Kano branch before the Nigerian Civil War in 1966. Both had worked in the same department and became close friends during a sales training course they attended at the Lagos corporate headquarters in 1962. Together they had dreamt of accumulating great wealth by working hard and getting promotions along the corporate ladder of success.

The civil war in the country had prompted Chibuko to abandon his position in the company. He fled to his home village and only returned to Kano at the end of the war.

By this time, Abba had resigned from United African Company. He had set up the nucleus trading firm that grew to become AAA International, Limited. At a chance meeting at the local post office, he had invited Chibuko back to his headquarters. Subsequently, the unemployed Chibuko became an accountant with the Abba's company.

"Good morning, Alhaji," saluted Chibuko as Abba sat on the chair next to the bed. "Did you have a pleasant trip?"

"Your telex was very distressing," he replied, beckoning Chibuko to sit down. "Tell me exactly what happened."

"Well, it's a long story. I'm seriously praying you could help bring these parasite politicians to their senses," Chibuko's voice trembled with emotion.

"I take it you'll be ready for us to leave for Abuja through Kaduna as soon as it is daylight. Right now, it's about 4 o'clock in the morning, and I must know the full story before sunrise. I think I have an idea what the problems are and what solutions we may require. But, still, I want your own side of the story."

"You're right. I doubt if I can have the strength to leave with you at sunrise. You see, I've not had enough sleep and without adequate rest, I can't function effectively." Chibuko paused for a while and coughed to clear his throat before continuing his litany of woes.

"The trouble started with the default on the extra money, or rather kick back. The Director of works had demanded more money on the last payment AAA received on the schedule F of the project contract agreement. The initial agreed kick back sum was to be five percent of the overall amount received. But the director demanded ten percent, stating that he had overlooked certain aspects of the re-engineered blue print in the building phase. In reality, this error is basically a minor difference in design; the correction of which is no big deal. I prayed for time, explaining to him you'll come to the site on time to hear and honor his demands. Time went by, and you didn't come to see him. He became furious and ganged up with the Area Administrator to threaten me at the project site."

The trouble came to a head ten days ago when I presented our bills for payment on the schedule "G" of the project and the Area Administrator bluntly informed me there was no funds with which to pay AAA. I asked to know why this had to be .I was told that it had to do with the Director of works request for ten percent."

"The fools! What right did they have to act so? Ingrates, why must they try to run AAA down? "Abba lamented.

"Allah will surely roast them in hell for their small mindedness. Bastards, all of them," he roared.

"Had I known this was the sort of trouble I was getting AAA into, I would have tried to bargain further with the Director of works. But as you know, we've been going through cash flow shortages since the battery manufacturing section of AAA closed down."

"Yes, I know it's a shame, I've not been able to get new replacement for the two Spanish engineers. I don't want to bring other expatriate engineers who would further rip off the operation like Juan and Antonio Lopez. For now, the battery factory must remain closed even though AAA is desperate for the extra funds"

"You're right. Of what use is it if a dishonest employee uses trusted position to liquidate one's holdings? Better the factory remains closed for the short term. I suppose it'll be best for AAA to find other means of raising cash for its construction project and other investment programs. "

"How is the situation with our banker?" interjected Abba. "Do we have enough cash to meet immediate overheads?"

"Our overdraft with Kano Cooperative Bank is seriously overextended above five figures. The Manager is very anxious and insistent that we pay some money before the next bank audit. It appears one of the bank directors is mad at you," Chibuko stated.

"Yes, I should have known that son of a bitch would try to squeeze me when he got back to town. I believe you know Hassan, the executive director. I threw him out of a dinner party in my London apartment for his drunken and disorderly behavior. This, of course, is his way of getting his sworn revenge."

"In that case, our position seems threatened from all angles. I wish we had early warning of the government's fiscal austerity. Your cousin should have warned us. Then maybe we should have abandoned the project months earlier, taken our money and ran."

Letting the thought of not being warned drift, Abba continued on a different tone.

"The times are tough, and everything requires thinking through to make smart decisions. It's a pity we had to mortgage all my four buildings to finance my Sharada Industrial office complex. My remaining debt-free property at the present is my home and the fleet of cars. Of course, I cannot sell my cars to raise money. The thought of doing so would kill me. Besides, not many people in this part of the world appreciate the exotic value of vintage automobiles. Assuming I can find a buyer, the entire fleet can only fetch below one fifth of its original value. The truth is, I've never faced financial crisis of this magnitude before. Come to think of it, with AAA's track record of success, we should never have had to face these obstacles. History, however, teaches that the success of all great men has always been as a result of overcoming seemingly insurmountable obstacles. Andrew Jackson had no university education and no exceptional advantage but used his setbacks as power generators to eventually win the United States presidency."

"I have read his biography so I know"

In a determined poise and staring fully into the eyes of Chibuko, Abba continued; "I'll need you to accompany me to Abuja. We'll leave in approximately two hours and make a stopover at my Kaduna home. There, I'll contact some financier friend with ideas to raise some capital."

"You forgot, I intend to sleep as I'm totally exhausted. I will of course, meet you in Kaduna in time to continue with you to Abuja."

Human beings would always relax in times of trouble except when their own house is on fire, Abba thought to himself. Aloud he replied, "Why sure, you certainly deserve to rest your old bones. You've been working too hard. Say we'll meet in Kaduna by tomorrow morning."

Pleased, Chibuko grinned. "Thanks, the sleep would certainly refresh my tired brain. I'll arrive at Kaduna in time so as not to disturb your schedule."

"And not to worry. I'm hopeful to find the means to reverse this cash flow scarcity. All things being equal, I should be able to have good news in Kaduna," exulted Abba, concluding the meeting.

CHAPTER SIX

The city of Kaduna is of great historical relevance in the politics of Nigeria. Starting as the power base of the British Northern Protectorate, the City of Crocodiles has grown into a place where all Nigerian rulers of the previous decades had spent their time. Thus, a statistical list of home owners in the exclusive residential quarter of the city would seem like viewing the current issue of Nigeria's "Who's Who." Kaduna is home both to the powerful and the struggling man. It is like Harlem and Brixton existing on the same landscape with Golders Green. The city was inhabited by Oxford educated millionaires and unemployed illiterates, both sharing the same suburbs. Contrasts and contradictions appear everywhere, reminding everyone that Nigeria moves to the rhythm of petro-money gushing from plentiful oil wells. Nigeria, reputed as black Africa's wealthiest nation, boasts of reasonable gross and razzmatazz.

Nigeria once the world's sixth largest exporter of crude oil, about half of which was bought by the United States. Only Saudi Arabia sells more oil to the United States of America. Nigeria's income from oil amounts to billions of dollars. Then, almost overnight the yearly income peaked to $9 billion. 1975, Nigeria had the prospect of a 5 billion dollar annual surplus. Suddenly the government drew up a 4 billion dollar development plan for the year 1975-1980, the most ambitious ever underwritten by a black African government. For Nigerians, no dream was too distant, no vision too expensive. Almost every Nigerian adult participated with extra-ordinary zeal to transform the ancient heterogeneous society into a modern, unified state. With huge national check book balance, capable and incompetent businessmen sprung up. Many emergency contractors collected millions of dollars in illegal kickbacks on massive projects. New national projects were planned. They included a new federal capital in Abuja, seven new universities, thirteen new television stations, three new international airports, among others. The minimum wage was doubled. The civil servants were granted an automatic pay raise of sixty percent back dated and tax-free for ten months. The independent trade unions equally got substantial pay increases. Everyone had a slice of the action. The national cake was seemingly equally divided amongst the ethnic groups.

Soldiers, politicians, businessmen and civil servants grew abundantly rich on mega salaries. Everyone had a price at which they could be bought. Foreign embassies and diplomats scrambled in Lagos. Multi-national corporations elbowed one another for influence, all painfully aware of the dangers ahead. They all knew that Nigeria was trying to go too far too fast. European statesmen knew with time, she would pay the price of depending on one commodity for its massive economic developments. The blessing of the oil would inevitably provide many inescapable curses. An exodus from the rural to the urban areas resulted in the neglect of the farms. This forced the once self-sufficient agrarian nation to import food at great cost. Therefore traumatic shock waves hit the population when the government discovered that demand for its oil had fallen below expectations. Government commitments to on-going projects clocked four times the available funds. The climax for Nigeria came when the United States fiscal deficit reached a reckless height. This prompted the Federal Reserve's Chairman, Volcker, to clamp down on global money growth, thereby inducing the Great Debt Crisis. The world-wide situation was bleak indeed and would have been disastrous except for Volcker's short term solution to defaulting sovereign borrowers. Either that or the nine leading United States banks would be forced into bankruptcy. The Mexican government, a participant, had to announce that it would not be making any further payments on its $90 billion in foreign debt. This act would, if left unchecked, precipitate a world financial crisis of the first order.

Kaduna's urban segregation was pitiful. The plight of the poor paralleled that of residents in "The Other Britain". A term used by London politicians to refer to urban deprivation in such cities as Port Talbort, Wales or Liverpool. The decline in living standard in these cities had been further accelerated by Prime Minister Thatcher restraint on government spending.

The Kaduna blue collar workers employed in the textile factories as machine operators were the first to feel the bite of the government' austerity measures. The daily paid laborers had only their jobs at the textile mills to keep their body and soul together. Lacking secondary education, they earned as little as five naira a day. Their lives were pretty dull and without much hope of future advancement. The expatriate management of the textile mills had an on-going war with the Ministry of Industries over the need to use local raw materials as substitutes for imported ones.

The never-ending battle for importation of raw materials with the Federal Ministry of Industries in Lagos brought serious restrictions on the growth of the privately owned mills. Industrial operations became hamstrung. The industrial effectiveness crippled under a formidable, all-embracing system of import license and control tightly wrapped in red tape. The feud between management and the control authorities became a classic example of people made corrupt in their bid to circumvent government controls.

The owners of the textile mills with their frustration and tolerance stretched to the limit needed very little excuse to embark on massive layoff of their factory operatives. On hearing of the government austerity measures, the factory laid off three thousand workers. The lack of any organized trade union denied the machine operators a platform upon which to press for betterment of their situation. They bore the pains of their retrenchment stoically. As each laid off operative retired to his nearby shanty dwelling in Kaduna South, the weak ones resorted to the habit of either staying drunk on the local brew of gin. While others became con men. Some would graduate to become dare-devil armed robbers. They would continue in this armed trade until caught and publicly executed. They further exhibit the jungle law of modern African society.

In the minds of the retrenched workers, there was abundant wealth in circulation, but far out of the common man's reach. The local musician's voice could be heard proclaiming "The Austerity in Air," as an evil force. It was conjured by the moneybags to wipe off the poor from the face of Kaduna soil. Soon the vibrant lyrics became a popular anthem amongst the inhabitants young and old. Everyone learned it by heart.

The devil is known to find shady work for idle hands, and so the local police station became busier with cases of petty crimes. The young and jobless school drop outs formed mobs. They vandalized luxury cars that came into their rundown neighborhood. They questioned how some people could afford opulent cars when most could scarcely afford two meals each day. Such a display of affluence in the midst of poverty had always been an enigma to them. Tempers were often at a boiling point and needed very little to ignite the time bomb.   One afternoon in the month of June, a young man drove his Mercedes Benz coupe' 1982 model into the neighborhood. The car stalled and refused to start. When the young man asked for help from the locals, they rained abuses on him. "Na dem chop all our money. Thief! Thief! Na dem chop all government money" became the battle song. Their anger was further fueled by Kazeem, the factory foreman, who had been laid off that very day. Kazeem was terribly bitter about his dismissal and the reasoning behind it.

In a fit of annoyance, he decided to vent his anger by leading the mob to brutalize the rich young man. Terrified at the mob's onslaught, the man ran for his dear life, abandoning his expensive car which was damaged beyond repair by the mob.

The victim went to the police and insisted on pressing charges. The police officer, Inspector Bello, bluntly informed him that the station's cell was filled with hungry looking characters. He pleaded with the man to retrieve his car and have his insurance company take care of the damages. Allah should be thanked for sparing your life. He further explained that the poor bastards were openly happy to be locked up in the overflowing police guardroom. That way, they reckoned to be fed by the government. Free meals twice a day and no rents to their greedy and overfed landlords.

The police inspector could reason with the angry mobs because they were of the same tribe and stock. With his monthly salary, Bello could still not reasonably feed his household of seven kids. His wife, he painfully remembered, had to moonlight at the Funky Costain Club two nights a week. This was to supplement the feeding allowance she received from Bello's meager salary. At first Bello had raved on the immorality of the whole business. He had tried to persuade her, but the woman was hell-bent on having her children well fed. Either he conceded to her nocturnal past-time or she would pack her belongings and move back to her home village.

There she would marry a village farmer. Life was indeed rough on Bello, especially when he remembered that his wife had become a pub crawler so that his seven children would have three meals daily. Countless times, Inspector Bello dreamt of a miracle that would take him away from his cursed inability to provide enough for his family. But somehow, the miracle failed to take place.

Inspector Bello had been with the police force for twenty-five years. He joined when life at the family farm became intolerable. As a young man, the city lured him away from the farm, and his career in the force was made possible by his uncle, Sergeant Peter Bello.

Now, after nearly thirty years in the police force, Bello had come to realize that being an inspector was not an answer to his poverty. Some of his mates who also did not have formal education had been promoted on the basis of godfathers. One of the beneficiaries of such connections, Bawa, was a top brass at the police headquarters in Lagos. He was very smart. A smooth operator. He worked hard to perfect his con schemes.

"Always use your Number six," officer Bawa chided Bello once when they worked together at the Kaduna police post. On further inquiry of what "Number six" meant, Bawa had explained."Number six "is the survival mechanism. A sort of sixth sense, which enables the cat find its way out of tricky situations. It is this "Number six" that top politicians, top army brass, top criminals, and also every Nigerian businessman uses. To be successful, one must use his "Number six" always. It saves one from ending up bankrupt, dead, or in a mental institution, deranged and beyond salvation till kingdom come.

Bawa further philosophized, "Me, I always use my Number six, and very soon, I go start to use my number seven."

Number six had worked for Bawa, but Bello did not have the knack for using this sixth sense. Bello believed that his inability to use this mysterious sense was the reason why life had been so unrewarding, unexciting, dull and hopeless. Lacking courage, he often assumed that his life was beyond salvation.

Contemplating the young man's ordeal with his beaten up face brought back bitter memories of the successful Bawa. Such imagination always sprang up in Bello twinges of jealousy. He knew envy existed in him, but he had never come to terms with. He was still lost in this deep melancholy when Martin Oban, the Mass

Communication graduate completing his National Youth Service at Kaduna South Police Station, walked up to his desk.

"Oga, what happened that you look so sad?" He asked innocently.

"Ah! Nothing, my dear young man, I was just feeling a bit tired. "How about the inmates at the Corpers' Delight?"

The 'Corpers' Delight" is the hostel and a hide-out of the members of the National Youth Service corps serving in Kaduna South.

"Wetin dey happen at Corpers' Delight"? Inspector Bello inquired.

"Well, sir," replied Martin, "Na only austerity everybody dey cry about. No one knows when it go stop."

"Yes, this austerity, my wife tells me that prices of basic food commodity are daily skyrocketing. A carton of soap detergent has doubled the usual price. To cook a pot of vegetable soup now will cost fifty naira. How can poor people survive this high cost of living?"

"Oga, it's true, I read in the newspapers that the city's inflation rate is approaching six hundred percent. My major concern is how I can get a job. You know I'll complete my National Service next month in the company of 40,000 other graduates.

"So twelve months is over, how time does fly! Maybe you can apply to work with the Police Force," advised Inspector Bello.

"I suppose I'll apply, but I don't see much hope. The government's embargo on employment will mean a slim chance for the likes of me. I've nightmares worrying about what life without gainful employment will be like. Some of my friends and I have decided on going back to the university for post graduate studies. But I reckon I've had enough of schooling. I want to be my own man, but tough luck."

"Don't give up hope. Your luck may still turn up fine and before you know it, you too will become a big shot."

"Yeah, I pray all day just for some lucky break. I don't want to end up begging for food from my relatives and family members."

Martin always dreamt of the summer of 1980. The year before he graduated from University of Lagos, marked an important milestone in .his life. It was his twenty-first birthday. The summer represented the best period of his life. Uncle Tunde, highly successful from his Abuja huge contracts, gave him a free round ticket to London and New York.

Tunde had studied architecture in Italy after which, he proceeded to Atlanta USA and majored in interior design. He also obtained a doctorate degree from a downtown correspondent college. On his return to Nigeria in 1978, he had barely finished his National Youth Service before going into partnership with a local contractor to set up shop. Their firm had won lucrative building projects in Abuja. Tunde worked tirelessly to execute many more projects in the new Federal Capital city. The payments had been prompt and immediate. This made it possible for him to immediately join the Naira millionaires club. With his business connection, Tunde bought enviable properties in London, Milan and New York. As more money flowed in, Uncle Tunde became more generous. He freely gave tickets to relatives to go on summer holidays.

Martin, armed with a round trip ticket, two thousand dollars' worth of traveler's checks, he set out to have a wonderful time in both London and New York.

The flight from Lagos to London had been packed. It was peak season for Nigerian trend setters roaming the world capitals. The plane stopped at Kano International Airport to pick up passengers from the Northern States. From a vantage spot, Martin did a mental study of the human cargoes. The description of the traffic fully represented Nigeria's various ethnic groups. Everyone was in such great hurry.

There were many middle aged corporate executives possibly making a trip to their alma mater to show off their recently acquired material possession. There were many emergency lady contractors and inexperienced smugglers who seemed to roam around the world in pursuit of illegal trade. There were about thirty colorful attired Hausa Imams bound for Mecca to pray to Allah for economic harvest for their benefactors.

There were uncountable pregnant women with bosoms swollen as if ready to discharge their matrimonial burden. The expected children would be lucky to be delivered in a London hospital. They would return to Nigeria designated as a "been-tos." There were also many noisy students of both higher institutions and secondary schools anxiously awaiting their first flight in the powerful Boeing 747 jet plane. They brimmed with hope of seeing for the first time the white man's paradise and the famous London

Bridge.

The wealthy minorities, the overfed civil servants, the ministers and recently elected politicians were all gracefully shielded from the foul odor of the economy cabin. Equally present in the first class section were the captains of industries as well as fun loving men who enjoyed globe-trotting. They all shared the singular pre-occupation of reaching London soonest. From thence, each would move on to own individual clandestine past time. They all were out to enjoy their naira power as the elite of the masses of the petro-rich nation.

Martin dutifully studied the peculiarities of the Nigerians on board the Nigeria Airways flight WT 880 to London. The journalist in him prompted him to see the situation as a suitable news features. Armed with his pocket notebook, he set about jotting down his observations.

A two hour delay at the Kano airport resulted in angry passengers. There were verbal assaults on the Nigeria Airways crew. Upon inquiry, Martin learned their flight was delayed for a minor mechanical tune-up. Meanwhile, the travelers' tempers boiled almost to the breaking point. The delay came to an end as passengers were seen going to board the plane. Nudging himself, Martin willed his journalistic mind to relax so as to enjoy the pleasant trip.

Finally, the plane touched down in London Heathrow, and Martin rode the London tube to Tunde's house in Stockwell. He spent the next thirty days enjoying English hospitality reserved only for those who had the monetary power. His friends in Stockwell introduced him to "Thursdays," and "Gulliver's," London's exotic disco clubs situated in the heart of London West End. He also visited the British seat of power, the House of Parliament. He shopped at New Bond Street, the famous Oxford Street, and took pictures at the Piccadilly Circus and Trafalgar square.

It was at Bond Street stores that he ran into one of the flashy Nigerian state governors. The statesman spent close to twenty thousand pounds sterling on silk suits. Of course, he paid cash with a promise to introduce his minister friends to equally patronize the store. Martin witnessed the senseless squandering of oil wealth and could not believe his eyes.

During his four weeks stay in London, stories of the wanton extravagance of his countrymen filled his ears. There was the shocking case of a Nigerian university student who left cash valued at half a million pounds in a London taxi cab. The driver made away with the bounty. Martin had kept notes with hopes of writing a story on the resultant doom that would befall the nation should men in high positions continue with such mindless acts. In fact, on his return to Lagos University campus, he had written a nice article with the title "My Words to The Winds." The article, true to its title, had gone to the winds because the newspapers would not publish it. One Lagos sub-editor openly told Martin that editors kill such stories.

"People in glass houses should not throw stones," the editor admonished.

Gradually, the situation grew out of hand. The economic gloom was only beginning to produce bitter effects. The austerity measures, it seemed, caught everyone unawares. Except the few ruthless men who had stashed millions of dollars away in foreign banks. Members of the "Man Pass Man" club were in such exalted position. Martin had been opportune to know of these trend-setters at parties he attended in London and in Long Island, New York. It was the last week of August, five days before he was due back in Lagos, his cousin; Wale took him to a wealthy Nigerian house warming party in Long Island. The entrepreneur merchant Prince Peter Abudu owned a Lumber Saw Mills in Sapele. He manufactured high quality wood for the lucrative construction industry. The booming business had motivated less successful men in the Sapele society to boast of owning real estate properties in the cities of London, Paris and Geneva. To show class, the merchant Prince had searched out a million dollar estate in Long Island. He bought the house in order to be numbered among those prestigious men in Sapele society to own a palace in a foreign land. He reckoned it was time to redeem his lost prestige. He took pride in outclassing the Joneses. Expensive Dom Ruinart champagne flowed through out the party to the amazement of everyone present. The story making the rounds was that the Prince had to bid higher than three Arab oil Sheiks in order to eventually buy the property. The selling price of the ancient and elegant mansion situated at the Long Island exclusive area, reserved for American corporate chief executives was worth well over six figures. The Prince, of course, paid for the house in cash.

The high point of the party was around midnight when seven

amazingly beautiful blondes walked in with a tall, princely man in his forties. He looked every inch like a successful black American actor from Hollywood.

Curious, Martin nosed around to learn the identity of the graceful creature. He was shocked when he discovered that the man was the popular Alhaji Abba Abdulmalik. This was the man made famous with the adage, "Let us have wine, women, mirth, laughter and soda water the day after." Numerous tales had circulated of the Alhaji's exploits, his blonde women, flashy, expensive cars and, of course, his international playboy reputation. Such was the seemingly incredible lifestyle and fable that spread across party folks. A lifestyle envied by all, especially students in University.

The loud whistle from the desk Sergeant sharply jostled Martin back from his day dream. He sat up, adjusted his chair in the Kaduna South Police Station and wondered what became of the popular AAA chairman. How was the famous Alhaji coping with the austerity? He wondered about the blondes and the cars. Many other questions filled his mind, and he realized that the good times had been just too good to last. No matter what Martin's future amounted to, he would never forget the great times he had in London and New York. Uncle Tunde had been his benefactor.

Poor Uncle Tunde; the austerity was becoming too much for his honest soul. His story was a confirmation of the saying that "those whom the gods would destroy, they would first blind with greed." It was greed that had driven Tunde to miscalculate the mood of the economy. He had set up a gigantic ceramic manufacturing factory with little knowledge in the practical financial requirements to make the outfit feasible. He had borrowed heavily. And had been unable to obtain the necessary import licenses required to import the machinery. Now the banks are demanding repayment on the loans and threatening to foreclose on his residential home if he did not meet up with the payments. The last news Martin heard was that Tunde had developed high blood pressure. The doctors said his conditions may deteriorate further with time. Capitalism without bankruptcy, they say, is like preaching the gospel without mentioning hell. Poor Tunde, but for him, the summer of 1980 would not have been possible for Martin. The best option for Tunde was to file for protection from creditors under the Federal Banking Act. The decision, however, to file for bankruptcy would not be an easy one. Aristotle was right when he stated that "there is a foolish corner in the brain of the wisest man." Poor, poor Tunde. Comparatively, he was luckier than the inhabitants of the Kaduna dormitory communities. The factory operatives were being put out of employment due to austerity measures. According to the police statistics, there was a corresponding increase in the incidence of alcoholism, mental disturbance and suicide. Like the poor in the American South during the period of economic gloom, the factory operatives, feeling ill-treated by the factory owners, had developed a deep-set sense of hopelessness. This was intensified by the government austerity measures. It was inevitable that a large scale emigration of the more able unemployed will begin. That was despite the ties of family and culture that bind the African natives to their home territory. The once Treasure Island nation of petro-currency was fast turning into a famine outpost. The feast has finally ended and all feared for the future. The country's best hope was to become a tourist center. However, even that had its varied pitfalls. It seemed unlikely that small businesses could provide the solutions. What was needed was the creation of thousands of small businesses to make up for the loss of jobs. This required massive inflow of foreign capital, like those stashed away in Swiss bank accounts by elite Nigerians. It would necessitate the combined efforts of both the government, patriotic Nigerians and the IMF to provide solutions to the crisis.

Either that or the future generations would live in an environment where earning a living would be problematic, to say the least. Rather than becoming energetic, the people would take a listless approach to life, never pushing too hard. Each day would be an obstacle and the struggle would last forever. Martin agonized over what fate had in store for him and subsequent generations. A man condemned to joblessness after working so hard to acquire university education and would live without hope. Their future would be blighted, filled with tales of woes and more austerity.

CHAPTER SEVEN

Pedro da Souza sat in his palatial office decorated with Japanese garden cottage and oriental screening. The placid atmosphere produced heaven's serenity. He opened the Newsletter story on "Nigeria and Oil: the feast, the famine and the future". Drifting into a relaxed posture, he evoked memories of that distant past when everything was so fresh, so venturesome, so surprising, so interesting. He was a witness of the events flowing from the vile passions of wicked men. Those shortsighted in good works. He reviewed the entrenched oligarchic manipulations of the Lagos "fat cats" and the corruptions of their degenerate descendants. Nothing had changed. They prospered in the same deep devilish animosity. These deceptive "demons" had only one motive. They fooled everything and everybody into an everlasting frustration. They ensnare the innocent in serpentine ambush. But for the grace of God, Pedro da Souza could have become a member of this mafia power brokers. He had taken the wise step of voluntary exile. The decision ended his being a victim. Wisdom had granted him discernment to see into the falsehood in the hearts of Lagos power brokers. He contemplated the appalling darkness. The bloody corruptions African politicians nauseated him. He nursed the burden to somehow make a difference.

To be repeatedly told that one's political future is blighted because of not belonging to the major ethnic tribe of a nation is like heaping a curse of Cane on an aspirant.

A born leader and man of the people, Pedro da Souza had,

58

from birth, a deep desire for authority. He had always wanted to direct affairs of state as Chief. He was born of Creole parents with Brazilian connections in 1913. His descendants were among the first white explorers to reach Lagos in 1840. This was before the European powers recognized Britain's claim to Nigeria during the Berlin Conference. The London-based Royal Niger Company was the first charter to develop viable commercial centers in the new colony. Pedro da Souza had served as a local missionary boy with the Lagos Island Catholic Diocese. The chaplain had noticed his brilliance. He favored him to be sponsored by the Irish Chapter of the African Missionary Society based in Cork, Ireland. They paid his tuition to study at the Fourah Bay College in Sierra-Leone. He had earned academic laurels and became president of the student union. The resident Monsignor Sean McGovern had personally paid for his three years study in Philosophy at the famous Trinity College in Dublin. For altruistic reasons, Monsignor McGovern worked relentlessly to promote his political ambitions. He became one of the first native legislators elected into the British Protectorate for Lagos Colony in 1930.

In 1943, the British authority was to appoint three indigenes to the newly formed Nigeria Executive Council. They were to be under the jurisdiction of the British Governor's Cabinet. Pedro da Souza, the great hope of the Lagos Island thought he would be among the three elites. The outcome of this election devastated him. Although he was abandoned by his mother at the age of four when his sailor father left Lagos for Rio de Janeiro. The church took over to provide him support and the chaplain became his role model. He superimposed a strong spiritual value system that enabled happiness to flourish in the young soul. He matured and manifested superior self-esteem. Pedro the politician saw the 1943 election as his take-off pedestal. He worked very hard in order to win the superior seat. Fate, however, had decided otherwise. Powerful oligarchic interests blocked him. The tragic comedy was Pedro's ignorance of the oligarchy. With the Moslem North and Christian South. With many tribal divisions and argumentative people, Nigeria at her independence was perceived as Africa's most ungovernable country. When the British arrived in the mid-nineteenth century, they found not a single, but several regional mini-nations. Each of the 250 ethnics were represented by the major tribes. There were the Hausas and Fulani's of the north.

They were of Arab descent .Their rulers; the emirs built empires with palaces of baked mud. The Yorubas of the west were self-assertive people. They worshipped more than twenty pagan gods and made up the majority of the Lagos population. The pastoral Ibos lived and spread from their homeland in the eastern region to become Nigeria's most capable entrepreneurs. They were the local money bags and easily given to self-praise. The British had forced the major tribes to amalgamate. The decision had potentials which were still unfolding. Ethnicity then became for some groups not an economic asset, but an economic liability. The ordained order for meritocracy to the basis of upward societal mobility was discarded for tribal considerations. Mediocrity became accepted policy thus making way for disorderliness. This malady grew with time, to corrupt the entire political system.

Pedro having failed miserably in his innocent attempt to win the executive seat became discouraged. He began his journey to moral ruin. He watched helplessly as mediocrity became the order of the day. Realism finally hit urn in 1959. He saw for the first time that he had no hope of actualizing his life ambition. He remained still a respected member of the political circle. He continued to serve his Lagos constituency in diminished capacity. He wept daily as he saw with disgust that the underpinning of mediocrity and tribal politics would with time destroy the peace of the nation. He knew that politicians who think only of the next elections were dangerous mobs. The true statesman thinks of the next generation and of Judgment Day.

Even though rejected, his experience and eloquence as a politician continued to command the respect of his grass root colleagues. He was their local hero. He was an orator who was both admired and feared for his hatred of falsehood. His loyal peers conceded that he could have become the most effective chief executive of the nation. Of course, all things being equal. But without the ethnic support to win any superior office he was abandoned to political limbo. He therefore lived aimlessly and prayed daily for divine intervention. The extreme wrong-headedness of the men at the helm of power overwhelmed him. They were lucky men without the foresight to know that being lucky without innate wisdom always end up a fool. It was their self-destructive madness that would drive the new country, black Africa's great hope to become besmirched with dark barbarism. Its institutions, a mockery. Its laws, a farce. The newly elected rulers of the realm exhibited prodigal childishness in the highest places with careless abandon. They became intoxicated with power. The curse of futility was upon the political buccaneers with their supine sentiments. Their vain glorious morality and sullen acquiescence promoted every form of corruption. Pedro had worked hard in the struggle to uproot colonialism and install political independence. After the victory, the country had become the passive prey of a democratic parody. The helpless victim of political scoundrels.

The writing of anarchy was on the wall and worse was yet to come. Guided by foresight and a penetrative grasp of ongoing trends, Pedro reached his conclusion. He concluded that political exile would best for him. He approached his mentor and bosom friend, Monsignor McGovern for advice.

Monsignor Sean McGovern was seated at the head of the small conference table--the biggest furniture in the priest's abode. His pale yellow skin revealed the old man was sick of malaria. He took a long drink from the glass of the Irish whiskey and his deep sea-blue eyes sparkled, lighting up his face.

Pedro sat to the old man's right. He smiled silently and picked up the whiskey bottle and poured more into McGovern's glass. "I'm glad you like old Irish cure for malaria fever," Pedro commented pushing the glass back towards the old man. "Two more glassful and you'll be cured," he assured the priest.

"Aha! Thank you. I appreciate your coming along with the bottle. Now tell me, how is politics? The newspaper reported you will act temporarily as the Minister of Trade for the next four weeks."

"Yes! I'm taking over from Adamu. He is going to London for surgery. Cancer, I believe".

"Well, I'm glad for you. It's your first real top assignment. With your talent, I know you deserve to go much further up." "I know and I'm grateful for all you did for me. "

"Come, come my boy. The praise belongs to God. Not a blade of grass moves but by His will. You ought to know about that, or have you lost faith? Father Bradley tells me you seldom come to Sunday mass these days."

"I know, and it's one of the reasons I'm here. I'm intending to back out of politics."

"I've been expecting this sooner. But tell me all about it."

"You know more than me, concerning the unsatisfied needs of the people, which cannot be politically ameliorated. Only God can turn the mess around."

"Yes, I think I'm aware of the oligarchy. It's part of the conflict of Northern Ireland. Life has taught me that there are no political reasons but political passions. Our convictions are only a particular view of our interests. It can be either practical or emotional. No one is a patriot for nothing."

"Did you say no one is a patriot for nothing?" Pedro asked puzzled.

"Exactly. Every man has his price. Mine is a bottle of vantage Irish whiskey. I'd not have spoken with you if you had not come with the bottle."

"Do you suppose I've been tangled up in the affairs of the public, pretending to be a patriot when in reality my passion is fake?"

"Fake passion? Who could accuse Pedro da Souza of nourishing fake sentiments? Certainly not me. I'm aware of your noble intentions. There is an Irish saying that 'the road to hell is paved with good intentions.' The truth is that you lack the ingenuity to profit from the petty crimes around you. And I've seen you agonize these past ten years. You lack the crude trait that enables ruthless politicians to survive these critical times."

"Should I quit politics?" he demanded.

"Now Pedro, I can't command you what to do. I've always believed you are capable of making your own judgment. And in time, you will come to know what exactly it is you want."

"Yes, Father, I suppose you've never forced any decision on me. Only this time, I do request you tell me if I'm making the right move."

"But Pedro, you're wrong. No one can tell if we make the right or wrong decision. Take my case for instance; I come from a family of bootleggers. My parents were shocked when I decided to take the vow of poverty. Even after sixty years, some members of my family still resent what I am. Looking back, I could have become a business man and probably made millions, but I chose otherwise. I've never and would never regret my decision. Very soon, I shall die and would hope that Saint Peter will deem me worthy to be admitted into the gates of heaven. To me Heaven is all I hope for. I hope and pray that I'll make it. That on the Judgment Day, I shall not be found unworthy. My quest has been that I may die a saint. To forever walk the streets of gold is my eternal desire..."

"In effect, we make our beds and lie on it," Pedro interjected.

"You're very correct. The Christian way is that one's career is not so important so long as one has worthy ideal. This compares with the amount of goodness one can accomplish in doing one's duty. We are to be our brothers' keepers."

"Can I accomplish more for my constituency outside politics? The population of this city is fast changing, and three quarters of the residents either want me dead. There is the language barrier, and I cannot mix well enough among these strangers. Within my peer groups, I'm respected, but when it comes to real political in-fighting, everyone abandons me. The brusqueness of these rejections depresses me for hours on end."

"These are no easy times and I happen to be aware things will get worse. I pray not to be around by then."

"Are you going back to Cork?" asked Pedro. He became sad at the prospect of his mentor leaving him forever.

"No, my little brother Danny wants me to spend my retirement with his family in Long Island, New York. He has done well for himself trading in crude oil. I think you should come and see me there when I'm settled in New York."

"So it's all settled that you will leave us all behind?"

"Yes, I believe I've served enough. Sixty-one years next April. I'll leave for New York in June, knowing God is satisfied with my career."

"I'm glad for you. You will be missed, especially my wife Angela and David."

"I still have six months to go, and soon you'll be busy with your Ministry of Trade and forget about missing me."

"Yes, the ministry is the biggest in the city. With our policy of rapid industrialization, we are in a hurry to develop our industrial base overnight. My main interest would be in the petrochemicals section."

"We hear Adamu made a bundle of money signing exploration contracts with American oil companies. My brother Danny confirms it. "

"Adamu is the type to take advantage of such situations. For my part, I do look forward to the foreign trips. Next week, I shall visit Geneva in Switzerland in connection with something to do with OPEC. The Organization of Petroleum Exporting Countries, the newly formed international cartel for oil rich nations."

"I wish you God speed in your trips. And always bear in mind that one's conviction of practical necessity is stronger than an abstract political doctrine. Seeing that the times have changed, it takes a wise man to change as well."

The huge grandfather clock chimed half past the hour, and the Monsignor rose to prepare for the evening mass. He instructed Pedro to pray awhile before departing.

The Monsignor's parting admonition remained with Pedro. His words gave him the courage to switch careers.

Ten days after Pedro's visit, the Monsignor's acute malaria fever worsened, resulting in pneumonia. He was rushed to the Lagos General Hospital where he died three days later.

Pedro spent the precious last hours with his benefactor. The priest that gave him his first real opportunities in life. The Monsignor's last words were that Pedro should be bold to live out his conviction. He specifically instructed him to try and meet with Danny. "The industry has a great future," were the very last words of the dying Monsignor. Even in death, he exhibited sacrificial love for Pedro compensated for the rejections, the young lad suffered. Love no one could equal.

Danny McGovern, the vice president of the Greenspoint Oil, flew into Lagos in his corporate Boeing 727 jet plane. He carried his brother's corpse across the Atlantic to rest finally in the family vault in Mallow County, Ireland.

Three weeks after the funeral, Pedro visited New York as the minister for industries of OPEC's newest member. Danny was at the New York International Airport to meet the Nigerian delegation. He brought Pedro to meet his family at his Long Island home.

Within a year, under Danny's expert high powered guidance Pedro saved sixty thousand U.S. dollars in a Swiss bank account. He used this booty launched Zeus Industries. In the summer of 1964, he bought the three adjoining properties on the area currently occupied by his palatial mansion. He remodeled the vast estate until the present noble San Marino emerged. The renovation was completed precisely on the 25th of December. He moved into the residence, leaving behind forever the curse of futility, which Lagos politicking had imposed on his ambitions.

Barely twenty months after his departure, had the major tribes begun struggling for power and control of the country's natural resources. Black Africa's biggest hope soon became its greatest disappointment. The Ibos and Hausas politicians formed a coalition against the Yoruba's. The ensuing conflict caused the civilian government to break down. Anarchy reigned everywhere. In 1966, five young southern officers overthrew the government. They killed the Prime Minister and other prominent Northerners. Six months later, the Northerners regained power by toppling the Southerners.

Northern soldiers chased southern troops from their barracks, murdering scores with bayonets. Screaming mobs descended on the strangers' quarters in every northern city, killing their victims with clubs, poisoned arrows and shotguns. Ten thousand Ibos were murdered in the crisis that followed.

The thirty-month-long civil war that followed these atrocities claimed a million lives. In its first twenty two years of independence, the nation had experienced three coups d'état and the assassination of two heads of state. The shattering of the masses hope and a comatose economy continues to repeat its malady.

"Ain't nothing changed. Nothing will ever change," Pedro shouted out loud in his reverie. He mentally pictured the disappointed Bulus, the Lagos wheeler-dealer lawyer. He recalled Ted Hunter's bleak analysis of Nigeria's future. It was insane to assume another revolution was about to re-occur. It seemed just a matter of time before the winds of change took effect .It will carry the potency of destroying everything that stepped on its way. So much for peace and tranquility surmised Pedro as he reached to pour himself a glass of St. Ives pure orange juice. Slowly he picked up the telephone and pressed Andy Lincoln's button on the intercom.

"Send Mr. Hunter in after five minutes, "he instructed.

"Convictions borne of practical necessity." The words re-echoed in the inner recess of da Souza's mind. The year was 1964 when Reverend Monsignor Sean McGovern expressed thought of worthy idealism. The amount of goodness one can accomplish by faith in God must measure up in good works. Pedro knew his life was the fruit of Sean McGovern's good works and only God turns human mess into a miracle.

What exactly did the old man mean? What is authentic good works? He forced his agitated mind to recollect Barrister Bulus' deductions. What did he mean by, The Feast, the Famine and the Future?

Zeus Industries was a feast and had a future. The famine was the unsatisfied need of the masses. The people whom Pedro had loved and originally intended to serve. The people in his former constituency in Lagos were now victims of the austerity measure. Like a great plague, it killed every minute of the hour. He reasoned that God would want him to reach out benevolently. Bulus had been used to awaken his conscience unto good works.

Pedro agonized over whether the resources of Zeus Inc would make any difference. He wondered if Zeus could let some ray of hope fall through the darkness for his plagued people in Lagos. Zeus, Inc. had a worldwide net income before taxes of $4.5 billion in the fiscal year 1982. This was no meager achievement. With prudent fiscal management it was enough to feed the entire population of Africa's three poorest nations for a year.

Pedro contemplated the numerous holdings of Zeus Industries while he awaited the entry of Ted Hunter. He recounted the different areas of industrial operations of the country then an idea began to form in his head. He spoke on his plan to help fight the economic austerity in Lagos. He planned a rescue operation. He recalled the American corporate legend, J.P. Morgan, who had a unique vision as a one man U.S. Federal Reserve Bank during the great depression of 1929. The vision of a one man gang flooded his mind.

CHAPTER EIGHT

Ted Hunter strode into Pedro da Souza's presence in exactly the five minute as requested by his host.

Time had matured Ted Hunter. His dress seemed a compromise between the demands of office and leisure fashion. It consists of a black lounge suit, a white cardigan and a pair of grey flannel trousers.

Pedro da Souza watched the oil consultant, and his eyebrows shot up. He snapped his fingers, indicating that the guest should sit down.

"Mr. Hunter," he began solemnly" I've read your analysis and I must congratulate your brilliance."

"Thank you," replied Hunter leaning forward to reveal his alertness.

"Brandy, Mr. Hunter?"

"Yes, Scotch if you may," he replied.

He rang the bell and the drink appeared for Mr. Hunter in an instant.

With pleasantries over, Pedro da Souza briefly summarized Hunter's qualifications.

I believe you've a soft spot for Lagos. Can you enlighten me further on this? I'm rather curious. Or is it a personal matter?" asked da Souza, stretching himself. .

"There is no secret in my love for Lagos. My Newsletter editorial has over the years shown my sentiment and loyalty to Africa's greatest nation. I come from a small town in Belfast. I visited Nigeria for the first time in 1956 while working for Metropolitan Newspapers. I was the editor and virtually fell in love with the people. I saw the great potential in the country but there was also the tribal divide that seemed to tear all apart. At that time I could not understand the natives' attitude of seeing themselves as tribes rather than as a nation. Lagos, then, was a hub for economic growth. Nigerians and foreigners jostled and hustled through crowds, sweat dripping from their brows. There were numerous dodging and honking cabs, each hurrying in New York style to their next appointment. There was no idleness, but every man worked hard, each at his own assigned task. I noted such was the quality of which great nations were made. When I returned back to London, I kept in touch with my Lagos friends. Naturally I moved to Geneva when I became an oil consultant. Nigeria has my loyalty in the OPEC caucus. Believe me sir, then, when I say I know the country like the back of my hand."

"You've a point. Your predictions on the future of OPEC are very bleak indeed. Do you not think you tempered your predictions with the realities of your fallibilities?"

"No, I don't think so. I've immense talents and I've equally enormous weaknesses, but I never exaggerate my facts and figures. Seven out of ten reputed financial analysts in the oil industry would support my arguments."

"Are you aware that the world has always survived endless prophecies of doom? All predictions of catastrophic damages of world institutions never occur, but that does not discourage the alarmists."

"If you mean 'The Great Debt Crisis' and the world wide induced depressions, then I can say that the predicted relentless damage of sovereign economies has started."

"My newsletter carried a transcript of Prime Minister R.D. Muldoon of New Zealand's article in the International Herald Tribune stating: 'Forty Sovereign Borrowers in Tribune.' Muldoon should know, he was a former chairman of the board of governors of the International Monetary Fund."

"The businessman in me tells me that Muldoon is a politician, whipping up public sentiments. I remember he said something that once about economic instability leading inevitably to political instability, which in turn leads to strategic instability ...," he trailed off.

"Muldoon is no alarmist. A lot of financial analysts respect him for his great ideas."

"But do you agree with his solution to the banks problems?"

"Yes and no. The solvency of the International Banking System remains desperately dependent on their ability and willingness to service sovereign debts. The bank loans to these countries still amount to 120 percent of the shareholders equity in the top nine U.S. banks and to more than 100 percent of equity in Manufacturers Hanover Trust, the most exposed lender I think. This figure compounds daily," he replied.

"I think Muldoon wants a new Bretton Woods-type conference to consider feasible proposals like greater symmetry in the balance-of-payments adjustments and a wider use of drawing rights. Hence, to move gradually over to the medium and long term solution of the structural problem. For the short term, the U.S Federal Reserves will either have to rescue major defaulters or get the banks to lend more to the debtor nations."

"What does Muldoon mean by 'enlightened self-interest?'" interjected da Souza, cryptically.

"Beats me," came the reply. "I can assume he means real compassion on the side of powerful nations ministering to the needs of the poor countries."

"Do you think that is feasible?" asked da Souza, his curiosity aroused.

Hunter remained silent for a moment, then picked up his glass of scotch and drained its contents.

"If there be the resources, backed by determined powerful will, for example, the US President, then I suppose the idea would be feasible. Different countries would then receive different cures. Not like the current blanket treatment advised by the I.M.F. Take Britain and Nigeria for an illustration. It is common knowledge that Britain will be in an unsound financial position without the oil from the North Sea. For the past ten years, Britain has been pumping oil from the stormy North Sea as though there is no tomorrow. Very soon, tomorrow will arrive with tough questions about where the petrol currency has gone," Hunter said.

"A historic opportunity would have been squandered. A large part of the oil reserves was used up to sustain personal consumption by reduced taxation and to foot the bill of over three million civil servants. European economists agree that Britain is without sufficient quality investments. It is true that the British manufacturing process suffered greater fall between 1979 and 1981 than in 1930's. A quarter of the steel and textile industries alone were wiped out in the period. Even with this gloomy picture, Britain may suffer relentless economic depression and austerity measures when the North Sea oil stops. But there will remain strong political and strategic stability. They have the serene climate necessary to attract massive foreign investment capital. A new economic rebirth will take place in Britain as was in Japan and Germany after the Second World War. Recovery and reconstruction of these war torn nations was made possible by huge American capital. A sick Britain would start picking up in time. The reason is that on a chart of foreign Investment Risk Matrix, Britain is ranked A1, same as countries like Japan, Germany, France and the U.S.

Nigeria, however, is ranked D2. The economic risk of foreign investment becomes unacceptable as you move down the chart. The biggest capitalist nation the U.S. will spend about $796 billion in fiscal year 1983, or about one-fourth of America's entire economic output. The U.S. government will borrow $281 billion in 1983 and by the end of fiscal year 1984, and the government's debt will amount to a staggering $1.3 trillion. That makes it about $17,000 for every taxpayer in America. Financial statistics show that the U.S. issued, backed or sponsored $848 billion in loan, which has not been paid back. These huge financial figures are a far cry from the African situation.

Earlier this year, the World Bank projected a likely disaster in the flow of capital to Africa. Unless additional capital is found, the net flow will decline from $ 11 billion in 1980-82 to $5 billion in 1985-87. Except the problem addressed by African leaders, foreign countries, private and public sectors and multinational institutions, the future will be very bleak indeed. Economic instability will result in political upheavals. African military coup planners would spring up, overthrowing established democratic systems. Jerry Rawlings in Ghana, Samuel Doe in Liberia. Guinea, Mali, Upper Volta and Nigeria are slated to follow suit," Hunter concluded.

"Another military coup in Nigeria?" exclaimed da Souza with animation.

He continued, "Nigeria chose a political system modeled after the United States. With a president and vice president serving four year terms, a Supreme Court, a Senate, and a House of Representatives. The country rejected Britain's form of parliamentary government, which is easy to topple through votes of no confidence from the opposition party. The American alternative has worked these past three years. I hope it will continue to work for the next five years," stressed da Souza.

"What it boils down to is that the US form of democracy and capitalism is not the best option for the people of Nigeria. What Nigeria needs is a strong government that would put national interest ahead of self or ethnic or religious interest. One that would implement a realistic, cost-conscious plan for the country's growth. The formidable challenge ahead is whether the soldiers will stay in the barracks while the civilian administration falters? Will oil revenue really be put to work to benefit the majority instead of a chosen few using tribalism to thwart national goals. I assume you know what I mean when I speak of the Lagos 'fat cats." The power barons with deeply embedded oligarchic interests. You will agree with me; that there is an urgent need to devise a way to make ethnicity an economic asset, not economic liability."

Hunter looked up at his host and could detect loss of poise. His guarded control seems to have disappeared. There was uneasy silence between them. Suddenly the old man's head jerked up and he stared back at Hunter. The gloom his eyes flashed like fire. The suffering of the years, all the humiliation and the full realization Hunter's force of words dazed the old man. He whistled and grunted. His choking voice panted. He put his hand to his head and sobbed. He was genuinely broken without shame or control. In his anguish, he repeated heavily, "Ain't nothing changed. And is ever going to change." Momentarily, he stopped sobbing and feebly wiped his eyes. Turning to the younger man he whispered finally, "Forgive my outburst. It must be old age and my feeble mind. You know I take pride that I weep for my helpless people"

Hunter watched him without moving. Many things had shaken him, but never like this. The blood in the veins of his face whitened. But for the professional in him, what he was seeing would have become too unbearable to endure. Outwardly, he appeared cool, calm and collected.

"I do understand, that you love the country," he struggled to reply.

A deep warm silence seemed to fill the room. The old man did not volunteer an answer. He nursed his melancholy

"How long do you think OPEC's current daily production of 17.5 million barrels compared to output of 22.7 million barrels a day in 1981 would last?" da Souza asked at last.

Wall Street financial analysts insist that worldwide demand for energy will continue to shrink into the next ten years. This is due to reduced industrial production in Japan, Europe and America. It means a slow but steady erosion of oil prices through the next years. OPEC's strategy is to limit output. That is to lessen production at the rate of 10 to 12 percent every year until demand picks up. By next year, OPEC's total production level should not be in excess of fifteen million barrels a day. A more realistic figure would be between 12 and 13 million barrels a day then prices would stabilize between $18-22 per barrel. Economic forecasts show that most members cannot keep to the output limit and would continue to increase their production capacity irrespective of what the cartel stipulates. I predict that in the next year, Nigeria will break rank with OPEC. They will cut their oil price to match British and Norwegians. Saudi Arabia for the next year will continue to adhere to its production ceilings to prop up the OPEC cartel. You know the Saudi's are the key players in the body".

"How long would Saudi Arabia continue to do so?"

"Sheik Yamani insists he can go on forever. Analysts forecast in the next twenty months that Saudi Arabia will grow tired of the cartel's cheating members. And if you can't beat them, then join them. When that day comes, the price of oil will be drastically reduced to $15 a barrel. It is a hard game. The jungle law reigns," Hunter declared.

"Zeus is experiencing a luster trading on the spot and non-contract market. The mood around Rotterdam is that price of contracts of future delivery of oil and other petroleum products will continue to fluctuate. For now, traders are reluctant to bet either way on oil prices. Nobody has a clear idea what might happen next. The stakeholders seem to have the fear that the spot market may collapse like a pack of cards."

"The oil spot market collapse? That will never be. The world has a vested interest to make sure that OPEC does not die. The U.S. is committed to safeguarding the world energy consumption. That is, until a more effective, reliable cheap source of alternative energy can be feasible."

"I hope for the sake of us all, you are right. And lastly, what do you think of Nigeria's chances in this great debt crisis?" da Souza asked calmly. He glanced about the warm study furniture of the oversized room. He noted the objects of pride, security, intelligence and peace. His home in Switzerland. His blood rose in irritation, perhaps at his inability to duplicate such serenity in his native Lagos.

Hunter seemed apparently lost in his own quiet thoughts, his face with an odd speculative expression. He spread out his hands in an eloquent French gesture. He shrugged and after a moment he said, "I've studied painfully to really understand the psychology of the Nigerian personality. I've researched every aspect of Nigeria's economy, but I fear I may not competently answer your question. I know Nigeria has a vibrant informal economy, which needs to be brought into the mainstream of economic dynamism. There is the urgent need to resolve the problem of capital availability. This means stimulating venture capital, divesting mutual fund possibilities, making the banks, the stock exchange houses more effective, and funding privately owned lending facilities to encourage private enterprise. This will stimulate financial intermediaries to broaden equity participation within the economy. The government must understand that excessive rules and regulation stifle incentives. It discourages the entrepreneur without whose unique contribution a nation acquires greatness. The government must also combat all forms of corruptions. It must pursue the policy to promote a lawful and orderly society. A way must be devised to make ethnicity an economic asset. Find a way to solve the above problems and Nigeria will be on its way to achieving real greatness."

"Do you think this utopia can be found?" da Souza questioned. His voice and face were smooth, yet expressing nervous anxiety.

"Yes." Hunter became thoughtful again. "Control the key factor input and the success of any project would be realized. In 1975, after decades of living beyond its means, New York City was on the brink of bankruptcy. That June, the Municipal Assistance Corp., a state agency, was formed to bailout the city. The bonds that MAC issued fared dismally at first. The first issue, though offered at a huge discount to the public dropped at an almost unheard of $100 for every $1,000 of face value on the day it hit the market. Today the MAC issue ranks as one of the premier bonds of all time. An investment banker Felix Rohatyn, a partner at Wall Street's Lazard Freres is still popularly regarded as New York City's savior. As chairman of MAC Rohatyn's financial expertise saved New York by bridge-financing a $300 million note due that June. Together with a loan of $1.3 billion, MAC finally raised the rest of $4.5 billion budgeted sum in 1978. In a cooperative joint venture, the unions, the banks, other financial institutions and MAC bonds made possible the issue of the biggest long-term Municipal bond in America. It is now thoroughly respectable. The Chrysler Motor Company used the New York's experience to create healthier financial structures and to make certain its present profitability,"

"Yes, it's splendid what Lee Iacocca did for Chrysler. And you tell me such a feat can be replicated in Lagos?" questioned da Souza.

"Yes, qualified by different variables, with adequate strategic planning. I remain optimistic of a favorable outcome. This is subject to the aforementioned problems being solved. An extraordinary strategy is what is needed," Hunter responded.

"What do you know about bond issuance for third world nations? I mean the foreign bonds?" asked da Souza, anxiously.

"I did a research with Dean Witters Reynolds in New York and spent fifteen months in the bonds marketing office. I keep up my knowledge of current issues by subscribing to the Dessauer's Journal, a fortnightly international investment newsletter published in Massachusetts. For issuers, bonds are attractive because they reduce borrowing expenses. Bonds carry risk protection of buy-back guarantees. They are issued on the financial strength of the issuer and reputable guarantor."

While Hunter spoke, da Souza rose and paced until the speech ended.

"I've a proposition for your consideration," the old man raised his voice to emphasize his demand.

Hunter turned and faced him quizzically. "What kind of proposition?"

"That you come and work for me. It carries a non-negotiable offer of four hundred thousand dollars paid in mutually agreeable installments. The project I have in mind is similar to Rohatyn's MAC. We are talking of a time frame of about twenty months" boomed da Souza. His confidence seem restored.

Perspiration glistened on Hunter's face. He stared at the arrogant old man. Apprehensive that the large sum da Souza had mentioned could become his, he repeated the sum almost inaudibly.

"Four hundred thousand US dollars…"

"A minor associate can temporarily handle your Newsletter, Mr. Hunter. Take my offer, and soon you will be free to enjoy the rest of your life in enviable luxury."

"I think you already know my answer," Hunter replied softly. His volatile emotion flared. He became distressed at what he considered his weakness in feeling as he did. He could not understand the process of the old man's thoughts.

Summoning up courage, he asked, "Is the ultimate objective to make more money for Zeus Industries?"

"I do it for power," said da Souza quietly. He leaned forward and put his clenched fist on the desk. Hunter backed away in his chair, smiling. He laughed with a touch of understanding derision.

"Power! I've always wanted power. When I was a child, I worked harder than other kids, and my mates grew up to hate me. As an adult, I grew up proud. I was not defective in any sense of the word. I believe the world is my oyster. I never lied or cheated. I had things worked out to be best and so be on top of my contemporaries. I became a politician in order to use my unique talent for the betterment of my people. But the political system became corrupt beyond redemption. In self-preservation, I came here in voluntary exile and went into business for myself. I hated the fat cats and city power brokers that ruined my political ambitions. In the last twenty years, I've worked ever so hard to gain economic powers beyond my imagination. I have vast foreign reserves that my foes lack, and I mean to use this power to accumulate political power in my home base."

Hunter relaxed as he digested the old man's logical rhetoric. "For a minute, I assumed you were the Mayor of Belfast. He daily repeats almost the same sentiments. No offence intended, of course."

"Then the Irish and I have much in common. Power, I've learned is the only weapon with which one can fully realize one's aspiration. Without power, man lives like a vegetable. Spineless like a worm. Power, however, is not my only desire, at least not for now. The strangest thing that ever happened to me was the death of my wife, Angela and only son David, on the 14th anniversary of my exile in Geneva. That was six years ago. The tragic loss makes it impossible for me to have any descendant to enjoy my vast fortunes. As a result, I have searched for a project to spend my last days on. I have researched random coincidences, luck, fate, predestination and unexplainable events that the cynical shrug off and the open-minded devour. I have tried to find a pattern, a reason. Cerebral types decipher them with intellectual scrutiny. Scientists set up experiments to re-create them and fail. Christian believers suspend logic and take them on faith linking it to telepathic psychic energy. Non-believers set about investigating with the aid of extra-sensory guides and tarot cards. I have not indulged in these crude interpretations, but have been intrigued by the eerie ethereal happenings," da Souza confessed.

"I've however, reached the irrevocable decision that I must do something for my former constituents in Lagos. And I do need your expertise to mastermind my economic package. I know the assets of Zeus can make some difference by providing foreign capital flow into Lagos."

Zeus has real estate holdings in the US and is conservatively valued at $1.5 billion; oil production and petrochemical production facilities are valued at about $900 million. Crude oil carriers are valued at about $540 million, while semiconductors, computers and engineering concerns valued at around $790 million.

Zeus's subsidiaries include banks, insurance companies, financial houses, and stock brokerage firms. We have department stores, pulp and paper manufacturing factory, publishing houses, cosmetic and fashion conglomerates. All of these combined add up to generate an annual net income of around $4.5 billion."

The silence that followed was interrupted by a soft knock on the door.

"Come on in," da Souza ordered. Andy Lincoln entered with a large box with ancient documents in his arms. He walked over to the desk and placed the box in front of the old man.

"Gentlemen, I believe you both know each other, at least by reputation," da Souza said, waving to the two to get acquainted.

The two grinned at each other. Hunter stood up slightly and shook hands with the Texan, Lincoln. The salutation complete, they both sat down and listened with rapt attention to the lord of the manor.

"In life, one has to be anguished to be inspired. Human beings tend to be complacent until a certain crisis fires their adrenalin, intoned da Souza in a voice of a born again leader. "I want the three of us to form an extraordinary team to accomplish my secret ideal. An ideal my late mentor Monsignor Sean McGovern would be proud of. I'm sure his spirit is watching even as I speak. Monsignor Sean was the priest brother of the famous oil man Danny McGovern, the Chairman of Greenspoint Oil Company. You both know Danny as one of the most respected in the oil industry and business world. Zeus Industries owes its birth and present success to the McGovern brothers. It was under their high powered guidance that I came to actualize my life dreams. Sean gave me my first insight, upon which my happiness and earlier achievements were based. He inspired my interest in political gamesmanship. This started my quest which I had hoped would have led me to someday become president of my nation. When my lofty hope was dashed and my life collapsed like a pack of cards, Danny readily came to my rescue. For ten years, I learned the oil business under Danny's expert eyes. I have, thanks to Danny, become rich beyond my wildest imagination. But the more I worked and prospered, the more I suffered the mental torture of my unfulfilled political dreams," da Souza said, reflectively.

"Six years ago, Andy was with me on that fateful night when my Angela and David departed this world in a ghastly car accident. I watched helplessly knowing all my wealth could not buy back their lives. Today, Zeus Industries is one of the great fortunes controlled by a private individual. If I were an American citizen, my name would appear annually in the Forbes 400. Had David lived, I may not be taking the steps to achieve this goal. I'm seventy and my doctors say I've cancer of the blood. I know that my time is limited. I intend to leave behind a legacy for the people whom I originally set out to serve. That way, I believe Sean McGovern's ideal would be accomplished. Then I may be lucky to gate crash past Saint Peter into Heaven."

Pointing to the box, he continued, "The contents therein are the necessary authority with which to liquidate the entire Zeus holdings. Every business subsidiary has a legally assessed value. My attorneys in New York, has been instructed to give you the necessary assistance. There are dossiers on top corporate jackals, bankers, consultants, contractors and vendors. The "fat cats" who combined to literally manipulate the Lagos economy. The wolf pack was eleven in number. These leading industrialists, disgruntled with the Nigerian Indigenization decree of 1972, set forces at work to manipulate the economy. When the explosion takes place as surely it must, I intend to use my vast resources to put a final stop to their activities. I want you to gather every available financial data on their businesses and personal activities. I want every incriminating detail of their dubious operations. Trace all their bank accounts, along with every illegal deal made, with whom, and dates. Gather this detailed information, and I shall have the ultimate weapon to schedule a meeting with the wolf pack," he boldly concluded.

"You mean to use fear to get them to cooperate with your plans for Lagos?" asked Hunter.

"Precisely, Mr. Hunter. And I bet you will not disappoint me with the details requested. Concerning foreign bond issues, am I right that foreign issues could rise as much as 30 percent in the next year, thus surpassing the overall gain expected of U.S. Securities? Moreover, should the strength of the U.S dollar wane, then foreign stock buyers will reap an additional bonus when they sell."

"I'm sure you're most correct in your assessments," replied Hunter.

"Yes, of course I am. I buy the best available information. I expect Andy and you to provide me with my precise details. Good hunting, gentlemen, and God speed."

CHAPTER NINE

The trip from Kano to Kaduna took two and a half hours. The driver's professional handling of the powerful Mercedes 450 SE ensured a smooth ride. Sitting in the back seat of the humming air conditioned car, Abba contemplated his plan of action.

It was true; he had never had to face so many crises all at once. But it was equally true that he had a tough spirit that had helped him reach his present life station.

At a very young age, Abba knew that he was a child of promise. He was bigger and more courageous than boys his age. He had been blessed with superior intellect. His physical height and intelligence made him the leader of his neighborhood gang. At the age of fifteen, he had mastered the Koran. The Imam who taught at the school prayed constantly for his destiny.

The Abdulmalik family was very large. It consisted of a dozen young males. The father of the house, Baba Abdulmalik, had started from a humble beginning. As a result of his successful industry, he had gained the confidence of both the native ruler and the white colonial overlords. His early education in the white man's school had given Baba Abdulmalik the foresight to acquire a vast expanse of cheap land. And as the city of Kano expanded, Baba Abdulmalik sold these lands. He used the capital from this to break the monopoly of the Ibos in groundnut trading in Kano. Gradually, the Abba's influence had grown in Kano, enabling him to erect the largest mansion as befitting evidence of his wealth.

In 1950, when the time for national politics came, it was Baba

Abdulmalik to whom intending contestants came for sponsorship. He gave generously of his time and money to the aspiring politicians. He believed he was above politics. He therefore endorsed the young men who would have been his own sons but for his wife's inability to bear him children.

He had married only one wife instead of the four stipulated in the holy book. His wife Hassana was barren. Instead of marrying other younger women to get offspring of his own, Baba Abdulmalik had insisted on keeping his one wife.

To fill the large compound, he had opened his doors to help the local orphans--Almagiris. He had given the young boys Islamic education and enough to eat. He sponsored the brilliant ones onto secondary schools. It was this early hospitality of Baba that had enabled Dogon Talata and Abba to move up in life's ladder.

In fact, many of the young orphan boys, who had shared the same humble roof with Abba during his boyhood were holding various important posts in the new civilian administration.

Abba recalled a drama which had occurred in his childhood days at Goron Dutse that was to reshape his life. He reminisced over this episode during his silent ride to Kaduna.

He had grown up to love and respect Baba Abdulmalik whom he had come to accept as his real father. The incident shook the very foundation of his loyalty to the Abdulmalik clan.

The boys had been playing the equivalent of the white man's polo game when he suddenly noticed a senile woman coughing terribly. Her body shook with spasm as if she were minutes away from death. He had been gravely moved. He was so touched by the pain the poor old woman was experiencing that he commanded his pals to stop playing their game. When Sidi Bala, his second in command, insisted that the game continue, he kicked him with great fury. He could not recollect when he landed a devastating kick on the skinny Bala. Bala fainted, but it was not him that he was concerned with. He hurriedly went to the aid of the dying woman.

After a drink of "fura de nunu"; a native yogurt milk that he had hurriedly purchased from a vendor, the woman regained momentary consciousness. Her eyes lit up and joy seemed to fill her countenance when she sighted Abba.

He could not help but notice the resemblance between himself and the dying woman. In fact, he was so moved that something deep inside forced him to call the woman, "Iya," mother. On hearing his voice, the woman smiled as if to say I've waited to see you just one more time. Thereafter, she gave up the ghost with an angelic countenance. Her transformed smile on the corpse contrasted deeply from the woman in agony whom he had initially set out to help. At that brief moment, she revealed a woman of certain beauty in her youth.

The incident left a deep scar on the thirteen year old boy. He decided, therefore, to carry out his own investigation concerning the deceased woman's real identity. He questioned his teacher at the Koranic school but none was any wiser about the woman's true identity.

His lucky break came four years later when he was student at the Government College, Hadejia.

The trip from Kano to Hadejia in the year 1955 was mostly by train. The train plied from Kano to Nguru. Passengers for Hadejia alighted at Mallam Madori and rode on donkeys for the remaining twenty miles to Hadejia. It was on the train that he had been recognized by the ticket collector and questioned about who his real father was.

Chance or fate must have been responsible for him losing his ticket. On questioning his lack of proof, the ticket collector had called him all sorts of names. He also threatened taking him to the local police station and from there, to prison. It was while he was pleading with the ticket collector in the staff cabin that the man suddenly stopped questioning him. Taking a closer look at him, the ticket collector inquired about his name, his age, and his parents. Surprised, he replied in a quivering voice that he was born in Kano. He was not exactly sure who his father was nor whereabouts of his mother. The ticket collector stood silent for some minutes, with mouth agape as though shocked by some potent symbol.

Gradually, his fears rescinded. He took a closer step to scrutinize the familiar feature between himself and the ticket collector. At that instant, he retold the story of the senile woman he had noticed exactly four years ago. Explaining in detail the similarity in appearance, he wondered if the dead woman might have been his real mother.

"My name is Lateef Isaq, and I've been looking for my elder brother, Ali Isaq. The last I heard of him was when he visited our home village in Bendel State with his Fulani wife. You see, we're from Etsako Local Government Area in Bendel State, Nigeria. Ali, a railway employee, had married a Fulani girl and came home to present his wife to our parents. Father became so angry that his first son married a non-native without his consent. He put a curse on Ali and his wife. Ali was then a ticket collector with the Railways and was based in Kano. He lived near the Goron Dutse quarters of Kano City. The curse must have shattered his life, for Ali was his father's oldest son. That was exactly seventeen years ago. And you say you lived in Goron Dutse - where this woman died four years ago? That must have been Amina. I remember her exactly, a very beautiful woman with the similar nose you have. The features match completely, especially the cheekbones."

He had listened to the ticket collector's story, but was not moved. This man must be mad, he reasoned. What else but arrant nonsense. His entire life had been spent dreaming that Baba would adopt him as his real son.

But his mind urged him to play along with the ticket collector if only to avoid paying the extra money for his lack of ticket.

Having made up his mind, he raised his voice and humbly replied: "I'll try and investigate all you're saying. I know definitely that blood is thicker than water. And if you're right, then you may become my uncle."

"In that case, let me play the role of your uncle. Not that I've anything to gain. My parents are dead and I'm the only male child remaining. Our compound has been taken over by our powerful neighbor. I'm also afraid to go home these days. The curse of our father is still upon our family lineage."

"Well I'm sorry to hear your sad story, but maybe if I can get your address, I can keep in touch so we could become friends," he replied. He was relieved he would not have to pay any fine. Besides, it is always good to develop a friendship with the ticket collectors.

By this time, the train had almost reached the last station. And prompted by emotional sentiments Lateef Isaq removed a ten shillings note from his bag of money and gave it to Abba. He also promised to visit him in school when he was free from duty.

Armed with the gift of ten shillings, Abba had started the glamorous life style that would earn him recognition as an international playboy later in life. From that day, whenever he was short of money, Uncle Lateef, now stationed in Mallam Madori, was always around to cater to the young man's need.

Back in Goron Dutse, he asked around for news of a man matching the description of Ali Isaq and was able to confirm such a man had existed some seventeen years back. Also, the woman whose features resembled that of Amina was reported to have gone mad shortly after giving birth to a baby boy. Baba Abdulmalik had offered shelter to the baby boy since the husband of the woman had died three weeks before the baby's birth. It was the shock of the man's death and the labor Amina had to endure that had finally driven her insane.

She had been left to roam the streets of Kano and had probably come to rest on a familiar spot that fateful day four years ago. Allah had thus made it possible for him to know his own true life story. It was no coincidence. Through the unfolding events that brought Uncle Lateef came into his life he became wiser.

After his investigation, he ruthlessly decided to opt for ignorance concerning the facts of history. He reasoned that if Allah had deemed it fit to make him an Abdulmalik, then so be it. Being crafty, his relationship with Uncle Lateef improved for the better. This was due to Lateef's knowledge of the affluent life in Lagos. The City of Lagos in the fifties was the biggest thing in the life of the nation. To have lived in Lagos was like having been overseas and enjoyed the white man's standard of living. Lateef was knowledgeable about Lagos. Abba's numerous visits to Lateef's house was in the hope of hearing more stories of the fantastic real-life characters who operated in the city of Lagos. Lateef also had plenty of cash. He was generous to the inexperienced youth. He came to gradually understand, the power he could wield with money.

Life at the Abdulmalik's compound also forced him to appreciate political power. Baba had authority over the politicians who were always pleading for his patronage. His respect for the power of money was reinforced by Lateef's tales of the first millionaires that operated on Lagos Island. Notable among those were the Greeks: Zarpass, Duramos and Leventis. Next came the Sierra Leoneans and the Liberians. Notable among these groups was the Liberian shipping magnate, Chief Dele Thomas Backays. According to Lateef, Ali, his elder brother, had been a close associate of the Liberians in the early twenties. Among the first Nigerians that joined the millionaires club was the big agricultural produce merchant and transporter, Mazi Ike Okafor from Onitsha Province. These elite groups lived a lifestyle of enjoying the best wines, wheels and women that money could buy. They lived opulently and were respected by the British.

The stories of the escapades of the first Nigerian wheeler-dealers became a motivating force in the brain of young Abba.

From Lateef, he learned of the Kreugerian saga. The story of Ivar Kreuger, the Swedish "match King" who built a world monopoly on matches. He was a seemingly successful giant who later became a spectacular business failure of all times. Abba was fascinated with the stories of this monopoly creator of a half-billion dollar industrial empire. This celebrated Wall Street lender of money to European governments became his hero. At night, he dreamt of the day he would become a millionaire. He planned to live an extravagant life with a huge mansion. He envisaged himself as one of Lagos "movers and shakers." He would show the bulk of the rich people how truly to enjoy wealth.

While his classmates continued with their education at the Hadejia Government College, his interests gradually shifted to becoming an active participant in the good life. He determined to abandon his Cambridge School Certificate Examinations. He opted to get out of school of his own accord.

With some travel money from Baba Abdulmalik, he set off from Kano Railway Station. He was happy to travel in the cold month of November. His destination was Lagos to seek his own fortune. His main contact in Lagos was Lateef Isaq. He was now stationed at the Lagos Railway Terminal. Baba Abdulmalik also gave him names of close friends to contact at Obalende, Lagos.

He had been lucky and quickly learned to speak the Yoruba dialect. He was also introduced to Mr. Brad, the British Manager of the United African Company by Lateef. Within two years, he became one of the top salesmen. The company, at this time, was embarking on the national character quota system .This was policy whereby Nigerians from the northern part of the country were given favorable opportunities. They obtained on-the-job training for future management positions. They were to become indigenous Hausa managers for the company's projects in Kano.

His tenure at the U.A.C. gave him extensive business management education. His Kano origin was a major factor his fast rise. He spent ten years in the company. The cumulative experiences he gained enabled him start up his AAA Incorporated. The going had been good.   However, the present austerity measures seemed to be threatening the very foundation of all his dreams.

A solution no doubt must be found. He prayed Allah not to let him lose everything he had labored so hard to achieve. He therefore drew up a list of possible power brokers resident in Kaduna whom he would contact. Looking out of the car, he realized they were approaching Ahmadu Bello Way. They would soon, reach his Katchia Road residence.

CHAPTER TEN

Abba's guest house in Katchia was beautifully decorated. He took pride that the grand design was his brain child. He also appreciated his planning the guest house to be strategically located on Katchia Road. The realization that his guest house was a comfortable place of rest and strategically located on the motorway to Abuja, lifted his sad spirit. It served as home away from home to top government officials posted to the Federal capital city.

The house usually came alive at one o'clock in the afternoon. That was the time for the powerful controllers of the projects in the new city visited. They relaxed and swam in the Olympic sized swimming pool. The building's interior decorations was superbly done. Each room had its own video recording machine and twenty-five inch Sony color television set. The video library had an enviable collection of assorted movies. The girls from the nearby polytechnic were always around in expectation of sugar daddy visitors who were generous with their cash.

As the Mercedes car approached the gate, he could see the profile of Idris Gumel in his "Baba riga" attire. Idris, the sales manager of the AAA motor company looked skeleton thin. His physical condition revealed his deep fears that his job was being threatened. The shipment of the month's batch of cars from Japan had been stopped due to non-payment for the previous batch. News of the import license being recalled by the government meant drastic consequences on Gumel's livelihood. This was apparent in his disheveled appearance. His face showed that he had been drinking heavily.

"Good afternoon sir," Gumel saluted, opening the door as the car came to a halt.

"Good day to you," replied Abba. "I hope you haven't started hitting the bottle again."

"Well sir, wetin man go do? All these bad news may mean an end to my career as your sales manager, "replied Idris Gumel in sober reflection.

Moving past him into the lounge, Abba asked, "Is anybody staying in the house? The Ministers from Abuja, have they not arrived yet?"

A genuine laugh bubbled up Idris' throat.

"Those crafty rogues. There is an alleged fraudulent transaction involving over fifty million naira." He added quickly, "We heard they are under police investigation. You know Lawrence Kamalo and Musa Kafin are now inmates at the Alagbon Close .Or possibly at the Lagos Maximum Security Prison Kiri-Kiri Quarters for criminals and public enemies."

"Have you gone crazy?" "How can you speak so harshly?" He asked fuming.

"Well, I'm sorry, sir. But I've been feeling a little bit funny since the beginning of these austerity measures. My spiritual guru tells me to pray seriously to Allah. The future, he says, is hazardous. But I'm equally worried for you too Alhaji."

"We shall survive alright by the power of Allah. And don't you go feeling sorry for me. Try the phone and see if it's in working condition. If so, call Don Cattorini. Tell him to come over here. Fast!" commanded Abba.

The meeting with Don Cattorini was essential to Abba's scheme to continue the Abuja project and offset AAA's cash flow crunch. Don Catto, as he was generally referred to by his close friends. He controlled three textile industries in the Kaduna. Rumor had it that as a native of Sicily, he had connections with the Mafia. He had lived most of his adult life in Kaduna. He also owned the local gambling Casino and transfered millions of naira away annually from Nigeria to finance his foreign businesses. His management style could be described as totally Machiavellian.

Don Catto in the past had pursued Abba to help him get his import licences. The sleek Don Catto had impressed Abba as a man that could depend on for future help. And so reposing absolute confidence in Don Catto, he had promptly taken action to obtain the licenses. On the trip from Kano this morning, he had decided that Don Catto, would be his financial agent. Therefore, he didn't call on the Cooperative Bank manager, after receiving the information from Chibuko. He also knew his company's credit at the bank could not be extended. Abba trusted he would obtain adequate finance for AAA's present need from Don Catto.

Two hours later, the front door bell rang and in came the sleek Italian. He displayed Sicilian sleekness beneath the impeccably tailored silk suit. The fifty-five year old Don Catto took great care of his appearance and could pass for forty.

He took a quick look round the room and sat down comfortably stretching his long legs.

"Well, Alhaji, I came as soon as I could. In fact, I've been wanting to see you concerning my Lebanese friends and my machinery spare parts."

Abba rang the bell to summon the house boy after inquiring what drink to offer the financier. The presence of Don Catto and his assured self-confidence brightened his hope of a possible solution to AAA's sinking fortune.

He wondered just how well informed Don Catto was about the present gloomy economy.

"Yeah, your Lebanese friends, it was a pleasure to do business with them that last time around. Say, what's their problem now?"

"It certainly has to do with their importation of raw material for their industries. There is this new flour mill Ben Abdullahi and his brother helped to finance last year. Their raw material for production will be exhausted in four weeks. They are running the mill at fifty percent capacity. That way, the material available will last a further two months."

These Lebanese all seemed to know just what profitable investment to put their money into, Abba thought to himself.

Aloud, he hedged, "You realize that the conditions for import licenses have become more difficult than was previously the case."

"You mean the austerity measure. Sure! Everybody has started feeling the pinch. The spare parts I need for my factories cannot be cleared through Port Harcourt. I'm told I have to pay duties of over five hundred percent. It is crazy "An unholy look seemed to glow on Don Catto's cheeks." In Italy, people could get killed for demanding customs duties like that. That is gospel truth," he concluded

Changing the tempo of the conversation, Abba pronounced, "I guess this is not Italy. We have our own ways in Nigeria. We negotiate through intermediaries. And it should be less expensive if you've the right contacts. You know the process"

Don Catto nodded." Thanks. I knew I could always depend on you. Your phone call was just the medicine. I needed to hear from you."

While he spoke, Abba's mind darted from one consideration to another. He mentally weighed how best to persuade Don Catto. He needed to raise one million naira, without arousing the Italian's greed.

"As I said, Don Catto, I can help both you and your friends. That is if you've the right sum up front, "concluded Abba.

"And how much do you think is the right sum?" demanded Don Catto in a conspiratorial tone.

Abba shrugged. "I've to be straight with you. I need the sum of seven hundred and fifty thousand naira. Common sense tells me, with such an amount of money we can influence any official no matter how highly placed." He paused to gauge Don Catto's reaction. *Mouse trapped?* He wondered and prayed that his anxiety would not be too obvious. He was really desperate for a million naira. He decided to throw in a little preparatory softening.

"Make a list of what licenses you and your friends want, to cover the seven fifty grand. Get me the list plus the money and rest assured that I'll deliver the booty. I have some friends in Port Harcourt who could help spring your wares for you at a reasonable cost. This is conditional to your lending me an extra two hundred and fifty thousand. I cannot give you any collateral. Of course, our agreement is based on gentleman's agreement."

Don Catto stood up and walked around the empty chair. Holding it forward, he stared intently into the roof. He had been dazed by the glib way his host had explained away his need for the one million naira. Yet his Sicilian logic made sense of the demand. It was like Abba had been from his native town. Business was considered business.

"One million naira won't be difficult to gather. It might take some time of course. Be rest assured that you're dealing with a man of honor. As you say, you're in need. I will find ways to help you raise the amount. I will of course, demand that you keep your own part of the bargain. "Don Catto paused, Well my dear Alhaji, I pray that our business friendship will continue to flourish. Prudence, however, demands that you hand over the title deed to your properties in Kaduna and Kano. I mean the residential homes. This is just my own way of ensuring that the million naira rests in trusted hands. I am sure you understand."

Abba hesitated momentarily. A pang of dread shot into his heart. Don Catto noticed the hesitation.

"But Alhaji, you must know even for a big Italian entrepreneur like myself, handing over the sum of one million naira to a friend can be too much. Also, the shrewd instinct in me persuades me to give only one third of the requested sum. The remaining two thirds will come in two installment payments after the delivery of my imported machinery spare parts from the customs officials in Port Harcourt." Don Catto summed and watched warily. He knew that time would reward his prudence. Abba grinned. He had to make a decision. He was confident Don Catto would deliver the initial three hundred thousand naira as soon as he got the title deed to his Katchia and Lamido Crescent homes. A sixth sense, however, warned him not to agree to the demand. The surrender of his homes was not negotiable. The odds were overwhelmingly against his ever getting the houses back. He sweated cold sweats and became lost in thought. Time seem to stand still as he mentally debated his response. Money had the power to make people do unthinkable feats. Greed, however made him think of immediate survival. He calculated the purchasing power the three hundred thousand naira would afford him. He would at least use the money to finance his immediate needs. He also knew that he would grease the palm of government workers and to continue to fund his lavish lifestyle.

Instinctively, Abba glanced at his solid gold wristwatch. The time was three o'clock. It meant Chibuko would reach Katchia Road at any moment.

"Well, Don Catto, you drive a hard bargain. I do really need the money urgently. Three hundred thousand would be exactly short for my needs. Suppose you increase it to five hundred and fifty thousand. And bring it all tonight in cash. I will have my lawyer drop in this evening. He will hand over the title deed to you. I will also throw in the Rolls-Royce Silver for good measure. One more thing I'll promise you is that your spare parts will be released from Port Harcourt. All I need is a clear line through on the phone to my friend resident there."

"Ok, Alhaji, I'll bring five hundred and fifty thousand first thing in the morning rather than tonight. I'll be here with the money before noon tomorrow. Prepare the title and bye for now, until tomorrow." Don Catto promised. He then made his exit.

So much had happened in half an hour. The fact that the deal was consummated in that brief time both appalled and elated Abba. And for the first time since the meeting at the Brussels Sheraton Hotel, he was relaxed. His happiness centered on the anticipated resources almost at hand. It will help him to battle the austerity plague. As always, it took money to make money. Sipping a dry martini, he decided he would have an early night.

Later in the evening after Chibuko had come and gone, he sat up to plan the Abuja trip before retiring for the night. Tomorrow he would commence the execution of the day's decision. While he worked, thoughts of a female companion to celebrate the occasion with crossed his mind. A pity, he was the only one in the house. Haruna Sule had gone off to visit his wife and children after dropping Mr. Chibuko at Abuja project site.

Chibuko had been surprised to learn that Abba had been able to find financial solution to stop the striking workers. He left, therefore, to go back to the project site. He would calm the workers, informing them that help was on the way. Together with the site supervisor they were to get the accounts straightened out. Abba would pay off the essential debt when he visited Abuja the following afternoon.

CHAPTER ELEVEN

At about 9.00 p.m., Abba was just slipping into a deep slumber when the phone rang. Cursing the inefficient long distance operator, he picked up the instrument.

"Hello," he bellowed into the phone.

"Dear! Did I wake you up, Alhaji?"

Martina's voice seemed so far away.

"Sorry. I'm in Kaduna for the annual Trade Fair. Right now I'm bored, my companion having gone to visit his family. I wonder if you are not too busy to take care of me for the night."

"My dear Tina, how are you? It's been quite an age! In fact, I'm all on my own. Some diversion would do my melancholy just fine," he responded cheerfully.

"My driver is away right now. Do pick up a taxi and come along. I suppose you can find your way."

After hanging up he dialed the local operator to inquire if his call to Port Harcourt was through. On hearing his name, the operator begged him to hold on until he was connected.

The personal call to Chief I.K. Madu was very brief. "How is your body?"

"Chief, I'm fine and okay. I want you to help my friend clear his consignment from the Port Harcourt Wharf ... I'll send the particulars to you by next Monday."

"Okay, tell your friend that there will be no problem! It may take some time. The customs boys are getting tougher. But still, no problem! I will let you know the expenses when I see you."

"Thanks, Chief, I knew I could depend on you." Hanging up, he hurriedly had a hot bath and after rubbing himself clean, felt fit to entertain Martina.

As the doorbell rang, he walked leisurely to open the door.

"What a beauty you've turned out to be," he couldn't help remarking.

Martina stood still, not too sure if there were other women in the apartment. Her past experience made her cautious.

Noticing her apprehension, he laughed. "You have always been a frightful girl. Feel at home; it is just you and I in the whole house."

A moment later they were both on the bed. He had never felt so good since his ordeal began in Europe. This was the way he knew to reduce his tension. Martina was very experienced in the art of manifold stimulation. Exhausted but happy, he slept and snored heavily. He would, of course, reward her generously. Abba reckoned that with Don Catto bringing half a million the next day, he would plan more strategically. Armed with that sum of money, he would be sure to triumph over the monstrous austerity measures. With resolve and determination to show the government officials he was a tough man to beat, he drifted into a comfortable sleep--the most relaxed sleep he had since his return from Europe.

When he woke the next morning at about seven o'clock, Martina had gone. She left a thank you message for his three hundred naira gift. Momentarily recollecting the events of the night, he smiled and woke into the new day to prepare for the hard tasks ahead.

He had just finished his breakfast when Don Catto phoned to say he would be around at exactly ten thirty. He had been lucky, he announced, to have gathered the requested amount. Abba's own lawyer had already visited and brought the title to the two houses. A formal handing over statement of the house plus contents had been drafted and made ready for Abba's signature. The papers for the Rolls Royce had also been looked into by the lawyer. Don Catto could have the car at his own leisure.

By noon, all the arrangements had been concluded. The customs bill of lading for Don Catto's spare parts was given to Abba. He promised to see to its onward transmission to the pirate chief's office in Port Harcourt. Don Catto also gave him the detailed lists of the request of his Lebanese associates and agreed sum in twenty naira denominations. In return, he got the title deed to the two properties, and the key together with the particulars of the Rolls Royce Silver Spirit.

The negotiation, no doubt, left both parties mutually satisfied. He saw Don Catto to his car and immediately set off for the two hour drive to Abuja.

The deal of raising the cash must have been one of the fastest in the business world. He was vaguely aware that the properties in Kano and Kaduna were both worth just below four hundred thousand. The Rolls Royce Silver Spirit model had a market value of under a hundred thousand.

"Somehow, I will find ways to help you raise you the remaining amount. I, of course, demand that you keep your own part of the bargain. "Don Catto cautioned."Well my dear Alhaji, I hope that our business friendship will continue to flourish."

CHAPTER TWELVE

The effects of the austerity measures on the new city were quite shocking. Where previously a teaming army of daily workers marched to and from the project sites, the sight that greeted Abba on this trip reminded him of the movie *'The Ghost Town.'* Almost every face had a peculiar hungry countenance.

Even his driver, who seldom spoke in his presence, was forced to venture in the Hausa language, saying, "There are a whole multitude of hungry people out here."

"Haka ne," Abba contributed. "Yes, there must be some powerful reason to explain this scarcity. Gloom and doom had taken over this city of plenty. The answer must, no doubt, be found in Lagos. "After all," he reasoned Lagos was still the capital of the country."

At the project site, the combined presence of Chibuko, the six site supervisors and the Project Manger helped to assure the angry workers that their money would reach them before nightfall. The workers, who were mostly bricklayers, had been meek and patient. They prayed for the success of the merciful Alhaji's undertaking. Their gratitude was justified as other contractors had merely abandoned their projects and workers and fled to God-knew - where.

After learning of the non-payment for their completed contracts, many of the contractors fled from the city. They abandoned the daily paid workers to their own individual fate. Notable among these was the contractor handling the project next to AAA's site. So callous was he that he not only refused to show up at the site, but got his thugs to beat up the site engineers that visited his Lagos office for payment of their outstanding debts.

The firm's equipment and building materials were still lying abandoned on the site. Meanwhile, the contractor took off for a six week holiday in Europe to burn some of his ill-gotten money.

After the payment to the laborers, the suppliers of the

building materials were next to being settled. As the amount owed was so much, Chibuko suggested that only fifty percent of the total sum owed such suppliers would be released. The other fifty percent would be paid as soon as AAA received payment in Lagos. The suppliers had initially wanted to rebel. But seeing the determination on Chibuko's face, they collectively conceded. This wise alternative, helped stretch the five hundred thousand naira or it scarcely could have been be enough.

Thanks to Chibuko, Abba was able to spend just three hundred thousand naira. He hoped that the spent money would be recouped in Lagos.

It was almost nightfall by the time the last creditor was paid. Leaving the rest of his employees to be settled by Chibuko, Abba strolled over to the Government Rest House, the elite club for the Abuja top brass.

On approaching the club, he was bewildered by the solemn silence surrounding the property. Usually, things would have started to swing by this time of the evening. But for all the noise he could hear, he might as well have been at the graveyard. The morbid inactivity was scarcely believable as the club was noted for its hectic disco parties.

Fortunately, the old barman was there to greet him, "Good day sir, Alhaji! It's been long since we saw you last."

"Yes, Bako. Tell me, where is everybody?" he inquired.

"Well Oga, "It is because of the austerity. The government has no money to pay contractors. It also reported that some directors of the project at the new city gathered together to steal about fifty million naira. Two days ago, the police came to arrest the people concerned.

They took them away for an official meeting in Lagos. We are bracing up for economic belt-tightening to combat this austerity blight."

"Is that so?" Abba whistled.

"That is so, "replied Bako."Oga Alhaji, I beg you, help me with some naira that I'll take to eat. Hunger has nearly killed me and my family."

Dipping into his trouser pocket, he came up with a twenty naira note, which he passed over to the bar attendant. And before the man could properly thank him, Abba marched out of the deserted club house.

Back at AAA's project site office, he left instructions with Chibuko to bring over all the vouchers for the outstanding payment from the government. He prayed that he would be lucky to collect the money when he reached Lagos the following Monday.

"I have all the papers ready here and also the bill for the extra expenses spent for the procurement of building materials since the escalation of prices. Alhaji Sule Maigari especially requested that we include it in our next bill. There is also the variation bill," continued Chibuko.

"The payment we made for the Abuja land to locate the brewery factory has been acknowledged. Alhaji Sule Maigari said all we needed was to erect a factory as soon as the paper reached your hands. He, of course, expects you to grease his palm. He assured me, he is not a greedy man. The standard pay-off is five percent of the factory project cost,"

"The damned idiot," Abba swore. "The trouble with this country is that the members of the Senate, the House of Representatives including all the civil servants indulge in practices that could be defined as anything from conflict of interest to cruel extortion. You may not know it, John, but the brewery deal has been put on hold by our German partners. Imagine how much I wasted in bribes to get this land for the building site. Now I can't even see someone to buy it from me. Yet Maigari wants me to continue to pay him money. The system really is sick."

"Yes, sir," replied Chibuko. "If only everyone wasn't so naira-minded. We all tend to worship the naira more than we care for our loved ones. Only God can rescue us from our worship of Naira."

"That is very well put. The white man says Nigeria is the 'Naira worshippers' jungle. Now, John, let me have the bills. Have you got any cash to last you until I return from Lagos? Something tells me I may be there longer than I intend to."

"The major problem is our two banks; they are on my neck. If only we can open an account with the African Continental Bank. I know the Kaduna Branch Manager. He might be able to help us. Chibuko advised"

"Really! Why did I not think of that? I think I will leave you with about twenty five thousand naira. Open the account as soon as the bank opens on Monday. Forward the document for my signature at my suite. Remember you're my front man, and I'll be depending on you now more than ever. I pray you don't betray my trust. But should you, Allah will reward your atrocities."

Aggrieved, Chibuko sharply protested, "Why! Sir, I've been with you since 1970.It has been over thirteen years now. Have I ever been unfaithful or disloyal? Why must you talk to me like this? I've served you well and will continue to maintain loyal service to you. Of course, I'm not a thief."

"I'm terribly sorry" Abba apologized. "The past four days must've been too much for me. The realization of the loss I've to bear, all on account of this austerity, must be my reason for acting so absent-mindedly. Do accept my apologies. I'll make up for this temper of mine when I return from Lagos. See me off to the car, John, and let's resolve to maintain our friendship. I'm returning to Kaduna tonight. From there, I'll drive to Kano tomorrow for some urgent business, ísha allah . I'll sleep in Lagos on Monday. Should any emergency occur, you can fly down to meet me at my hotel suite."

"Okay, sir," replied John, not fully recovered from Abba's unexpected onslaught. "Good bye sir, and God bless."

CHAPTER THIRTEEN

Dr. Richard sat up late into the night engrossed in the Lagos Monthly report about the increasing number of corporate bankruptcies in Lagos. The figure for the second and third quarters of 1983 will increase greatly. This was according to the statistics from one of the nation's largest accounting firms. The year would end up perceptibly worse than the last year. Small companies were the hardest hit with half the failures in the construction and contracting business. He reasoned he was experiencing the worst moments of his life and business career. In fact, his once successful life had taken a dramatic downward turn since he returned from London the previous Thursday morning.

At dawn on Saturday, he decided to send his wife and three children away to his parents in Ondo State. He believed that his parents residing in Akure, the capital of the state will have the good cheer of entertaining their grandchildren. This was a gesture he did not particularly care to accord them except when situations became unbearable in his Victoria Island residence. To coax his wife Sade, who had initially refused to go on the trip, he offered his newly acquired symbol of power, the Mercedes 500 SEL aerodynamic and his trusted driver of three years to take the family to Akure. The bait of the car had motivated Sade to hurriedly pack, and they left the house around noon. No doubt the opportunity would allow Sade to visit her own village where she could show off her husband's Mercedes. Richard could not help but laugh at the childish showoff.

Before their wedding, Sade's father had been against the marriage. Because he was relatively successful as a trader, he had wanted his daughter to marry into the merchant class. Richard, the eldest son of the farmer Kemidare was certainly not rich enough for his only daughter. But Sade stuck to her guns by running off with Richard, and on the wedding day, there was not enough to eat and drinks did not flow. The humiliation suffered by the newlyweds had moved their guardian angels to show mercy on them. Being of a brilliant mind, Richard had saved to study at home for his Cambridge School Certificate Examination. After passing the examination with flying colors, the resident politician helped Richard obtain tuition sponsorship for a year from the government of the Western Region. Thus, in 1960 at age 28, Richard set off on the ocean liner "River Niger" from the Lagos Apapa Wharf for Belfast. As a black student in the Northern Ireland city of Belfast, his life had not been easy. He had survived, working as a cleaner in the ship dockyard. He worked the midnight shifts and hours to supplement his tuition fees.

During Richard's second year in the city, he was able to bring over his wife Sade who worked at a local textile factory. In fact, while he studied for his geography degree at Belfast, he worked at the dock yards learning the business aspects of the shipping agency. It had then been his dream to set up his own corporate freight forwarding agency once he returned to his motherland. After ten years at the University of Belfast, he had obtained his Master's Degree in geography and duly returned to Nigeria with enough money to set up his own shipping agency. Time had been benevolent, and the agency had grown over the years.

The poverty that smothered him as a young man had gradually run away from him and his immediate family. His numerous investments would leave him with enough to live comfortably, no matter what fate brought his way, or at least he always thought.

The news unfolding after the President's announcement of the austerity measures all seemed to conspire to shake the very faith he had built up in the capitalist system.

True to his promise to Binta Lilah, he had investigated the state of the nation's economy through his trusted friends. The truth of the matter was that the shock of the revelation had been too much for him.

The first call he made when he reached his home on that Thursday morning was to his cousin, an accountant with the Arab-Nigerian Merchant Bank. Bola Lawani had remained silent on the phone and said he would drive over on his way home from the office.

Shortly before six, the doorbell rang, and Bola briskly walked in. He carried six bottles of cold imported Heineken beer. In the course of the hours that followed the beer was consumed.

"The joke of it all", according to Bola," was the fact that the Lagos Reserve Bank was not aware of the extent of our foreign financial commitments. The bank's foreign currency reserve was falsely recorded to be in healthy surplus. The actual figures were very much in the red. The reason for this discrepancy has, of course, never been checked out. In a Western country, heads would have rolled over such carelessness but not here."

"Also, the fraudulent issuing of import licenses to greedy middlemen enabled these ruthless capitalist merchants to purchase luxury goods in vast quantities. Goods which, as a developing country, we would be better off without."

'Speechless", Richard begged Bola to continue.

"Another important factor was the huge amount of money transferred from the country to pay for properties in the Western capital cities. The politicians and the rich businessmen were the main culprits in this crime." "Over-inflated "Form M" from the banks allowed manufacturers to have surplus foreign exchange. This promoted capital flight and satisfied their individual whims. Let's not forget a lot of Nigerians today own a fleet of very expensive imported cars. I know three of our customers in the banks have their own Gulf Twin-Star engine planes. In Kano, about ten indigenous businessmen own their Boeing 727 planes. To get to London, all they need is to ask their captain to take off anytime, any day. There is no hassle of waiting for scheduled flights. These planes are also used to export millions of naira currency. This was exchanged in European cities for as little as three naira to one pound sterling.

With such a low exchange rate, the speed to build the new capital city created a lot of loopholes for devious contractors to make away with uncountable millions. It would be normal for a city of that size to have taken between fifteen to twenty years to be fully commissioned. Not so for Nigerians, we are so much in a hurry. The Abuja city would, when completed set a new world record in the building of new capitals. The politicians aided by storing huge amounts of both foreign and local currencies for the next election. They reasoned it is best that they invest the money abroad. Switzerland has always had a certain attraction for this illegally acquired funds belonging to politicians from African countries. The Swiss banking system generally safe guards this ill-gotten wealth. A case in point is da Souza. Even if the army should take over the government, it would be impossible to recover these funds. We hear tales of da Souza's massive wealth every day. The cost of acquiring appropriate technology can be classified as costing the country a huge sum of foreign reserves. The Board members of the nationalized industries comprise of incompetent mediocrities and mostly parasitic party members enjoying comfortable sinecures. Thus, vast sums of money are expended without the resultant return in profits or efficiency."

"Yeah, the case of these incompetent gradually displacing brilliant minds in organized institutions has always been a universally accepted practice." replied Richard. "In fact, the principle has been in existence even before the birth of modern democracies. I believe it has to do with trust and loyalty."

"That reminds me, "continued Bola Lawani, now on his fifth bottle of the cold lager beer. "I've not enumerated the external factors contributing to this belt-tightening austerity." With anguished eyes, he stared intently at the last remaining bottle of Heineken as if begging for more.

Taking the cue, Richard shouted across the large room for the house boy to bring more Heineken beer.

Smiling, Bola took a long drink and lapsed back into the conversation.

"The external cause for this austerity has been brewing since the oil crisis of 1973.Since the past decade, Western scientists have been moving gradually towards the utopia to develop viable alternative to oil. But they have not been lucky enough to make any meaningful progress. Sensing this failure, the various governments pressed on for conservation of energy."

The Western governments' inability to find cheap alternative source of energy further fueled them into pressing for energy conservation from their consumers. The result of this campaign has been a net reduction in the need for oil in the Western countries. Examples are fuel-efficient cars, the computerization of production factories, robots building cars, and various other quality products limiting energy wastage. OPEC must suffer the consequences of the resultant world oil glut. Having less demand for the OPEC oil, Western countries, no doubt, have finally achieved the perfect weapon to disorganize the cartel. Countries like Iran, short of foreign currencies, have thus started reducing the standard OPEC price for their light crude oil. The Central Bank of Nigeria's statistical figure for the past weeks showed that our major American customers have limited their buying from Nigeria, thus creating further scarcity of foreign exchange. Their argument is that their capacity is full for the present. But, I suspect, they are probably refusing to buy in the hope that we would lower our prices. But for now, I do not think it would be in our best interest to lower any price. This is currently the position government is taking. So, our oil market is virtually at a standstill, disallowing us the use of needed foreign exchange."

"The activities of the Western bankers also have a major impact on our present problem. Back in the early 70's when the demand for oil from the OPEC nations was at its all-time high, American bankers relentlessly pursued the Finance Ministers of the OPEC cartel enticing these ministers with bribes in order that they convince their respective governments to borrow money from the Wall Street banks."

"So anxious were these American bankers to lend money to our country that they underestimated the risk of default. Their major pre-occupation was to have dormant funds working for them and earning very high interest. Today, the situation has changed, and the current debt situation of countries like Argentina, Venezuela, Brazil, Mexico, Poland, Chile, Peru and Nigeria all add up to over three hundred billion dollars, increasing daily with interest. Some of these countries do not, at the moment, have enough foreign reserve to even pay interest on the accumulated amounts owed. Yet they must still borrow more in order to pay interest on the outstanding debts."

"The enormity of the debt crisis is posing serious problems for the capitalist system of government. In fact, I believe that short of a miracle, the debt situation could well bring about the end of capitalism as we now know it."

"But for the wasteful mismanagement and bad luck, which the present oil glut brought to Nigeria, we could have been in a better position than either Mexico or Brazil. Inflation in the two countries is now over two hundred percent due to food shortage and black marketeering. Ours is rising and will yet reach over three hundred. The short-term remedy is that Nigeria must submit to the orthodoxics of the International Monetary Fund. This will further result in massive cuts in public spending and huge drop in the importation of essential commodities. Also we may be forced to devalue the naira. These punitive measures must herald untold human sufferings and for how long no one can predict."

"To conclude, the President had no choice but to introduce the unfavorable austerity measures. The depressive business cycle will in time create hyper-inflation, and I'll be surprised if massive unemployment especially at the graduate level does not become rampant in the next six months." Lifting up his glass of beer, Bola drained the remaining contents saying, "The beer has helped carry my memory along."

Glancing at his wristwatch, Bola stood up, regretting he had spent more hours than he expected. "I must hurry home or my wife Bisi will be furious. I'll look into your corporate finances at the bank and will come over next Saturday evening. Possibly by that time, you would've digested fully how the austerity will affect your business operations, especially your new shipping line." Bola concluded.

Seeing Bola to the door, Dr. Richard felt disappointed that the young man had not thought it fit to discuss his own business tonight.

Aloud, he replied, "Take your time, but make a detailed search to see what leverage I can use with my other investment bankers. It has suddenly occurred to me that I may be forced to move out of this apartment. It's very expensive, and the current lease runs out at the end of this month. Good bye for now, and drive with care. Greet Bisi and your son for me."

CHAPTER FOURTEEN

The next morning after Bola's visit, Dr. Richard visited his merchant bankers who were handling the new Kemidare Tire Manufacturing project. The news he received from the Bank Manager helped to confirm his fears. The rising timidity on the part of private banks was exacerbating the effect of the austerity on the Lagos business community.

Mr. Taylor, the manager, had forcefully voiced his inability to provide further finance to the Kemidare Tire Company.

"The point I'm stressing, Dr. Richard, is that your tire project is constrained by the current scarcity," he stated emphatically.

Dr. Richard replied that the tire industry would be in great demand in the country. "The potential for export into the Economic Community of West African States and other African countries is also very high," he concluded.

"Yes, but Nigeria is such a high cost economy," the manager elaborated. "Our high labor cost will always undermine your ability to achieve a high record for exports. At least not for local tires. You will have to compete in the tire market with Lagos based multinational firms like Dunlop, Michelin, not to mention the numerous illegal imports from abroad.'

"The present austerity will also escalate the cost of natural rubber, I know that license for machines and spare parts will be nearly impossible to obtain. Another headache is the government's directive to manufacturers to sell tires at a standard price and not to increase prices arbitrarily. These uncontrollable cost variables plus the special skilled labor needed to ensure viable profit, would definitely make it unrealistic for my bank to continue to finance Kemidare Tires. A further piece of prudent advice, Dr. Richard, is for you to liquidate all your high capital expenditures. I know certainly that pioneering into high technical enterprise will worsen your financial security in these months of austerity. Take my advice and trim your investments. By that, we want you to become lean, mean and smart. That is what survivors do when the going gets tough. Concentrate on the proper management of Kemidare's impressive range of commercial and residential properties. Evaluate new property development, but do not start building anything. Then wait and see for the next nine months. Your shipping firm I've heard is about to fold up?"

Mr. Taylor paused in his monologue and stared at Dr. Richard to see how he was reacting.

"That tire industry is my next major interest after the property management company. It's like my entire future depends on bringing it to life," Dr. Richard replied. "As you know, the new ocean liners I bought will have to be re-sold in order to pay the custom duties, and no buyer has come forward yet. So I'm entirely dependent on the tire industry. To borrow the bankers phrase, 'I may boom or burst' on the tire project. I cannot abandon it now."

"The reason I'm telling you all of this, Dr. Richard, is that I've more facts than the entire economic research staff of other banks. Also I've taken a deeper interest in the tire factory since we became your merchant bankers. After all, I was intending to invest heavily in it myself, but we must be pragmatic for now. We can re-start the project at a later date. But with this austerity and the mediocre policy of the government's economic management team, one would be best advised not to venture into any risky business. Do you understand me?"

Dr. Richard nodded. "Perfectly, and thanks for your advice all the same. I'll need more time to plan and re-strategize. It'll be like reducing myself to total unemployment. The tire project has been on my mind for over six years. I had hoped it would compensate for selling off my ships."

Dr. Richard left the bank's building slightly relieved. For better or worse, he decided, he must reduce his investments in the tire plant. The conversation with Mr. Taylor, therefore, made him happier than he had previously been. He was satisfied, he had made a major decision.

But his happiness was short-lived. Soon after leaving Mr. Taylor's office, he called on Tunji Miller, his stock broker. At Miller's office, he learned that most of the shares in his investment would not be paying dividends at least until the next year. Most of the institutional investors were short of working capital and had started unloading shares of manufacturing-based industries.

These manufacturing firms had problem of inadequate raw materials. In the past, they had to buy import licenses from middle men at highly inflated prices. But with the current austerity measures, even these licenses had all been recalled. The bad news about his shares, mostly in the manufacturing industries, was all Dr. Richard needed to have a heart attack. In the past, he had reckoned that with the income from the Kemidare property company, his annual income could be the envy of most small corporate chief executives. He had therefore cultivated the habit of investing surplus sums of money in the Lagos Stock Exchange. The annual income from these secured his invested capital. The dividends provided the main stay for him and his family, leaving his other incomes for further business investments.

The four bedroom apartment he leased in Victoria Island was paid for from the dividend, which the shares provided. He knew the lease would expire very soon and the sum of one hundred and fifty thousand naira must be handy in order to re-negotiate another three year contract. Failing to renew the lease would mean that the Kemidare family would become homeless, deprived of their elegant residence on Victoria Island.

The information that the expected income of about one hundred and eighty thousand was not forthcoming became too much for Dr. Richard that he slumped into the nearest chair, panting heavily. His feet seemed too weak to carry his weight. His mouth opened wide, too overwhelmed to speak for several minutes. A strange dejected expression crossed his face. All seemed lost, like all hell had burst open.

"Damn it!" Dr. Richard shouted, finally finding his voice. "They should have informed us of this at the last annual general meeting."

"So they should, but even the Board members were not aware that there was austerity in the air. It certainly is not their fault," responded Tunji Miller.

"How do I raise enough to cover my expectations? Now, don't tell me you can't find buyers for my stock holding," commanded Dr. Richard.

"Yes, I suggest you sell most of the badly affected shares, though the market is depressed right now. But if you will give me four weeks, I shall try to dispose of them. You'll have some losses, of course, just state exactly which batch to sell and how many, after which, I should be in a position to come up with the money this time next month. Four weeks is the least amount of notice I can guarantee. The market is very depressed."

Picking himself up, Dr. Richard swore not to allow his emotions get the better of him.

He tried to manage a smile on his face, but the sad countenance remained. Deep down in the marrow of his bones, he knew he must do something drastic. Either this, or he would certainly be dead before this austerity blew over.

At precisely six o'clock on the appointed Saturday evening, Bola Lawani rang the bell and Dr. Richard opened the door to let him in. Appearing more sober than usual, Bola came to the point.

"Sir, I have studied the whole accounts and checked up the mortgage on Kemidare building, and my conclusion is that you must put a stop to the tire industry at the present. Our bank's lobbyist to the government and the Senate told me in confidence that it would take between three months to a year before any new import licenses for new industrial equipment can be issued. You also must contract out the management of Kemidare properties. The Knight and Queens Company, an international property management firm, has expressed interest in the Apapa office building. It is the only property not mortgaged to any bank."

"Your evaluation is quite impressive!" Dr. Richard's tone was reserved. "Just carry on, but do not command me on what to do."

"Thank you, I've been working at it since my last visit, sir," Bola chuckled and then stopped, becoming aware of Dr. Richard's generally sour mood.

"Anything wrong, sir?" he asked.

"Yes," Dr. Richard replied absentmindedly. "Everything seemed to be wrong. Suddenly all this economic gloom is becoming too much for me. Never in my wildest dreams could I imagine any of the unpleasantness I have had to cope with these three days. It's like I'm being buried before my time is up. If I had known, I would not have invested in that tire industry. Also I would not have bought those six ocean liners. It's as if the gods are all out to do me in. To pay the customs tax alone, I must sell all the ships and at the end, I'll wind up with huge losses. You know, I have always seen myself as a shrewd businessman. I thought with all the connections anyone would envy, I could do all things. But this austerity is showing me the extent of my powerlessness and limitations. I especially regret my inability to evade the customs excise on the ships. The worldwide recession now makes container shipping the worst business to invest in. You remember the beach site portion of land I was hoping to buy on Victoria Island last year. I had to use up over thirty thousand naira in bribing the city council officials, but I could not even get it. And now with this austerity, you can be sure my ambition to own a property there will be dashed forever. To obtain a current Victoria Island certificate of occupancy costs about two hundred thousand naira after the standard pay-offs. Yesterday I suffered severe trepidations that disturbed me so much. I am fearful that I don't seem to have enough money to continue to maintain my present standard of living. This Victoria Island apartment has become too expensive for me, and I do not know how to tell Sade that we must move back to a poorer neighborhood. Do you think I can make a good politician?" he asked suddenly, noticing the young man's uneasiness.

"Well, sir, I never thought of you as a politician," replied Bola.

"Yes, I didn't think seriously of politics until this morning. I've had to send my wife away so that I could coldly decide what to do with my life. I prayed to God, and suddenly a voice said to me that maybe I ought to go into politics. It was also the same way when I decided to abandon teaching geography at the Iddo Grammar School and go into business. I think it's high time I withdrew from business into politics. In the past few days, I have made decisions leading to a loss of over three million naira to the Kemidare Holdings. The calculation is mine, of course I assumed the cost of all the equipment already purchased on credit and those on their way from Hong Kong, the custom duties of which I may not be in position to raise. A loss of this proportion certainly must warrant my leaving the business world all together.

I am sure that the banks will be happy to foreclose on the mortgaged properties and sell them cheap. Ralph Waldo Emerson who said, "Commerce is a game of skill, it is a game of great intricacy and subtlety that every man can play, but which few men can play well." I have between now and a month to sell up all our 28-thousand-ton ships at a loss. That is, after I have paid off the crews, then I shall be left bankrupt for life."

Not exactly sure how to respond to the old man's neurotic

state, Bola Lawani solemnly expressed his sympathy. He excused himself and   promised to visit again. Outside the apartment, he paused to lament the greed that had precipitated Dr. Richard's bankruptcy. It was pure greed that had made him overextend his credit so much that the banks will certainly sell off four, if not all, of the Kemidare office buildings.

Had Dr. Richard been wise, he should have repressed his dream of owning a tire industry. How could a single man hope to compete with the multi-national corporate resources of the likes of Dunlop Tires or the famous Greek Shipping Magnates and the Nigeria National Shipping Lines? All the same, maybe if the austerity had not struck, just maybe... but who knows. God certainly has a way of maintaining equity in this world. Only God can help the nation from this greedy businessman intending to become a politician.

CHAPTER FIFTEEN

The twelve-thirty local flight from Kano to Lagos on Monday afternoon had on board Alhaji Abba Abdulmalik. He had travelled back to Kaduna, from there he drove to Kano where he spent the weekend. He maintained a prayer vigil to Allah with Imam Fulani. He had also gathered a group of ten prayerful Imams whose prayers had been focused on begging Allah's goodwill. Abba was expected to pray and fast for the next fourteen days. It was a discipline he found impossible to pursue.

This was necessary to avert the impending tragedy. The omen envisaged by the Imams was not in favor of their benefactor. Imam Fulani had not told all he foresaw. He feared the negative reaction he might receive from his benefactor.

Imam Fulani calmed his restless spirit and had given him four specially prepared incantations with talisman for good luck. He also personally saw Abba off to the airport on the Monday morning. He would, of course, continue his prayers with the other Imams. Already, arrangements were under way to include Imam Fulani's name and ten other Imams for the next pilgrimage to Mecca. A trip to the Holy Land was necessary to present Abba's sacrifices to Allah. His presence was also specially requested. Come what may, the date with Allah in Mecca must be fulfilled by Abba. The Imam had warned of dire consequences if he failed. He would risk Allah's wrath.

For the present, he was worried about how he would be received in Lagos. His conversation on phone with Alhaji Dogon Talata the previous night had impressed on his mind the great turbulence ahead. Dogon Talata had stated that most of the government's high personnel had all been caught unawares by the austerity. It was like they had been exposed to the naked light with their pants down. He emphatically informed Abba that it would not be right for him to make unrealistic demands. He further advised that it would be better for him to strategize how best to straighten his financial mess, without laying blames.

. Dogon Talata further promised to help Abba the best way he could.

Appreciating the logic of Dogon Talata's argument, Abba had promised not to cry wolf. At least he would keep calm until he met face to face with the powers that be. The telephone conversation had then ended when Dogon Talata promised to meet him at the Ikeja local airport. He was happy that the government vehicle would be on hand to pick him up as he would not be able to survive the infamous Lagos traffic.

Over the decades, the rural exodus had increased the population of Lagos from three hundred thousand to more than four million inhabitants, and the city was bursting. The over-population helped to make traffic congestions more intolerable. This was further worsened by the fact that most telephones didn't work. Business men must therefore make appointments in person. It became worrisome that a thirteen-mile trip from the Ikeja airport to Victoria Island's L'Hotel Eko Meridien may take up to two hours.

In order to alleviate the sufferings of the residents of the city, the government devised a policy. The cars whose license plates ended in an even digit were allowed to ply the roads every other day. Wealthy Nigerians circumvented the restriction by buying both even and odd numbered license plates for their vehicles. This further made cars to become a socially accepted form of investment, and thereby creating more "go-slows" on Lagos roads.

Punctual as ever, Dogon Talata was seated with his driver in a special numbered V.I.P. Mercedes-Benz limousine. He humbly stepped forward to greet Abba as he alighted off the plane.

Inside the car, Dogon Talata wasted no time but went straight to the point. "You've been jetting overseas for so long, you've forgotten how we behave here in Lagos. Here the future is never calculable. We make one plan today, and tomorrow we start on a completely different thing. We always assume, of course, our foreign partners would think like we do and therefore respond accordingly. A heightened reflex and ability to change fast to whatever demand is required is the only way of operating successfully in Nigeria. The Italians are very good at following our disorganized trait. The British, Germans and Americans will never adapt. So they always miss out on lucrative deals. Next to the Italians are the Indians, Pakistanis and of course, our old mentors, the Lebanese." Smiling contentedly at his superior analysis, Dogon Talata paused to closely examine his cousin.

"Haha! Abba! What the hell's been happening to you? The last time we met, you were exactly the replica of the Prince Charming; the envy of all the ministers who attended the London conference. What has been happening to you?"

"It's these austerity measures. They have wiped out all my investment dreams overnight," he gloomily replied.

"Well, I know. In fact, four of our close party supporters have killed themselves."Talata remarked frankly. "Anyway, your fortunes cannot be that bad; everybody is experiencing hell in capital letters."

"Yeah, it's very bad, and the worst thing is that I'm equally up to my neck in debts in London, Paris and New York. I'm sure my London creditors have already started screaming for my neck."

"Is that right? This deserves serious thinking. I've an appointment with some of the top ministers this evening. Maybe by tomorrow we can sit down to discuss with a view to finding solutions. Only from the little I know, the situation is pretty difficult. I hear even the big Chief himself swore by Allah not to give any license to anyone even if his mother's life depended on it. All the same, have hope, for you are considered a big influence on the international scene. Remember that last party you gave when the top brass of the administration visited London. Everybody was very impressed and happy over your lavish entertainment. Even the big Chief enjoyed every minute of it. It certainly must have cost you a fortune."

"Yes, it did. The champagne parties did cost me over three hundred thousand pounds sterling. And the truth is, the administration was supposed to reimburse me, but to date, nothing has been discussed to that effect. Also, some of the London hoteliers thought it was AAA International that was to settle the bills for six ministers' accommodations. Thus, instead of giving the bill to the accountant general of the party, the bills were forwarded to my London office. Always trying to be the nice guy, I promised to look into it. From what I hear, these austerity measures will probably make it impossible for these hotels to be paid. The debt will then hang on my neck." Abba postulated.

"I'm sorry for everything. Uneasy lies the head that wears the crown. You operated as a roving ambassador without any accreditation. If only you were not so independent, we could have found a way to give you all the diplomatic rights when the going was still buoyant. But I reckon all those are too late now."

"Had I known, I would have taken your advice. It is too late now. I will always live to regret not taking your advice. In view of my present situation, that would have been like life insurance. But not to worry, I still need help now, but I will not be fully dependent on just you.

For starters, I'm grateful you could spare the time to pick me up at the airport."

"Forget it," grinned Dogon Talata. "After all the fun you introduced me to in Europe and Latin America, I'd be a damned fool not to return my own little appreciation when I can. The Rio carnivals in Brazil, I'll never forget. I especially dream of the blondes. It was an occasion of a life time."

By this time, they were approaching the Marina fly-over. Dogon Talata gave the driver instructions to drop him at the Federal Secretariat, the seat of the Federal Civil Service. Abba was to be chauffeured wherever he wished.

As soon as Dogon Talata dropped off at his office, Abba had the comfort of the air conditioned car to himself. He needed time to evaluate the valuable piece of information he had just gathered. The only piece of permanent residence he had in Lagos was his suite. It cost about five hundred naira a day, a heavy sum of money to spend during this austerity period. But to keep up appearances, he decided it was the only place to be. At the very least, the prestige and comfort of the hotel would stimulate both his confidence and ego. The amount in his briefcase was approximately over one hundred thousand naira. He surmised he could survive some weeks before the money finished. Somehow, he would have to raise more money.

He had the remaining balance from Don Catto's five hundred thousand. The cash deposit on the license promised Don Catto and his Lebanese friends must be paid for from this cash balance. Also the pirate Chief would expect payment for greasing the palms of the customs personnel in clearing Don Catto's consignment of industrial spare parts. Abba was determined to live frugally to restrict his extravagant tipping of the staff at the hotel.

Further calculations revealed that the precise amount on him could only enable him to survive on his usual grand style of life for a very limited period of time. That is, assuming his commitment to pay for the deposit and bribe for the licenses were not to be honored from his present funds. To complicate issues, he could not calculate exactly how much more the officials might ask for before issuing the licenses.

From Dogon Talata's information, he painfully acknowledged that any new license would be conditional to further economic improvement in the nation's oil earnings. All hopes seemed lost for that moment. Still, who can tell--maybe luck would be on his side. Things sometimes worked when all hopes had been abandoned. He read that "When the going gets tough, the tough gets going." Yeah, most probably this was a true proverb. That being the case, a bit of craftiness might be needed to survive the difficult period.

Raising his voice, he asked the driver to take him to the Victoria Island address of Dumba. A chat with him might be helpful in the long run, he reasoned.

Luck was with him, for Dumba had just flown into Lagos from the Mid-Western City of Benin.

Sam Dumba greeted Abba with a beaming smile as he opened the vehicle's door.

"I've been thinking of getting in touch. But I've been ever so busy. The maniacs in government have removed the bottom from all our aspirations," Dumba lamented.

"I know, but you were never in any meaningful business since the new administration came into power. I heard you joined the wrong political party."

"That is correct. My tough luck, you'll say. Only it has helped to save me from the blood pressure I might now be experiencing. You see, because I did not belong to the party in government, I didn't share the optimism of their party stalwarts. Hence, while they hurriedly expanded at the beginning of the boom, I was left to operate from my lean base."

"Their over expansion must now be curtailed by this economic recession. Believe you me; I've been through the whole Mid-Western State, and what a sorry sight my business associates are in. I heard the banks have started demanding that they sell even their residential homes to pay outstanding bank debts."

"You can have your laugh and call their woes retributive justice if you must, but I'm in a hell of a mess myself. So much that I'm wondering if you can give me some advice."

"Ah! What are friends for? Whatever it is you need, I will contribute. Now tell me all about it." Dumba volunteered.

"With all due respect," Abba started, careful with his words. "I've heard a lot of stories about your business dealings. I've known of your Mafia associates in the city of London, Messrs Bob Ashford and Roger Baston. I know they specifically received money from some Alhaji is on the pretext of investing on their behalf. But they never invested anything at all. When the money was demanded, your friends blackmailed their victims into shutting up."

He paused as if expecting violent reactions from Dumba, but none came. Looking rather bored for all his care in the world, he smiled and asked him to please continue.

"Yes, of course, I can see from your looks that it is all true. My interest is how you make it impossible for these victims to feel revenge. Or at least try to silence you when you visit this country."

"You certainly are asking for a lot," replied Dumba. But I don't mind. The trouble is, I know you've been manipulated just like I was used by the boys in power. Only in my own case, I could understand their greed and can entrap them before even I'm caught. Thus, I can always escape whatever deadly scheme is planned for me. My strategy for self-survival is to get sufficient 'insurance' from my so-called victims. By insurance, I mean incriminating evidence that I can later use to compel them to reason my way. It's, no doubt, a very dirty business, but I don't mind since it's my British associates who take care of the dirty aspect of our deals. But nonetheless, I know how it's done, and I use the method because if I don't, someone else will. But using this method will ensure that I will not be a victim or prey to such entrapments. Remember also that most of these so called victims have the real power in this country. The way they exercise their power is the reason these austerity measures has been forced down our throat. But enough of self-praise, you did not visit me simply to discuss my unholy business ethics. Did you?"

"Yes, not exactly. I wanted to see if you could find a way to recover what was legally mine from our friends in power. It's a fact that I'm terribly over-extended both here and abroad. It becomes imperative, therefore, that I find a way to force their hands or else I may have to go the Ivan Kreuger way."

"You mean the infamous Swedish match magnate? God

forbid such utterance, Alhaji! I'm certain we can find a way. If not here, then maybe abroad. I know some powerful group in London who will underwrite any amount, should one decide to run in the next election. That is assuming one has certain hope of winning. I am currently here to investigate if I should not take the plunge myself. I suddenly find that age is creeping in on me. Besides, my base in London is not as safe as before. I will also be in a better powerful position if I can get into the Senate in the next election."

"With your perseverance and persuasive skills, I'm sure you will be successful. All you need to do is obtain your foreign friends money and throw a lot of it around. People always respect the man with the naira power. For my part, let me be the first to congratulate the Honorable Senator Dumba and wish you the best of luck."

"Thank you, Alhaji, and I'll think over your request tonight. Before next weekend, I'll make contact with you. Remember, it would not be right for me to be seen with you. My reputation does not permit that. So I'll call you up then we can fix a place to meet just the two of us."

"So long, my good friend. I'll be expecting your call." The chat with Dumba left Abba in a serene mood. He was as a man whom when pitched against the ruthless system decided to meet the competition head on. Such would demand an eye for an eye. Alone to himself, he wondered if he was capable of the sort of callousness Dumba was reputed to have. Maybe and maybe not. Only time could reveal that.

A storybook he had once read said something about one's inner self. It was this inner self that took over from the conscious self at the moment of extreme tension. The self's instinct aids survivability for the individual when cornered in a very tight spot. It was necessary for the alert mind to seek the help of this instinct when in grave danger. Silently, he lusted to possess this elusive, but superior energy with which to carry out his survival schemes. Not being a man of prayer, he doubted that Allah would listen. He surmised that Allah would at least hear Imam Fulani's intercessions.

Interrupting his reverie, the driver asked if he would be permitted to go and pick up his boss. A glance at the car's clock stated it was almost time for Dogon Talata to leave for home from his office.

"Do kindly drop me at the hotel, it's only a minute's drive from the Federal Secretariat," he instructed. Three minutes later, the car stopped in front of the majestic hotel in Victoria Island.

Not wanting the customary attention his entrance would have created, he strolled through the staff gate into the reception hall. The receptionist looked up and informed him his suite had been prepared and awaited him. Reaching for the keys, he instructed the receptionist to bring his luggage from the waiting limousine.

On the elevator ride to his suite, a further glance at his eighteen carat gold wristwatch told him his appointment for six o'clock with Barrister Bulus Musa was about to commence.

Inside the elegantly furnished suite, he switched on the air conditioning system and picked up the phone to request a bottle of Campari and bucket of ice from room service. This was the favorite solace Bulus. For himself he ordered the house specialty, a Chablis dry French wine. Terribly expensive, it sold for ten times its usual price in Europe. Such was the hyper-inflation one expected in Lagos, one of the world's most expensive capital cities.

CHAPTER SIXTEEN

Exactly ten minutes after entering the suite and settling down comfortably with his first glass of the French wine. There came a knock at the door and Bulus' voice requesting for permission to enter.

"Sorry I'm late," apologized the conscientious Barrister.

"Not to worry, after all, this is Nigeria," was the prompt reply from Abba.

"Yes, I always forget we keep African Time." Walking over to the liquor cabinet, he lifted the bottle of Campari and swiftly helped himself to a large drink. He exclaimed, "My first real pleasure of the day. In fact, it is the best way I know to cope with the harsh realities of these unfortunate times."

"Your telephone call to Kano yesterday, the lines were so bad, I could not catch up your lines of thought. What was it about your client's jetty?" Abba asked.

"You mean the pirate Chief's jetty?" replied the Bulus. Oh the facts are straight forward. Chief Madu's four jetties were among those affected in the austerity measures. The government has banned them from ever functioning. Ironically, a license for their functioning was granted only three months before this forceful closure. The amount paid for each license a hundred thousand naira. The four jetties therefore, cost the Chief four hundred thousand naira. This amount does not include the sum I personally had to offer to the government boys to quicken their slow pace," Bulus said while swallowing another gulp from his glass.

"Only four hundred thousand for the lot? That I'm sure is a very low price compared to the huge gains the Chief must make from his piracy business," Abba voiced out.

"His gains are not my immediate concern. What I'm mad about is the principle. Our powerful friends who gave this license in the first place should have honored the contractual agreement before foreclosing on the jetties. Oh Alhaji! My life has been disoriented since the beginning of these austerity measures. Almost half of my clients are on the verge of bankruptcy. One killed himself the other day, and my friend at the Central Bank tells me the worst is yet to come." Bulus was silent for a moment while he took another sip of his Campari. "Why did we elect these incompetent packs?" he asked.

"That answer is beyond me, but as the saying goes, in the land of the blind, the one eyed man reigns supreme," replied Abba.

"Possibly, but maybe not. I'd rather believe the man who said if 'Papa' had been voted in, the bulk of the timber and caliber gangsters would all have perished in prison. Now the poor masses of this country must burn in hell for the sin of the mediocre politicians."

"Your analogue is getting too far," remonstrated Abba. Besides 'papa' lacks the credibility of ever gaining federal power. His image as an ethnic leader is all he can ever hope to attain in life."

"Am I too serious, or is it the effects of the Campari? Come to think of it, I've started drinking heavily these days. But forgive my harsh statements. My energy these days is spent practically crying out loud sentiments against the suffering of my clients. For myself, as a renowned lawyer, my share in the pie of the capitalist system is always assured. Whichever way the economy goes, I shall always get enough to feed comfortably. I've recently been witnessing the anguish and miseries of my former clients. Their main crime is their entrenched entrepreneurial activities, which should have been rewarded in other countries. Here in Nigeria, they're rewarded with bankruptcy and poverty while their efforts could have netted them billions, had they operated in the capitalist European countries or America," Bulus corrected.

"Yeah, I know the feeling. Was it not Andrew Carnegie who stated that pioneering does not pay?" Abba quoted in his role of devil's advocate.

"Yes, I believe he said so," replied Bulus. "But his pioneering did pay, not only for him and his posterity, but pioneering is what got Britain and America where they are today as powerful nations." Filling his glass to the brim, Bulus took a sip and continued. "Defend your friends as you like, but I'll advise you to watch out. Their callousness would soon spill on even to your very self. Then you will understand why I'm so embittered. With time, I'm sure you too will suffer the ill-effect of this austerity. But enough of my emotionalism. On sober ground, I've scheduled this meeting to ask if there is any way you can help my clients.

"Not anymore, Alhaji Marnman Taofik is now in charge of the Ministry of Importations. Taofik has the explicit authority to personally endorse all import licenses. He is the only man to approach. Anybody purporting to be representing him would only be faking his authority."

"Well, well, well, what a surprise! I hope he is your friend?" Bulus chanted, his confidence seemed to be returning.

"I didn't exactly say that, but I reckon Taofik and I will try to reach favorable agreements. If you'll excuse me, I've to meet Dogon Talata at the Ikoyi club in an hour's time. Do keep in touch. You can stay behind to finish your drink if you so wish. I must hurry, so as not to be late"

The roof top restaurant at the Ikoyi Club was crowded as usual with the wheeler-dealers in the government circle. It was about nine o'clock when Alhaji Abba Abdulmalik was ushered to the table occupied by Dogon Talata. Also seated at the table was Alhaji Ibrahim Yardoya the minister in charge of the new capital construction projects. Abba exchanged greetings and pleasantries, after which, Yardoya started the conversation.

"Your manager, Mr. Chibuko had been denying me my dues. Now that you are here, maybe you will remedy the situation," Yardoya said seriously agitated. "My patience has been overtaxed by the obnoxious Ibo man."

Abba frowned at him. "It is a pity you misunderstood Chibuko. Also, the present austerity does not seem to have touched you. The times are not as they used to be."

"What exactly are you trying to say? Yardoya shouted, his anger already seething. "That will be enough for now," commanded Dogon Talata. "I didn't bring the two of you together for a boxing contest." He paused to examine the two adults and then continued.

"I believe Abba here is being owed outstanding sums of money as a result of the austerity. Your department is not willing or in a position to pay at the present time."Talata parried.

"Yes, that is correct," replied Yardoya. "It came as a great shock to me. If I had known, I would have helped Abba get his outstanding balance before this austerity. If only Chibuko had not been too cheeky."

"Well the past is gone and we are here to see how we can help

Abba. I understand the amount is nine hundred and fifty thousand for the schedule "F" payments," continued Dogon Talata.

"That doesn't include the schedule" "G", which has now been completed," added Abba. "In fact, I have the bills here."

Taking the bills from Abba, Dogon Talata checked through the figures and passed it on to Yardoya remarking, "The addition of the "G" schedule will bring the total sum to around one and a half million naira. What I'm proposing therefore, is that Yardoya will take these bills and have them processed. Then you will make sure AAA's billings are placed at the top on the list of the payment vouchers. You should be able to get all the paper work done by next week. We will wait until the government order for payment commences. Is that understood?"

"Sure," answered Yardoya, "I'm only doing this favor for your sake. As a matter of fact, I would have been able to authorize payment if the figures were below forty thousand. What I mean is I had the power before a recent directive, stipulating that any amount higher than ten thousand must pass through the office of Alhaji Mamman Taofik. He seems to be laden with all the powerful duties in the Administration."

"You mean Mamman Taofik?" asked Abba.

Yardoya nodded in appreciation, "Yes, Mamman Taofik is gradually taking over the most sensitive duties. He is bringing in new trusted men from his tribe to deputize for him."

"The other members of the cabinet refer to Mamman Taofik as "He who would be king," replied Dogon Talata. "But then, it must be in his destiny, for he comes from a lineage of Fulani king makers. His uncle could easily have taken the highest position in the country. Only his timidity prevented him from mounting the throne."

"Now Mamman Taofik is scheming to succeed where his elder kinsman failed," Abba deducted.

"Why shouldn't he," Yardoya enthused. He had spent most his life preparing for the highest position this nation can offer. After his secondary education at Government College Keffi, the British Colonial Administrator gave him scholarship to study International Relations at the London School of Economics. He also obtained a Master's degree in Economics, before he returned to Nigeria in 1957. Since then, he has served in the most privileged positions in the civil service and in other strategic government establishments. His track record has genuinely earned him the respect of the whole cabinet executives. The political power he has, therefore, compliments his integrity and intellectual dedication. At the start of this economic gloom, the Senate jointly picked Mamman Taofik. He won their unanimous confidence as the man to restore economic stability in the administration. He belongs to the species of noble public servants. He thinks only of the good of the nation. He frowns at the political immaturity of his colleagues in power. His efficient performance as Minister for Importation is the main reason why no fraudulent license has been issued since the austerity began. I know other ministers would have had pitied their suffering relatives and released their licenses. Mamman Taofik is reported to have sworn that he would rather allow his blood brother's business to liquidate than issue him a license to import machinery spare parts for his glass factory in Kaduna. It is also the determination of Mamman Taofik that no license will be issued to anyone until the country's foreign reserve position improves. Only at the threat of dire consequences did he concede two licenses to the big Chief. Even then, Mamman Taofik swore there would not be a second time and there had not been any repetition since."Yardoya said.

Abba could hardly restrain his exuberance."Sure, this is the way the cookie crumbles," was all he could find to say.

"What do you mean?" Yardoya asked and then nodded in understanding. He worked hard to restrict the wide grin that was spreading across his face. "You are right. I will bet my house in Kano that you'll never be able to get anything out of Mamman Taofik."

Dogon Talata sat back brooding. "All right, Yardoya, stop your silly grin. Abba here understands that Mamman Taofik is irrevocably not a part of us. We do not have his Fika tribe's innate discipline, neither do we leave one of ours to suffer like a dog. Among the two of us, we must pressurize Mamman Toafik to help Abba. It will not be easy. But we shall try our best." Talata admonished.

Yardoya nodded, "As I said in the beginning, I will try to help Abba even though I'm not sure what his chances are. Mamman Taofik hates Abba's flamboyant lifestyle. I remember that trip we all made to London. Almost all the ministers enjoyed the blondes provided by Abba. Personally, I had a wonderful time. Everyone but Mamman Taofik resented the show of opulence displayed by Abba. I could remember hearing him swear to cut off Abba's life support system if he ever had the chance. And from all the available facts it seems Allah is just about set to reward Alhaji Marnman Toafik with his ambition of destroying Abba." Yardoya admitted.

While Yardoya spoke, Abba seemed lost in thought. He congratulated himself with this audacious tactic of pitching the Kano ministers against the Fika clan. It was to be an all-out battle. A fight between godly and the not so godly.

He recovered just in time from his deep thought to hear the finishing sentence from Yardoya's speech. Raising his glass of French wine, Yardoya proposed a toast stating, "Confusion to our detractors and may Allah guide us safely to successes."

Concluding the meeting Abba repeated the favorite words of the late Sir Winston Churchill. "Let our enemies do their worst and we shall do our best." Even as he spoke, he doubted his ability to do his best. The hard times was slowly making him both victim and fugitive of his flamboyant life style.

CHAPTER SEVENTEEN

Binta Lilah, resplendent in a navy-blue suit, waited impatiently on the visitors' room. She sat outside the Exchange Control Office at the Central Bank of Nigeria, Lagos Headquarters. Her anxiety was as a result of the call she received from her son in London on Monday night.

On Thursday morning, she had decided to abandon all her other commitments to solve the problem with the bank authorities. At stake was her children's education in Britain. Two of her sons were studying for their ordinary and advanced level Oxford General Certificate of Education. Bala, the eldest, had phoned to say the Barclays Bank cheque she had given to their school bursar had been returned unpaid. The Bursar had threatened therefore, to send Binta's children out of their hostel and to stop them from attending classes.

Binta had requested the school principal's phone number and had promptly called the principal at the very late hour.

The distressed man had sleepily promised the insistent Binta that school could wait a further ten days for the money to arrive, after which, the children would be thrown out of school. Thanking Allah for the ten days' grace, Binta had moved into high gear. She planned her best strategy to get the exact sum in pounds sterling to keep the principal off her children's back. She therefore systematically called on all her rich boyfriends. She was informed each time that the austerity had robbed her ever-so-generous lovers of their capacity for being easy with their money. Only two had promised to give Binta three thousand, the currency would be in naira and not the equivalent pounds sterling she requested.

Not having enough naira in her own bank account, Binta had collected what she could and left Kaduna the following Tuesday at noon. Now after two days in Lagos, she still could not be sure if she would be allowed the customary foreign exchange allowance for business travelers, a small sum of fifteen hundred pounds. The waiting line was a long one, with many people intent on seeing the manager.

When it came to the turn of the man after whom it would be Binta's turn, she pleaded with the equally anxious man to be allowed in. And before he could reply, she gallantly sprinted past the man into the manager's office.

The manager, Albert Johnson, greeting was hilarious, "Hello Binta. Have you been waiting long? Why didn't you phone? I should have met you outside." "Don't you worry about me; I have had a lot on my mind." replied Binta. "My problem is how I can get a foreign exchange draft and express service."

"That will be a major problem, but if you are really desperate, I'll advise you to see some of the top brass upstairs. They can help you better than a small manager like myself" he responded, wishfully eyeing the beautiful Binta. He lusted, imagining what fun she will be if engaged in bedroom theatrics.

Standing up and hurriedly making for the door, Binta paused to appreciate Albert. "Albert, take that shameful grin off your face. You had your chance once, but you blew it." Not waiting for his reply, Binta stepped out of the office and shut the door with a bang.

She had taken Albert's advice and one of the top men with board-room connection had indeed listened. An appointment at his Victoria Island guest house had been kept and Binta was again free to smile.

"Have bottom power and you'll travel" "she kept repeating to herself. She relished what a smooth operator she could become when faced with emergencies.

A pity, she thought. There was no female offspring to continue in her footsteps. Maybe she could still have one. There might still be time, she dreamed. Occasionally Binta resented being a sex tool to be used by all the powerful men that crosses her path. No matter how much power the fairer sex thinks she possessed, the male still has the requisite charm to manipulate her out of realistic sense. This explains why the female could become so devilishly possessed when she is head over heels in love with a Romeo.

Binta had married Jacob Kajetan for the above reason and had continued to love the hopeless drunkard after all his betrayals. Jacob had been the local hero in Makurdi at the time of their marriage. Everyone thought he had ability and would go far in the

Air Force. Only Binta knew that Jacob did not have much brain to warrant him becoming a top ranking officer. He had limited imagination and technical capabilities but had been pushed along the promotion ladder by his maternal uncle, a top military brass.

The harsh realities of Jacob's life only started to surface after his uncle was killed in the battle front. At the funeral, Jacob had been so drunk that twice he almost fell into the grave. It was with the support of his flight lieutenant pals that he was able to stand at the funeral. The two able-bodied men stood by his side during the whole ceremony. Initially, Binta could bear the burden of Jacob's drunkenness.

The situation worsened when Jacob started bringing other women into their matrimonial bed. Once she had complained, and his anger had been so furious that she was lucky he did not shoot her with his pistol. Friends advised her to leave, but blinded by love, she had remained in the hope that he would change.

Fortunately, she had a secure job in the local government's office and was the Personal Assistant to the Permanent Secretary of the State's Ministry of Commerce. The pay was barely enough to keep the two children she catered for. Life was rough and tough. Daily harassment had become the practice since Jacob took to the bottle. The sordid poverty made her forever depressed as she labored painstakingly and constantly praying that Jacob would change. Rather than sober up, Jacob had gone from bad to worse. The Air Force directorate had no choice than to cut him off entirely from their payroll. Binta knew it was time to move on without Jacob.

Due to her sensuous beauty, she had admirers throughout Makurdi city, and it was to Alhaji Hassan Kubut's house that she decided to run to. Hassan had been understanding and had rented her a luxury apartment in Kaduna. He opened a convenience store and drinking bar for her. He also set her up as an emergency contractor. He showered her with money and had taken her on her first trip to Mecca. Afterwards he made her change her name to Hadjia Binta Lilah, to symbolize her conversion from Christianity to Islam. Thus, Hadjia Binta Lilah became a convert of the Moslem order.

Unfortunately, nine months after Binta moved permanently to Kaduna, Hassan was killed in a ghastly motor accident on a business trip between Makurdi and Kaduna. With his death, Hadjia Binta Lilah, as she had generally become known in Kaduna, decided never to have a man to boss and lord it over her again. She became, therefore, the dominating boss in her own life.

The booming economy made her business more successful than she had ever dreamed. With the security her earning power provided, she had different men at her beck and call. Whenever she became lonely, it was to one of these that she went.

The events of the past week had rekindled her need for a permanent man. A man to call her own was becoming too urgent for Binta. Maybe it was because of the overpowering austerity, but her dream in the nights constantly focused on the happy months she had spent when newly married to Jacob. He was there on her waking and she slept in his arms at night assured that Jacob was hers for life. As far as Binta was concerned the security a man offered a woman was the one thing lacking in her successful life. Often she wondered what type of man could fulfill this need. She had searched, but always ended up disappointed. The men she knew were only out to enjoy themselves without accepting the added responsibility, which invariably a woman must demand. Men, she reasoned, were certified bums of the first order. From a distance they seemed responsible enough, but the story changes as one gets a deeper insight.

A year ago, Albert, a Senior Manager at the Central Bank had been her constant companion. They had met while she had business in Lagos. Albert appeared a perfect gentleman and had informed Binta that he was separated from his wife, Risi. The truth was that Risi had been the power behind Albert's progress in life. Albert loyally respected Risi's influence in making him successful. He could therefore not bring himself to separate from her. He feared losing his privileged position in the Lagos society.

Binta had been kept in the dark about the real facts of Albert's life. When she found out the bitter truth, it was almost too late to back out of the relationship. She began to withdraw from Albert, but she had not reckoned with the fury of his Ijebu wife. Risi was reputed to possess witchcraft powers. Binta's friend had warned her to beware of the angry Ijebu woman. Risi was a brawler and would not hesitate to use her devilish powers to harm Binta. The gossip column of the "Lagos Truth" publication had so much to report on the scandal over the Albert Johnson's women-Binta and

Risi.

The shrewdness in Binta enabled her to abandon the deceptive Albert, when he became a source of embarrassment. She concentrated, therefore, on her growing business, taking time to enjoy men in her business circle when in good mood.

On the higher level of the Lagos business circle was Alhaji Abba Abdulmalik, a connoisseur of glamour, elegance and good times. Binta had tremendously enjoyed the elegant grace of Abba Abdulmalik, a legend of his time. They had met for the first time at the London Savoy Hotel and had since then spent a couple of times whenever chance permitted. It seemed like they had a sense of timing that allowed them both to literally give way to animalistic instinct of immediate gratification. Binta momentarily relived the first time they were intimate. It had been within an hour of their meeting each other. She had abandoned herself to her desires and he had been exceptional in making her fully gratified. Not many words were spoken. His silence spoke to her of the need for mutual enjoyment. No promises. No commitments. No responsibilities. Just have fun and enjoy the good times while it lasted. Often when alone, Binta gave thoughts to the serene relaxation with Abba afforded her. No man had been able to satisfy her that much, not even her first love Jacob.

Lost in her love thoughts, she envisioned Abba as a special man with deeper motivations. An insight misunderstood by most people who saw him as merely a flamboyant international philanderer. "Superbum," to quote the words of Barrister Bulus Musa.

Bulus had been chasing Binta for years and resented the knowledge of Abba being Binta's secret Lover.

Once, Bulus had lost his cool by phoning Binta and blasting Abba as a good for nothing son-of-a-bitch. Angered by the onslaught, Binta had equally replied that Abba was more of a man than any other man she had ever come across. He was a compassionate, sensuous man, a real -life Romeo. She pointed out that these were character traits that made men great. Rare factors, of which she was much aware the lawyer wished for but would never have. She had banged the phone on him. Since then a cold war had ensued between Binta and Bulus.

Engrossed in her urgent need for a companion to give her

warmth and comfort, she wishfully hoped Abba was present in Lagos. Impulsively, she picked up her address notebook and under the alphabet "A," she memorized Abba's phone number. Picking up the push-button phone box, she called Abba's L 'Hotel Eko Meridien suite. The receptionist answered saying that Alhaji Abdulmalik was in residence but was not in at the moment. Leaving word with the receptionist to inform him of her call, Binta hung up the phone, praying for him to call her back.

Smiling contentedly, she drifted into her day dreaming. She dreamed of the first time with Jacob. It was the greatest thing that ever happened in her inexperienced youth. She was so madly in love and had given all she had to please Jacob. Poor Jacob!! She wondered how he was coping with the austerity. She made a mental note to send Jacob a bank check for five thousand naira if her present situation improved.

The call from Abba to Binta did not come through until the following Saturday. Rather than the emotional dialogue between lovers that Binta would have preferred, the tone on the phone was formal and urgent In fact, it was a downright request by Abba for Binta to come along to his Eko suite that Saturday evening.

Changing her tone to the business-like manner response expected by her caller, she answered that she might just make it.

The fact that Abba did not waste time on irrelevant formalities worried Binta. The unique aspect of the playboy's style was his charm at making others feel his care for their well-being even if not genuine.

Analyzing their conversation further, Binta surmised something must be terribly wrong. She wondered what might be bugging Abba? Could it be the austerity? Or perhaps he had to pay outstanding debts. Binta had been prudent. She had stopped honoring all her extra financial commitments. The new house she was erecting for her junior brother in Makurdi had been stopped. Furious, her brother had rained abuses on her. She had not minded, for it was either she continued and then suffered heart attack when the debtors started demanding their money. She also stopped all her unnecessary expenses. She sold her new Mercedes-Benz 350SEC when she found their maintenance bills too high. The only extravagance she was allowing herself these days was her expensively furnished apartment in Maryland, Lagos. She paid twenty thousand naira per annum. The apartment was next to London, her major place of escape away from Kaduna. Her stay in Kaduna no doubt had become unbearable these days. The people who had subcontracted her Abuja building projects were yet to be paid. Their daily disturbances and harassments at her house made her remain in Lagos, hiding away from their morbid abuses. Also, it was in Lagos that she will be informed when payment for contractors was to commence. Meanwhile, her bank balance was fast depleting since she withdrew funds for expenses without replenishing what was taken out. She did not want to be poor again, but saw the austerity measures as a sure way of bringing everyone to poverty lines except for the few men in higher places.

Silently, she rained curses on the people responsible for bringing the austerity plague on the nation. God must see it fit to punish them.

Her thoughts went back to Abba. She wondered if he, too, was terrified by the austerity. Whatever must be wrong with her lover boy, she resolved to find out when she kept the Saturday evening's appointment at the L'Hotel Eko Meridian. The vanity in Binta took over as she started to assemble the exotic dresses that would help make her more presentable to prince charming.

CHAPTER EIGHTEEN

Abba spent the three days analyzing how best to tackle Mamman Taofik. The meeting at the Ikoyi club's roof-top restaurant provided him the ideas that formed in his head. He jotted down valid points and felt the need to discuss them with a trusted ally. Dumba, the man of many parts had then been invited to help him work out the logistics.

Dumba had no fear. He nurtured profound relish for change. He arrived on the appointed day and sensing Abba's sagging spirit. "Need a lift, old timer boss?" he joked.

"A lift? What is a lift?" He innocently answered.

"Oh! man, you do look like what the cat dragged in. I know just the right stuff to lift your spirits."

"You do? Well, what is it? Let me see," replied Abba. Dumba took out a gold vial from his pocket and turned it over in his fingers. He tapped both sides of the vial and a white powder filled the plastic top.

He held the small injector and placed it in one nostril, pressed the bottom and snorted. He repeated the same process in the other nose. Almost immediately, his eyes lit up and his face glowed as he spoke with elated bombast.

"This is the true aphrodisiac. Cocaine is like a hot wave hitting all the parts of the body at once. This is much better than alcohol, marijuana, or hashish. Cocaine is made from the leaves of the coca plant that grows in the Andes of South America, while Bolivia, Peru, and Colombia are countries where it is mostly grown."

"Yes, cocaine! I've heard of it, though I never tried it. Isn't it the same thing that almost killed one Black American comedian?"

"Not quite! What the comedian suffered from is called free-basing. This involves removing the hydrochloride and other additives by introducing a strong alkali to the crystalline cocaine. Then heating it to its evaporation point. The cocaine base that remains when smoked sends the drug almost instantaneously to the brain. The stuff I've here had its potency reduced by adding agents like procaine, amphetamines and strychnine. It still however, retains the effect to create an orgasmic high when introduced to the body. Here, try it." Dumba held the vial up to Abba's nostril.

"Snort," he commanded, pressing the plunger. Abba obeyed and quickly did the same with his other nostril.

He held still for a minute, then turned to Dumba. His eyes wide and shinning. "I felt it go right up to my brain. It makes me warm like I'm going to explode in a state of euphoria. I think the drug is so powerful that it can override and eventually replace the act itself."

"You may be right. But you should know that it is a very expensive habit with a high dependency rate." Dumba admonished. "The *Newsweek* magazine last month reported the arrest of James Loran, the automobile manufacturer. He was nabbed last month for conspiracy in a $24 million cocaine deal. I think it is a risky habit"

"Yes, you're well-informed. But I assure you I know many cocaine dealers all over the world. It provides huge profit, and I would not mind participating in the trade myself. A new challenge it will be for me."

The two men then sat down to plan their conspiratorial strategy. This took them almost three hours.

"Well, I've set the ball rolling," Abba laughed hoarsely as he hung up the phone.

"Yeah! The journey of a thousand mile starts with the first step," philosophized Dumba. He stretched his long legs on the chair in which Barrister Bulus occupied on his last visit to the hotel suite.

Abba had just finished speaking with Binta. She was a part of a plan worked out by the two men. From the information received, the one way to deal with Mamman Taofik's stubbornness was to entice him with an opposite sex. A society lady, one of elegance and sophistication. Abba had searched around, and Binta was the only person fit enough to undertake such role of Delilah. She could, if properly motivated, use her considerable charms to con Mamman Taofik into trusting her. A stage would be set for Mamman to be cornered into a compromising position and pressured into coming to terms with Abba's request. Blackmail was indeed a weapon Dumba fully understood.

Dumba beamed with mischievous enthusiasm. "Marvelous!" he voiced out. "It is about time Taofik realized that the game of survival is based on jungle laws." He enthused mischievously.

"Don't let your imagination carry you away. At least not until we've sufficient ground to believe we can do what I've in mind and get away with it, "Abba admonished.

"Anything you say, old chap. I'm with you all the way," replied Dumba.

"Yes, and remember, this is not London. We've our own ways of making a man do things he ordinarily would not have done. In Africa, we do not use blackmail, but witchcraft to achieve our goals."

"Damn right you are," confirmed Dumba. "I regret to say I had started thinking of bugging devices and hidden cameras."

"Bugging devices are in order, but I cannot accept hidden cameras. In fact, a powerful tape recorder with tiny cassette tapes to last three hours would be more precise." Abba answered to Dumba's suggestion.

"I shall search around for it. If I don't find a suitable model, I'll have one sent by couriers from London. We shall have all the equipment within the next ten days."

"Good, and thank you. I knew I could depend on your technical competence in these matters. Be kind enough to deliver the equipment, and I'll handle the rest. You appreciate this is to be kept top secret."

"Yes, of course. There exists a certain honor among thieves. Besides, it is the same system that we both fight against; only I've been anti-system longer than you. It'll give me pleasure if we both work to avert the disaster that would almost certainly strike should you fail to convince Mamman Taofik."

"Yeah! We don't make the rules, we only play the games. Get me the recorder and tapes, and I'll reimburse you someday soon."

"Forget it, what are friends for? Goodbye and blow kisses to Binta Lilah. She is a swell dame. A pity I don't have time for amorous pleasantries."

"Then you do not know what bliss on earth you miss. Except

I now understand your chemical source are more dependable. Can I keep your gold vial? The content will help me pass the turbulent days ahead in a more relaxed frame of mind." Abba employed.

"Alright, but do however, be careful with its usage. I hope the content can last you long enough. I have another vial to last me until I get back to London."

"Oh! Thanks. I'll wait for the equipment as you promised. Bye for now."

On Saturday afternoon Abba ordered the chef of the hotel to prepare a menu for the gastronomic pleasures of the expected lady. His august visitor was Madam Binta Lilah. The supper consisted of poached artichoke hearts, salad or radicchio and sweet corn, millefeuille of king salmon with mousseline de mer.

Shortly before Binta was to arrive, Abba called the desk receptionist and gave instructions that all his incoming calls were to be held until the following Monday. His intention was to spend Saturday through Monday morning with the ravenous Binta. It would take approximately that length of time to sufficiently motivate her to go along with the specific role he had mapped out for her to play.

It was necessary that Binta accept the part of enticing Mamman Taofik. She was the only person suitable on account of her being a desirable, sophisticated woman. Additionally, her visit to Mamman Taofik's office will be considered legitimate and on purely business grounds. Being an active member of the political party in power, she can bring influence to bear on the minister. He being a gentleman, will be nice to the lady, knowing she had a certain amount of political clout.

The last reason for Abba's expectation of Binta was the fact that he will be killing two birds with one stone. He could have invited his numerous girlfriends. Their inevitable demand for huge amount of money was incompatible with his survival instincts for the present. Besides, these girls were at best parasitic mercenaries. They went to the highest bidder.

The man who gave more naira obtained more of their feigned affection. Binta, on the other hand was an experienced woman who knew how to give lasting pleasures with unique vital statistics. If he remembered correctly, Binta was a performer in the bedroom duel. She was a compassionate tigress and selfless in the art of deriving mutual benefit all at the same time.

Checking his watch, he quickly showered and put on his new "Cecil Gee's" silk shirt. He splashed on cologne to match his expectant mood. The sharp rise in his breathing told him he would not be disappointed. Walking over to his suitcase, he took two tablets from the super-strength vitamin bottle he had bought in Albany, New York. The extra power would aid his energy for the next forty eight hours.

He had just finished swallowing the tablets when the sharp knock on the door informed him the quarry had landed. Shouting aloud across for her to hold on, he went to the bedroom mirror and momentarily studied his handsome figure. A glorification to the cult of Narcissism.

"Well, well, well, Binta Lilah. This is all for your weekend's enjoyment," Abba spoke into the mirror.

Walking out to the living room, he beamed in anxious anticipation, like an infant expecting some candies. His heartbeat quickened as he opened the door and gallantly swept Binta off her feet, carrying her directly into the bedroom. He knew with Binta, time wasting formalities was unnecessary and besides there would be time for those later.

Over the long weekend, Abba learned the life story of Binta. He was shocked to know the real, simple -hearted woman operating in the tough business world. Seeing Binta, at a glance, one would only perceive the shrewd woman she was. The Binta now unfolding was someone to sympathize with.

Midway through the tales of her life, she smiled hopefully towards Abba. Her gesture demanded if he had anything to add to complete her happiness.

Rather taken unawares, Abba had stammered negative reply. The cold hard look of the business woman she was returned to her countenance. She remained silent for long moments, apparently hurt. To placate her, Abba had pitched himself resolving to go along with the game until she got sufficiently interested in agreeing to act as his intermediary to Mamman Taofik. Cajoling her a little, he gave the best satisfaction his vast experience could allow. Her tenderness then gradually returned, and she again seemed like a child. A baby whose only need was Abba's love. An amulet with which to survive the harsh realities of the world. Recognizing this need in Binta, Abba continued to pour numerous delight into her all night. With time, her inner satisfaction reached the peak and she was ready to assume the position of his slave. Halfway through her climax, she vowed she was his tool to be used as he wanted. She thus revealed in that statement the extent of her vulnerability.

Nodding with amusement, Abba had allowed her to drift into a self-satisfying sleep. It was in fact, one of the best she has had in years. In her sleep, Binta dreamed she was back to the good old days with Jacob.

She relived moments of their exotic pleasure that had preceded the birth of her wonderful twin sons. In her imagination she had loved Jacob loyally and would do all she could to avert the destructive behaviors that Jacob was getting himself into.

Only on waking up did Binta behold Abba lying snoring at her side. He seemed to wear a worried expression on his tired face. The expression on Abba's face gravely troubled Binta. Her woman's instinct told her that whatever was the cause of Abba's trouble heralded a great pitfall ahead unless she helped him. The look on Abba's face was similar to that of Jacob she had seen in her dream before his downfall manifested.

Snuggling close to Abba, she kissed his forehead muttering she would fight tooth and nail to help him. All she would need was for him to ask her help. Anything he might request she inwardly made up her mind to try her best to provide. Thus, with her mind made up to stand by Abba, she again drifted back into deep slumber and slept soundly with only the faint recollection of the happiness Abba had given her. God keep Abba, she prayed.

It was not until the early hours of Monday morning that Binta was able to persuade Abba to tell her the extent of his problems. Somehow he had dodged the question, but something told Binta he would only be too happy to confide in her. Thus, she had pressed on until he agreed to tell her everything, leaving out nothing.

"Promise me you will not pass judgment on my follies," Abba demanded before he commenced the story."

"Well, I promise on Allah, I shall do no such thing. The real truth is I've fallen in love with you, and the devil in you has taken power of my will. I'm all at you command," she assured Abba.

"Yeah! The story of my life. But where exactly do I start?" Anyway I'll be brief. Here it goes. My chance meeting with Lateef Isaq in 1945 and the subsequent events that unfolded before I arrived Lagos made me believe I have a role to play in life as a flamboyant naira millionaire. Lateef had impressed upon my mind the dourness of the first Nigerian millionaires and I had silently sworn that should Allah give me the chance, I'd be one of the most glamorous members of the monied elite club. Luckily for me, when I moved to Lagos and started at the U.A.C., my Scottish boss liked me so much. He made me study every night to improve my education. The manager instructed me that there were two types of education: one was received from others. The other, and most important, was from yourself.

He also introduced me to one of the American writers on self-motivation and positive thinking. Reading these self-motivational books helped to improve my salesmanship and thus my chances to succeed in life.

He recommended me to be sponsored by the company to three management seminars in England. These courses helped my ability to market myself, and I improved rapidly along this line. On my return from the third London School of Business course on human management, I was made the assistant Manager in Jos. From there, I was made manager of the entire U.A.C. operations in Kano, all within a period of 20 years in the organization. No doubt Mr. Brad, who had risen to a powerful position within the firm's corporate hierarchy, helped me. The truth was, I had the brain to burn and I worked like hell to merit all the good fortune that came my way.

After many years as a junior and supervisory staff, I was really blessed to become a manager at a very young age. In comparison with other U.A.C. managers. Being of Kano origin ensured that I had a very bright future to advance further in the corporate ladder of U.A.C.'s employment. I was saving money and neatly acquired many lands. I sold these for the initial capital to branch out and start up on my own. Thus, it was that by 1968, I had grown tired of being an arm chair manager.

The Kano of those days was producing a lot of wild-eyed businessmen. The Ibos had all gone, and the civil war was at its peak. The Kano indigenous businessmen were gradually acquiring merchant skills to take over the monopolies previously enjoyed by the Ibo traders. At that time, my friends in the army informed me that the war would soon be over. The consequences for me were that the upper management position opened at the U.A.C. would gradually absorb the Ibos who would in time regain their former managerial positions. This time, only the Yoruba's were firmly in control. Anyway, I thought to myself if I were to start up on my own, it was now or never. So it was in 1969, I gave up my position as the U.A.C. manager for Kano State.

With the money I had saved, I set up a furniture workshop. From there, I became an army contractor. Later, I started my own hotel business. As though cursed each time, I got fed up with any business, I sold to my friends. I started my own auto-mechanic workshop where I planned to assemble my own cars, but later, I gave up the whole idea. As though pursued by destiny, money kept within my circle. I had a lot of friends who were in the military, so getting contracts was no problem. Life became a game of easy come, easy go. The army boys loved the good time, that being around me meant to them. They were generous with their contracts. Mutually, we both enjoyed each other's company. I had money coming from executing military projects nationwide. Meanwhile, my serious minded competitors and contemporaries were consolidating so much that I gradually became a laughing stock to them. By this time, the army was almost packing their baggage to go back to the barracks. Before the military vacated from the seat of power, I was wise enough to stick with the political party I was sure would win. I gave generously to the key men and aspiring politicians with hope of riding into prosperity with them. It was all a matter of time."

The short economic downturn in the last year of the military boys, I was confidently informed, would turn around to boom as soon as the civilian administration took over the reins of government.

Thus advised, I staked my whole worth on the party's bandwagon. Once in power, I was requested to come into the government as a junior minister, but I bluntly refused. My strategy was to use my considerable foreign connections in London to stimulate good public relations for the party on the international scene.

For the necessary operating fund, I was promised issuance of unrestricted import licenses for any product my AAA organization was interested in bringing into the country and for as long as the government was in power.

That was the reason why AAA's International Limited had to have offices in almost all important world capitals.

As the political party's Chief Public Relations Consultant on the international scene, I helped to boost the morale of the visiting party members. I arranged reputable diplomats to meet them whenever they had business abroad. Little did I know that what started as a game on my part would now put me and my company in debts totaling over two million pound sterling. Not to mention AAA's half completed manufacturing factories, for which I owed the banks another three million. He paused to gauge Binta's response and was glad at her sympathetic misty eyes.

Cuddling her closer, he continued, "Yes, the austerity caught me unawares. The worst thing is, I was just about mapping out alternative source of funds from Germany before the clamp down came. Already I've set up factories, half way, to manufacture assorted fast-moving consumer goods. The story is the same with each and every of these factories. At AAA's confectionery factory, most of the equipment are yet to arrive from France. AAA's engine-motor plant to be based in Kaduna was in the process of finalizing technical arrangement with the Japanese Toyota Group. All my projects are only half way complete. So it is either I had 'carte blanche' in getting my import license re- issued or I'm doomed for life. The above are the unholy facts."

He seemed to have spoken for over an hour, but Binta's sharp interest focused on his eyeballs. Getting out of the bed, she poured two ice cold martinis. "This will cool you off," she said, handing a glass to Abba.

He took the glass graciously and moved to sit down on the sofa. Binta walked up and sat on a chair directly opposite the sofa. She held up her glass. "Here's to Abba's new life. And may he have the gut and luck to carry it off."

Abba held his own glass up. "I think with your co-operation, he'll have what it takes. Cheers!" They drank, draining their glasses.

Binta looked up at Abba. "Just tell me what exactly you require of me and by Allah, I shall try my best to accomplish it."

"I guess I want you to sound out Alhaji Mamman Taofik for the renewal of my licenses."

"You mean Alhaji Mamman Taofik--that son-of-a-bitch? The pompous Minister for Importations. I've heard a lot of bad things said about his high mindedness. How he bullies with his words."

"You're right, Binta. He has all the power to make or break me. But let us forget him for now and get yourself my special affection,"

"Yes, sir, you know I never say no to your goodies." Moving closer, they both bounced back to the comfortable cushioned, king-sized bed.

It was as if the pledge by Binta to aid his cause was the sole reason he had kept his energy intact. Immediately after that, he felt powerless to continue anymore. A deep slumber overtook him. He allowed his soul the rest it deserved. He slept deeply aware that the first stage of his strategy had been successful.

CHAPTER NINETEEN

The sharp ringing noise of the phone startled Abba at seven o'clock on Monday morning. Cursing, he lifted the receiver to hear Sam Dumba's voice demanding to know the position and outcome of the weekend's game plan.

"Everything went fine, and did you speak with Roger in London? And what is the position of things with regard to the equipment?"

Dumba replied that Roger had promised to check around but could not guarantee their delivery to Lagos until the next weekend. Dumba completed the conversation stating that the hardware would reach Abba as soon as practicable. When Abba hung up, Binta was staring intently at him with anger seething in her eyes.

"Who was that on the phone?" she asked. "And what is this talk of hardware?" She questioned alarmed.

"Ah it's, my friend Sam Dumba. The equipments were meant for the recording of some drama I was thinking of arranging for Marnman Taofik."

"Just what exactly do you mean?" asked Binta, her voice getting shriller. "Haha! Alhaji, do not tell me you allowed yourself to be conned by Dumba the super duper. Allah will never forgive you for wanting to dirty your good name with the likes of Dumba."

"Well, Binta, it was not like that," Abba parried, shocked at the fierceness of her emotional outburst.

"Please do not lie to me," continued Binta, "I have listened to your desperate situation, and I'm willing to do everything favorable to getting you the license. I'll use all my woman's ploys to trick Mamman Taofik, but I can't agree to use Dumba's criminal method. In fact, I've heard a lot of Dumba's blackmailing escapades and I think his very sight stinks. But what do you know, Abba? How are you sure he'll not turn around to use his dirty method on you someday? I know he'll not blink an eyelid to betray even his own mother. And such a character of a man is who you think you can trust. I can go on and on telling you of friends of mine he had duped. He has not only duped them, but still retains incriminating evidences with which he could force them to death if he so wishes. Never allow yourself to fall into his devilish traps. He is a man never to be trusted."

"Okay, so you have a point," Abba lamely consented and continued. "Alright I'll not have any further thing to do with Dumba, at least not in tackling Mamman Taofik. However, can you guarantee your charm will be enough to make him see reason?"

My physical endowments are enough to charm any man out of his senses--that much I know." boasted Binta. "The snag is that I think you've bitten off more than you can chew. Remember Dr. Richard?" she asked.

"Dr. Richard, the clearing and forwarding doctor? Yes, I remember him. In fact, I think he was on the London flight with us two weeks ago." Abba replied quietly.

"Yes, that is him alright. Dr. Richard has vowed to give up business life after losing well over three million of his investments. Rumor has it that he bought six 28-thousand-ton ships without calculating the exact amount to be paid for import duties among other things. Also the cost of paying the expatriate staff became too much when the boom of our overseas container trade was cut short by the austerity. He is reported to be going into politics. According to the BBC news report, the cause of the austerity is beyond the power of Lagos politicians. It is a result of the world debt situation plus the fact that our oil revenue has been depleted. Our importations must therefore, be reduced to the barest minimum. It is said that there will be no hope of recovery until the world oil glut ceases to pose the problem it currently does. Price cutting by some of the OPEC has also resulted in the consuming Western nation's refusal to stock pile with the hope that the cartel will be destroyed. I have researched with some bankers to confirm this version of the austerity in the strictest confidence. This boils down to the point that if there are concessions to be made, it has to come from Mamman Taofik. I shall try my utmost to get it, but on my own efforts. I do not need the machinations of Dumba to utilize my bottom power. Neither do I need his stinking tactics to charm Mamman Taofik into changing his stubborn mind."

"Okay, so I'll leave you to do it your own way. Only I must impress upon you that all my hopes rest on your success," replied Abba and took her hand and pressed it to his lip.

"Yes and no," Binta promptly answered back. "I'll try my

best. Meanwhile, meet Yardoya and Dogon Talata to see if you can get paid for your Abuja contracts. When you get the money, my director friend at the Central Bank will help you to convert it into pounds sterling at the official rate. That way, you can build up your currency reserve in London. The trick is to plan on three or four different scenarios so you will not be putting all your eggs in one basket. You must be pragmatic. Okay"

"Yes, I have no defense. I yield to your wisdom. Thanks for all your meaningful thoughts. Somehow I knew that with you on my side, the problem might become easier. I give you my promise to get Dumba off his dangerous scheming. At least I'm no longer interested. However, let it be on record that there was a time when I would not dare to violate another person by blackmail. But this economic doom like a burglar has stolen so much from me. I make my vow to do as you say. " He reached for her arms, holding her helpless. He knew, by the eagerness of her surrender that she wanted to be taken.   Suddenly he moved, separating himself apart, Abba walked toward the bathroom. He beckoned Binta to come along. "The clock is past noon. Let's shower and go forward with courage.

After their bath, room service brought a tray of Continental breakfast consisting of omelet, bacon, toast, coffee and orange juice. While they had breakfast, Abba again lapsed into his reason for involving Binta Lilah to corner Mamman Taofik for him.

"Also I had my reasons for bringing Dumba into the plan," he stressed with a big bite from the toasted bread. "You must wonder why a man like myself, who has achieved nationwide popularity, should become so desperate as to become criminally minded. I, of course, see a correlation between myself and the austere businessman whose careful plans in life became destabilized by circumstances beyond his control. He has become desperate enough to want to kill or be killed. Thus, I must become fraudulent to avoid extinction. My life's unique drama portrays me as a rich and successful international man. To continue this life role, I must have my licenses renewed. I may be a big fool for not envisaging this austerity in time to prepare myself to face it. The reality is that I have to face the present. Necessity demands that I scheme in every way in the hope that I can convince Mamman Taofik to renew my licenses. Everything I contemplate is done in this great hope. When that hope becomes baseless, my life will fall into disgrace, and death will become the necessary end."

Pleading with Binta not to interrupt, Abba continued, his voice getting more emotion-laden. "Yeah, I've tried to fix a meeting with Mamman Taofik but he keeps dodging me. He is always engaged in one meeting or another. His personal assistant says he does not wish to see me. Also Yardoya and Dogon Talata tell me the money for my Abuja contracts will be paid, but it will take perhaps two months. Time will be needed before the government generates enough resources from selling its oil. Meanwhile, I'll wait until you can bring me favorable news from Mamman Taofik. It is of great importance to me. I'll dwell in hope until then. There comes a point in a man's life when he must decide to live or not to live. I believe I'm approaching my own moment for such a decision. Whichever way it goes, equally happy will I be in accepting my fate."

When they had finished their breakfast, Binta took her leave. She promised to track down Mamman Taofik whatever the cost. Before she departed the hotel suite, she swore that Abba would be duly informed of what transpired at the meeting.

Binta recognized that to get Mamman Taofik, she would have to pass through her Uncle Abel Idoko, who was the Junior Minister for Monetary Controls. As an important member of the Kaduna wing of the ruling party, Binta had the right to call on important party officers holding key positions in government. She therefore made her exit from the L 'Hotel Eko Meridian in a hopeful mood of being a "Daniel-come-to-judgment" for the desperate Abba. Little was she to know of the eventual turn of events. Good intention alone never accomplishes a task. Good intentions never conquer in the world's rat race.

Binta was not fully aware of the impossibility of her mission to turn Abba's wheel of fate. As an incurable optimist, she hoped that she would try what best she could for the despondent Abba.

CHAPTER TWENTY

Immediately after leaving L 'Hotel Eko Meridian, Binta requested her chauffeur to drive her directly to the Federal Government Secretariat. The urgency of Abba's need to meet with Mamman Taofik could not be underestimated. The feeling of love, which Abba seemed to have inspired in her provided the motivating force that propelled her into Uncle Abel's office. Though Abel was her maternal uncle, she had in the past sworn not to approach him for any special favors. This was on account of Abel's previous meanness to her. The Catholic missions had sponsored his education up to university level. He graduated with top honors. This had enabled him to climb the corporate ladder of one of the local banks where he worked hard to amass great wealth. His corporate position and money power had made Abel so arrogant that he forsook his immediate relations. He believed he was no longer in the same class with those of his clansmen who had been raised in abject poverty. The villagers and Abel had therefore never agreed on anything. This animosity grew to the extent that the local juju priest made a public declaration in the village that Abel's carcass would not be allowed to rest in Idoma land, his native town.

Lady fortune further advanced Abel, when he wrote and published an economic bestseller. His economic theories seemed to be in tune with those of the budget administrators in the civilian government. The Lagos party power brokers showed their appreciation for his financial ingenuity and therefore offered him the position of Junior Minister for Monetary Controls. This was a privileged position that made Abel an eminent person in the country's economic matters.

Binta's intelligent mind rightly concluded that the best way to get Mamman Taofik would be through Abel. And she prayed that Abel would be in the right frame of mind to receive her. Mindful of the fact that his arrogant uncle might be too busy to invite her for a chat, she apprehensively wrote her name on Abel's visitor's book.

The messenger, taken by Binta's smooth beauty, apparently rushed in to present the name to his master -the honorable minister.

A minute later, Abel personally came out of his huge ministerial office to usher her into his office. "Thank God, you are in," said Binta on seeing Abel approaching.

"I've been worried; you might have traveled out of the country."

"Quite right. In fact, I'm scheduled to leave for New York next Wednesday in search of financers to borrow money from for the country. You heard the news that we are broke. We are less well off than Ghana, that is, considering the debt factor," concluded Abel. He was radiate in his cream colored Italian, silk double-breasted suit with Gucci shoes to match. His wrist displayed the latest Seiko quartz in solid gold. His whole attire must have cost millions of Italian Lira at the Santa Margarita Fashion Shop in Milan.

Abel's flamboyance could best be described as very loud and ungracious. That is, if you consider his stomach, which was protruding as though requesting to be delivered of its content.

"Well, do come in, it is not every day my most beautiful niece comes to say hello to me in my office," beamed the happy Abel. Binta got over the shock of the unexpected welcome, walked into the office, the floor of which was decked with the most expensive Persian rug she had ever laid eyes on. Sitting down, she requested for some cold Coca-Cola to cool herself off after the heat of the burning fiery sun.

After Binta drank to her satisfaction, Abel commenced with the opening question.

"Now tell me, what has brought you to the condemned man's office? You heard the villagers told me not to start building a house in my village. How absurd! What they don't know is that I'm pressuring the Federal Government to provide vital development to our village. They include huge infrastructures- roads, hospitals, electricity, and even an irrigation dam to enable the farmers have bumper harvest. In fact, all the construction contracts would have been given out if not for this empty nest syndrome. Though not to worry, the economic austerity will not last forever. As soon as we get the economy on its feet again, our villagers will have all these things and more. That I promise you or my name is not Abel Idoko. After the town is provided with these amenities, then the villagers will beg to make me a Chief. You know, of course, that the title of Chief before my name will greatly increase my standing in the government circle and in the political party."

"I have no doubt that a chieftaincy title will suit you just fine. It is a shame you did not reach this conclusion sooner than now." She said sternly.

"Ah! You have come with your cynicism. For a woman with your beauty to be given such ruthless intelligence is always a rare combination. Okay, so you are right. I should have coerced the people a long time ago but I did not. The reason being I was too busy ladder-climbing, but I will make it up if only to become a Chief of Idoma land. I am sure that is not the reason for your coming here. Now tell me what can I do for my dear little niece?" Abel asked in his minister's V.I.P. Baritone voice. He bowed humbly. This training he had received as a banker he combined to flatter unsuspecting clients.

"Yes, I had wondered if you would never ask," Binta replied. She stared at him incredulously. "I called for two specific things. The first is that I want detailed information as to why the present inflation in the country is now over three hundred percent? And second, what does the austerity really mean? "What hope do we have? My business lies in ruins. All my plans have been blown sky high. It is my belief that as the whiz-kid Minister for Monetary Control, you will have an ample opportunity to know more than the other tin-head power lords of this administration."

"You want to know the cause of this austerity?" asked Abel, his mood changing from mirth to deep thoughtfulness. "The austerity, in a nutshell, is the consequence of our over- dependence on foreign oil buyers for our economic growth. Our import capacity and means of earning foreign exchange depends heavily on our ability to sell our petroleum. We are yet to have any other alternative source for regular foreign income.

To explain further, I shall take the case of Zambia, which is also totally dependent on copper for her foreign earnings. In 1972, there was a boom in copper prices with price peaking in April of 1974 to over three thousand naira per ton. By the end of 1974, the price started falling and reached an all-time low just one thousand naira per ton. Zambians had all their budget and economic projections calculated on the higher earning rate per ton. They never in their wildest dreams imagined that disaster could strike the way it did. Being heavily dependent on imports, Zambia's volume of foreign imports therefore, fell to almost sixty percent of their budget. The dislocation caused by this uncontrollable internal budgetary plan meant tragic shock and unimaginable human sufferings for the entire population. The fluctuating prices for basic commodities must impact optimism in calculating future earnings. Our plans were geared towards increased earnings on our crude oil. Little did we imagine the action of our desperate OPEC associates, and the world oil glut." Abel spoke miserably.

"You mean to tell me that your ministry has no way of monitoring international issues?" Binta questioned in a disturbed tone. She was displeased with the smooth and impersonal tone Abel had used to explain the calamity that had the potency of claiming the lives of people like Abba and hundreds of other businessmen.

"Not at all my dear," continued Abel. "We do have a computer for making economic judgment. Our economic forecast tools are of course, not the best in the world, but the international pressures are not the basic cause of the present human shock that the country is experiencing. The main cause is the internal distorted distribution of the national wealth. Now, do not quote me on this. It is of course my own personal opinion. My theory is that Nigeria is at the elementary stage of capitalism. Historically, this is a stage of what is called the accumulation of naked power. A country is created, but it degenerates into a system in which society operates in a "Man Pass Man" crudeness. The enlightened few must chase after naked power for all its worth. It is either they get enough power to live respectfully or they die. In such a system therefore, the enlightened members must struggle endlessly to acquire this power. In our Nigerian society, the naira is the symbol of this omnipotent power. Thus, we have a spiral web of 'Naira Worshippers' ranging from the messenger to the man occupying the highest position in both public and private corporate organizations. Salvation goes to the man who accumulates the most. Law and order must respect the almighty Naira overlord. This trend will continue until a stabilizing stage can be reached. That is when powerful economic barons will then gather themselves in a cartel to give protection to the masses. They set new societal law and order. They know that is the only way they can keep and maintain their fraudulently acquired wealth. I know that you as a contractor were forced to include an extra ten percent in your tender bill to enable you pay off the government officials who will sign your contract. The government officials in this position are ripping off the system in two ways. He is officially paid by the taxes of the people and his ten percent is also ripping off the people. His crime is, of course, greater than that of the armed highway robber because the robber is not an elite member of the system. Therefore, while the robber must be shot if caught, the official must be protected by the elite members in the government. The corrupt official takes solace in the fact that everyone else is doing it. Their accumulated wealth therefore, becomes a power base, from which their children derive their security in life. Their respect in society remains guaranteed as a result of their parents' luck to have illegally enriched themselves. I repeat, the guilty of our times are lucky to escape without punishment. The reason is that almost everyone is stealing from the same source. Our society exits at this point in time when you cannot prosecute thieves in high places. This explains the corruptions of our time. With time, our educated elites will demand for us to be more responsibly aware of our civic duties. Then we may learn to give loyalty to our government before gratifying our immediate pocket. Most of the developed countries have institutions bent on fighting corruptions."

Abel waited for Binta's comment and when she remained silent, he earnestly continued. "Personal power in Germany is not dependent on individually accumulated wealth alone. Thus, the people can expect to be justly treated and judged alike. Therefore, should a politician or minister commit a serious crime, he is more likely to be punished as would an ordinary criminal. Justice is then seen by all to be done. That is a stage, which I'm not sure we'll reach for a long time to come."

Abel paused to check the effect of his long speech and to give his niece the chance to contribute. Looking at her, she seemed more subdued than when she came in. Possibly something was bothering her.

Abel reasoned, but decided to let her be.

Looking downcast, Binta took a long drink from her glass of Coca-Cola and nervously grinned. "You mean to say, there is no hope of remedying what is going on? If that is the case, we, the powerless ones should go jump into the Lagos lagoon. Tell me, what is this international debt crisis all about?" she asked.

"The international debt crisis? That is a topic that has been bothering my ministry for months. Though we are indebted to the tune of over thirty billion dollars, our case is much better than that of Brazil. Our case compares with Mexico's as we are both members of the OPEC. Our indebtedness is gravitated by our stupid belief that the oil price will always increase annually. We therefore borrowed from the American banks at interest rates sometimes over the prudent rate of 12 percent in order to carry out necessary development projects. Our economic forecast gave us hope to pay back the loans in time without fear of default. The case of Brazil is associated with deficit financing by certain American banks to reduce the OPEC oil price increment shocks. The third factor was the flat money system which the U.S. Treasury actively encouraged in the early 70's. This led to higher interest rates worldwide. It brought about the resultant world-wide attitude of consume now and pay later. You and I know that rising expectations for improved standard of living not matched by productivity will always spell trouble in the long run. This is what is gradually becoming manifest. It is my professional opinion that the only way out of the international debt crisis is for the United States Government to step in. They should take over the privately owned banks and the responsibility of the developing countries debt. The U.S. Government can then reduce the interest rate repayments on these loans. They should at the same time be prepared to run significant trade deficits with the developing countries for as long as American trade budget with these least developed countries remain high. It is my strong belief that unless some of these drastic measures are implemented, the global debt crisis will open up a lot of unpleasant tragedies in the years ahead."

"Okay, so what will happen for now? I'm seriously in trouble over some manufacturing concern I am arranging with some foreign partners. I therefore, need some import license. How can you advise me so as to favorably achieve this?" Binta asked.

'My advice to all captains of industry in Nigeria is to wait, hope, and pray. There is no optimism or pessimism on my part. But as the Minister for Budgetary Controls, I can assure you, we are trying our best to get the foreign loans to continue with important government projects. Our request to foreign banks to lend us more funds are being contested. In fact, this austerity measure has been imposed on us by the International Monetary Fund. They do not care about the untold hardship that we, the men in the government have to suffer through imposing this belt tightening austerity. What do they care about developing countries? They sit on their fat asses and command us to impose sharp human shocks on our citizens and we oblige because we have no other hope. When we request for substantial loan to tide our economy over, they reply that our mis-distribution was the reason that got us into trouble in the first place. What they never seem to realize is that Nigeria is far better run than most African countries. And for that matter, America and England, at the early stages of their history. Corruption in high places will always be. Why IMF must force us to eradicate ours in the immediate now is what beats my educated belief in the gradualness of things. Good things, like the evils of society must take time to be made better. Aha, I'm going to this World Bank meeting next Wednesday and I can assure you I'll give them hell. But the necessary paper work for the loan approval would make it difficult to get any immediate result until maybe at the end of the year or next year. There will be no immediate solution that much I know. Abel spent a long time lecturing on his familiar subject. Now he turned his attention to Binta. "Concerning your import license, you can discuss that with my friend Alhaji Mamman Taofik. A fine gentleman, if ever there is one. Mamman Taofik is the only non-mediocre member of the administration. That is, apart from myself. Do you want to meet with him?" Abel asked with enthusiasm.

"Yes, I shall be happy if you can arrange for him to see me. It is of great importance, at least for my corporate survival," stated Binta in a matter of fact tone.

"Anything I can do for my niece to make her happy. I protest you do not come to see me often. Maybe I could have helped you get some contracts in the new capital city. With regards to Mamman Taofik, I know he is a very busy man. Not that I blame him. I did in fact, help recommend him for his present job. Part of the activities of the ministry for Monetary Control overlaps into controlling the issuance of import license. The need to have strict control over imports necessitated putting a minister of high repute and honesty into the position. It was my belief that Mamman Taofik is the most disciplined person to man the post and he has not proven me wrong. A pity, of course, he had created a lot of enmity between himself and the other easy-go-lucky members of the cabinet. The position exactly needed a tough minded Fulani of integrity to stand up to the hawkish mediocrity who give the administration its worst image. I shall phone him tonight when I know he would be less busy, to arrange a meeting between the two of you. I must warn you not to make unrealistic demands. It is a good thing that you came to speak with me first. You are now as knowledgeable of reasons of this austerity as any member of the executive cabinet. Call me tomorrow morning, if you are lucky you may be booked to see Mamman Taofik by the end of next week. As a favor for getting him to see you, do help me inform the village head that I have plans to bring huge prestige to the village. Tell him I will begin to deliver my promises as soon as this austerity is over. Bye for now. I have to hurry for an urgent meeting at Ribadu Road. Do give me a ring tomorrow morning to know when to see Mamman Taofik, and remember my message to our village head."

"Of course, I'll pass your promise to the man himself when next I visit our home town. I'll call you tomorrow and thanks for your time."

CHAPTER TWENTY-ONE

Two weeks after Binta's visit to her uncle, Mamman Taofik's personal assistant called her Maryland home. He confirmed her appointment for the next Thursday. Binta reckoned she had eight days within which to prepare. She therefore perfected her strategy to alleviate her lover's sorrow. She was starting to feel anxious about Abba's mental health and slept the night longing for his comforting arms. She kept away from the hotel for fear members of government intelligence service might see them together. They would then pass the information to the honorable minister's security details. When she could no longer bear the agony of the lonely nights, she insisted that Abba come over to her Maryland apartment. He bluntly refused, stating it was best that they stayed apart. Furthermore, he declined to leave the hotel suite for fear of missing any important phone calls. His anxiety was making him become neurotic.

There was real fear emitting from his voice each time he picked up the phone. His speech sounded distant with a bit of stammering. It was like his whole personality was undergoing drastic changes. From the telephone conversation, Binta could deduce that he was afraid she might bring him negative news. Such negative news would blow the light out of his already diminishing existence. His sense of significance and self-esteem had taken a lot of bashing since the austerity measures. His presence at L 'Hotel Eko Meridien before the economic burst, attracted many crowds. He took delight in frantic range of champagne party orgies. Parties were organized by Lagos social elites to impress him. They took turn to compensate him for previous parties he celebrated on their behalf. They each labored to repay the international playboy for the good time he gave them in his leisure palaces in the exotic capitals of the world: London, Paris, Rio de Janeiro, New York etc.

The ill effect of the austerity measures had put a stop to the champagne parties. A solemn mood was prevalent in the city. The hustle and bustle of the money bags had ceased in the hotel.

To his unstable mind, he saw this partying irregularity as an evil omen. Superstition becomes in times of uncertainty, the bedrock of the powerless. His powerlessness worsened with each passing day. Also his decreasing purchasing power adversely affected his mental stability. Such was his dependence on his naira power for his happiness that his melancholy increased as his cash diminished. He therefore stayed locked up his suite refusing to go out of the hotel for weeks. He became vulnerable and his phobia became more acute when the hotel manager informed him his unpaid bills were mounting. The knowledge that the funds may not be available to pay for the suite sickened him. The possibility of being thrown out combined to make his fatalistic mood more desperate. He became frozen with fear and daily consumed cocaine to get high. He watched pornographic video tapes and drank a dozen of 'Moet et Chandon' champagne. Gradually, he started to display the classic syndrome of the impotent male. He became recklessly frenzied, and spoke of nothing but suicide. He was terribly sick.

"All is lost forever and all is hopeless, "he retorted, when Binta had taken the courage to visit him to announce the appointment with Mamman Taofik.

"I am meeting with the minister on Thursday and until then we keep hope. You must not allow yourself to go into a rotten state of mind. You have not shaven for days and no doubt you've been drowning yourself in 'Moet et Chandon' champagne. The content of the very expensive wine will do your constitutions no good." She protested vehemently.

"Aha! But it gives me solace to pass the day. I suddenly realize I've been a bum all my life. I made money my god. I lived only for money, sex, inconsequential powers; and the vain commodities of life. Now I know all is lost. I mean lost for good," he shouted in fury as though possessed by a devil. He raved on and on.

Binta pleaded with him to calm down, but to no avail. Finally, accepting defeat, she sat down and studied her once flamboyant lover. Abba presented a frightful sight with unshaven face. He was all bones like a matchstick, a far cry from his previous healthy weight. The foul breath from his mouth stank like the odor that oozed from open sewers in the filthy Lagos slums. The transformation was inexplicable. Binta wondered how she had cared or loved the strange looking creature that appeared to represent Abba. He looked and ranted like a mad man.

When all her pleas to him were completely ignored, Binta packed her vanity case and went back to Maryland. Her mind resolved to try her best for Abba. She prayed to the gods to give her the wit to influence Mamman Taofik and to bring solace to her lover turned monster.

He was stolid black and stood five feet, five inches tall. Not a very tall man for the important position Allah had bestowed upon him. His acute brain power compensated for what the man, who would someday be king lacked in height.

He was dressed in simple native attire, which comprised a white top shirt "dashiki" He wore a white matching fine trouser, an embroidered cap that loosely decked his slightly bald head. His head's massiveness was accentuated by egg-shaped dome of a forehead. The internal contained an impressive data bank as on a human computer. His large brown eyes were hidden behind a pair of gold-rimmed spectacles. His personality accentuated his intellectual importance in the affairs of the realm. There was no doubt his brilliant utilization of his massive memory bank had afforded him the compensatory position of national honor.

"What can we do for such a charming Eve? I believe the name is Binta Lilah. Your uncle Abel Idoko said to give you our very best. Just acquaint me with your desires, I will cooperate accordingly." He spoke softly.

The crisp fluent English combined to persuade and disarm Binta. She reasoned that this was indeed a likeable man of rare intellect. The extent of the shock she felt at this realization was exhibited in her wide open mouth. For a split second, she sat mesmerized on her seat. She did not expect such a manner of greeting from the man intent on making a martyr of her lover Abba. The welcome was the reverse of her mindset. Here was an intellectual, a worthy ambassador of her country. He served honestly in a very powerful position lacking the high minded arrogance which had condemned the likes of Abel Idoko.

Dumb-founded, Binta cleared her throat to regain her composure. She graciously replied, "Well, put it this way, I've been pleasantly surprised at your simplicity and humble style in a very high office. I'm afraid I was expecting you to be rather arrogant, crude and unsympathetic."

"My apologies for disappointing your expectations. On the

other hand, I am glad you appreciate my so-called humble disposition. A lot of people would never equate my exalted position with the ascetic discipline I've subjected my entire life to. But I hope I don't put you off by my colorlessness or my innate lack of glamour. Yes, I'm a simple man with a simple mission. I work hard to serve my country as best as I can, even if it means fighting my not-too-inspired contemporaries. What a better place Nigeria would be if all were as conscientious as Mamman Taofik in carrying out official duties." He spoke with deep passion.

"If all men were like you, Alhaji, life would indeed be very dull, for beautiful creatures like myself. Some of us need a lot of affection from the powers that be in order to continue to be healthy. Stories have it that you are indifferent to all women. Your stoic discipline is commendable and intimidating"

"Not so, I may have class. I'm choosy with the type of women I permit into my busy life. But what's that to do with you. I'm sure you don't need such a bore as myself. I can hardly measure up to your handsome types. I mean the international playboys who have enormous physical powers as well as the financial powers to give you the world. I do know there must be many of those all waiting for your signal to give you paradise on earth."

"Oh! Don't be so cruel, Alhaji. The admiration that I have for you, may be quite different from the physical lust, which I may feel for what you call the jet-set fun men. For you, I may develop respect for your simplicity and intellectual faculties. Depending on how you respond, it may become something higher than love. It might simply mean needing you and reciprocating with my tenderness and emotional caring. All of course depends on whether you are interested enough."Binta flirted shamelessly.

"You have wits and I must not be deceived by your charms. You must have an active brain to have carried you from rural beginnings to the here and now," replied Mamman Taofik. "What can I do for you? Abel mentioned something to do with import license. If that be the case, I can assure you we shall remember you as soon as the economic situation changes. When that will be, I don't even know. It may be months. It could even last till the end of this administration. The situation is quite hopeless. When I took over this ministry at the beginning of this austerity, I demanded a full report on why we have to undergo this terrible human suffering. The full report is yet to be completed." He coughed, cleared his throat and continued. "The little authentic information I've gathered is enough to make any responsible adult weep at the ruthlessness of those who loot the national treasury. These same parasites lament my being in charge of importation ministry. But can you imagine what the result could have been if one of these immature-at-head and heart ministers were in charge? Allah knows, license could still have been issued to their blood relations. These irresponsible officials do not give a hoot whose death their action brings about so long as their bank balances daily increases. These are the men who would sell-their very own souls if only to make profit. And why I must have all these rotten individuals to sabotage my every effort is what shakes my belief in Allah. They should all be locked up in prison with the key thrown away. During my discussion with Abel, he stressed that from historical perspective the situation will soon be worse. But we sincerely hope it does not get worse than the present or we'll need a constitutional resolution to remain one nation. The army will then have a field day."

"What you mean to say is that no import license can be issued earlier than next month," Binta asked with anxiety, the desperation in her tone showing.

"Let me start by stating that our country's problem can be traced to poor management of the economy by past governments, tolerated or elected since our independence. It was poor management that made us permit fixed low interest rates and overvalued exchange rates while experiencing double-digit inflation. We promote harmful industrial policies, abandoned our agricultural productivity and increased our external indebtedness with foreign commercial banks. I have been under pressure from the powerful members of the Manufacturers Association of Nigeria. These are the various captains of industries whose numerous offensives I daily contend with. They have threatened to close industries and leave thousands unemployed. And I told them to go ahead. I can't approve import license for even the water authority to bring in necessary chemical for water treatment. The Lagos water engineer tells me, their supply will run out in a week's time, after which, our drinking water may become contaminated for lack of necessary treatment chemicals. Many people, I'm sure, will die from drinking untreated water. But the International Monetary Fund insists our monthly import requirements be cut to the barest minimum. Either we maintain this financial prudence or we shall not be able to satisfy the conditions for the World Bank loan we are currently negotiating. As far as my ministry is concerned, our control over import license is total. The only import avenues opened to fraudulent citizens are the airport and seaport. Those bribing the customs officers and smugglers can bring in necessary commodities. The only snag is that the inflationary price for these commodities may well reach five hundred percent before our economic situation can improve. What I may promise you is that when our foreign exchange earning situation improves, and we are in position to re-start issuing of import license, I'll personally make sure yours is on the top of the list."

"But Alhaji that will not be enough. In fact, I may even be forced to desperation, if I don't get the import license before the end of next month," cried out Binta. She was terribly shaken at the turn out of events. His stern firmness disturbed her. The bleak picture he painted was tragic.

"You speak of desperation. I see that every day. I meet those whose legacy of greed has contributed to our economic mystery. " Mammam Taofik waxed eloquent. "Ah! That reminds me, I got news yesterday that a party member Abba Abdulmalik is on the verge of insane desperation. But my advice to you should be not to contemplate ever doing that. You can reduce your life style. Cut short your expectations, exercise some frugality and obtain money from you richer friends to help tidy you over if you must. The austerity may be over in the next nine months or more, but a disciplined living standard would help make you a better human being. A great pity, self-discipline is what most human beings lack. This will be the reason I shall not be surprised if many take the courage to finish their life. You see, I have known about Abba Abdulmalik during the army regime. He lacks any sense of priority and has squandered more fortune than any captain of an industry in the country. A born sycophant, he had grown up into deceiving himself that the world owed him a living. He had been lucky enough to become rich. Abba Abdulmalik's foolish impression that Allah made him specially to be ministered to will trigger his downfall. How unfortunate! Generally, people of such disposition do not live long. They can never reap what they had not sown. Abba Abdulmalik has sown nothing and he will reap nothing." He spoke venomously.

"You sound so bitter over Abba Abdulmalik," commented Binta. "You must hate him so much as to wish his demise," Binta stated, disguising her concern.

"Not that, but his life style is exactly the opposite of mine. The root of my annoyance is that it is people like him who gave this country the reputation we now have. You take a trip to Britain and on the mention of the fact that you come from this country, every shopkeeper assumes you have the oil wealth in your pocket. They erroneously coax even men of better judgment into believing it is good publicity for the country. Only I know better. I studied there and I can imagine the innate contempt the average English shopkeeper has for pretentious African nouveau riches. I don't hate Abba Abdulmalik, his fate could have been mine but for the grace of Allah. I owe my life style to my strict upbringing. What I despise is the notoriety, the likes of Abba Abdulmalik have brought on this country. Their opulent life style in faraway cities like Rio de Janeiro has contributed to our present economic gloom. Every article of worth in Abba Abdulmalik's possession must have been bought at such expensive shops like the Harrods of the Western cities. The foreign exchange difficulties we are currently experiencing could be understood in the light of activities of men like Abba Abdulmalik. May Allah forgive him for his inability to comprehend the dire consequence his princely life style has on the economy of this nation. The joke of it was that some powerful members of the party were bent on giving him a government position as a salaried international consultant with diplomatic privileges. Common sense had prevailed at the last minute when Abba Abdulmalik foolishly declined the offer. The only sensible thing he ever did.' Mammam recalled how that the present administration is unwilling to accommodate the likes of Abba. He was convinced that the best solution for Abba was to terminate his life. While Mamman Taofik spoke, his energy was consumed towards destroying evil, he failed to notice the subtle transformation in Binta's countenance. Binta's anguish made her sweat profusely, but she continued to sit still while her lover was verbally chewed to death. She mentally conditioned herself to play the role of a disinterested third party. That was the best strategy and posture to assume in order not to give her secret away. It would serve no purpose letting the honorable minister become aware that she was Abba's emissary. To do that would kill the personal interest the powerful minister had in her. Call it curiosity or female bitchiness, but Binta was intelligent enough to appreciate Abba's seemingly impossible task of staying afloat. As a woman who had stood the test of difficult times, she believed that the laws of survival meant that the winner takes all. The loser was doomed forever to become a relic of the past. Losers must suffer alone as everybody hated failures. Binta was no exception to this universal law. She had resolved since abandoning Jacob to move ahead, always pitching her lot with the winners of the world.

She therefore coldly calculated the fondness the honorable minister felt for her. She weighed his promise to help her when the economic situation improved. Prudence demanded therefore, that she switch her soft-spot for Abba. She would not allow the unique opportunity to slip by.

The business woman in Binta led her to conclude that Abba was doomed. This was an irreversible fact, which no one had the power to avert. She therefore, made a decision that all was lost as had already been envisaged. She however, had her life and twin boys to think of. The dreamer in her took over in comparative analysis of the minister's power and capability to bring her to satisfaction. She was an incurable optimist. After all, Binta believed that any feat was attainable if one set one's mind to it. She knew her imagination would be possible, if she worked very hard.

She calculated what new horizons to accomplish when the time came for Taofik to fulfill his promise of import license to her. A home in Switzerland would then be possible—perhaps even a home on the River Rhone. With time, everything would become possible, she kept on reminding herself.

CHAPTER TWENTY-TWO

Six months after the trip to Switzerland, Barrister Bulus Musa's life had never been the same. The Old Fox's blunt refusal to consider the merits in his presentation unnerved him as never before in his long successful career. Often he lay sleepless at night, reviewing the high points in his arguments. It was not the question of money, for the Old Fox was considered the richest black African with the exception of Mobutu Sese Seko, the ruler of the Republic of Zaire. The outcome of the meeting was not what was expected from the cunning "Man of the people." Bulus wondered if the death of his only son and wife in a car crash had not served to drive the Old Fox insane. Still, he reasoned it was not logical, for the man appeared in full control of his senses. The only sensible conclusion Bulus reached was that the Old Fox was planning a surprise. Bulus rested his hopes that da Souza would in time show his hands. Only with time will the Lagos populace know of their wealthy son with the power to match the benevolence of a Rockefeller. And who's better to benefit from such immense overflow than the erudite lawyer. The thought of the future profit from da Souza made Bulus smile wolfishly. He sat down dreaming of the mansion to build from his share of the booty.

On the next Monday, however, discouragement filled the profile of Barrister Bulus Musa as he sat in his Broad Street Law chamber. The penthouse law firm was superbly furnished to suit the high tastes of the successful legal practitioner. The contemporary Italian furniture and interior decoration cost a fortune. The office furniture consisted of superior leather finished in ornate black coloring. Even the wall was beautifully clad with exotic oil paintings, imported from various European countries.

Seated at the high chair, Bulus thought about his life and career. The precarious austerity, he reasoned was spilling over to threaten even the expensive standard of life he provided for himself. The austerity had dealt serious economic blows on his affluent Lagos clients and the effect was beginning to tell on his law firm's bank balance. His thoughts were directed to the three o'clock meeting he had scheduled with Dr. Richard. The meeting certainly would be a rough one and Bulus must depend on his analytical ingenuity to aid him survive Dr. Richard's hawkish onslaught. Dr. Richard had phoned the previous day to fix an appointment in order to demand extra financial benefit for the sales of the Trans-Atlantic Ocean liners registered under the recently bankrupt Kemidare Lines.

Bulus' Greek client, who was putting up the fund to purchase the ships from Dr. Richard's bankers, had bluntly refused all further financial obligations. That was apart from the initial one already agreed upon by both parties.

It was Bulus' duty to tell his friend, Dr. Richard, this piece of bad news. Bulus had been a prime mover in the deal having initiated the meeting between the Greek shipping brothers and Dr. Richard. Had he foreseen the outcome of events, he would never have agreed to bring the two greedy parties together. He regretted gravely the unfolding episode.

Bulus' sympathy as a loyal friend was essential for Dr. Richard who had apparently lost all his life's fortune. Bankrupt and desolate, Dr. Richard had decided to go into politics. He might, with time, possibly recoup his losses from politics, but one very much doubted the chances. His bad luck was triggered first by his excessive greed in purchasing six 28-thousand-ton ships almost on his own. This was a very foolish decision to make in the erratic industry of ocean transportation. It became only a matter of major bad business deal before the banks demanded their money back. Dr. Richard's bad decision was helped by the slump in shipping trade, precipitated by oil glut and world recession. Add these to the effect of the Federal Government's austerity measures, and the nail to Dr. Richard's corporate financial coffin was sealed. Had he been luckier, the enormous risk would have catapulted him overnight to become one of the richest men in the country. But such was the nature of caprice. Dr. Richard's luck finally ran out on this spectacular venture. Experience taught Bulus that Dr. Richard was finished as a businessman and he doubted his chances in politics.

Come to think of it, despite all said and done, Bulus had done fairly well in life. Born of a Ghanaian father and Kafanchan mother, Bulus grew up in the tin mining town of Jos. His father, Kofi Mensah, had served the resident mining engineer, Mr. David Rosenburg who was said to be a native of South Africa. Though

Rosenburg was a very difficult man to serve, Bulus' father served his master with all his soul and pride for two decades.

Mensah spent almost all his life in service to Mr. David Rosenburg. He served as a steward, messenger, driver, laundry man, you name it, and Mensah was it. He gradually gained the trust of the difficult South African. To show his satisfaction, Mr. Rosenburg promised to see Mensah's twin sons through their college education. Thus, it was that Bulus and his brother Bitrus collectively joined Mensah in administering to the white man's domestic needs once they reached their 10th birthday.

Mensah's living apartment in the staff quarters of the Rosenburg gigantic mansion comfortably accommodated Bulus and Bitrus as they grew up. They had only their father since their mother had died of pneumonia when the children were barely three years old. Nurtured by their father with the help of Mr. Rosenburg's female maid servant, the two boys grew up healthy and happy. Encouraged by Mr. Rosenburg, Bulus gained admission into the local Roman Catholic Primary School and gradually learned to appreciate the wisdom of education. His house chores over, Bulus bent his head in reading all he could lay his hands on in Mr. Rosenburg's huge library. The young boy's hunger for knowledge, drew the attention of the indifferent Mr. Rosenburg to the studious boy. And as he finished his primary school, Mr. Rosenburg personally requested the District Officer in charge of the British Colonial office in Jos to ensure Bulus admission into the Government College.

The Jos Government College gave much enlightenment to Bulus, and it was while at the college that his mind focused on becoming a lawyer. Gifted with an early intelligence, Bulus utilized his time to increase his wealth of knowledge a hundred fold. The ethnic population of the college was such that almost all the other boys had specific future life mission.

The life of the average boy was so planned that each knew of his specific role as a future power broker when the colony became a country. Being children of important native chieftains, the British had enticed them to the white man's college. They assured the parent of their sons' bright future after gaining independence from Britain.

Not belonging to the elitist society, Bulus distanced himself from the boys and became a recluse. Often he stayed on his own and gave himself the education, which the other boys never had time or capacity to assimilate. By all standards, his educational ability when compared to the next boy in his class revealed substantial difference, but this was not the case.

The authorities had different motives in awarding academic grades. The school's politics and policy overshadowed the unknown boy from Ghana. They promoted unashamedly the sons of the soil. They were destined for great things in life. In his first semester examinations at the college, Bulus had been shocked to learn the first place he had worked so hard for was not given him. Instead, his class master had rated him in the fifth position out of a class of sixty.

Young Bulus was angry and could not understand the reason behind the class master's action. Bulus had protested to Mr. Rosenburg. He threatened to give up college education and to join Bitrus in the mines. Bitrus, due to inadequate intelligence had earlier been absorbed to become a pit boy in the mines. His story of the adventures in the mines had served to wet his appetite. Bulus therefore planned to abandon his secondary education to become a miner.

However, Rosenburg would not have any of that.

"Pay attention, my young lad, "he stated in his savage voice. "It is costing good money to fund your education. But I'm gladly doing it because Mensah has served me faithfully for twenty years. I'm the person who brought your father from Ghana to Nigeria I encouraged the marriage between Kofi and Hassana your late mother because, I believe Nigeria has better hope of economic survival than Ghana. Someday, maybe in the next fifty years, your offspring would bless the day I brought your father away from Ghana. Concerning your education, I am not worried about your being discriminated against. I have seen worse where I come from. It's a price you must pay to become accepted. That was the reason I advised Mensah to give you the name Bulus, reflecting the local dialect on the English name Paul. And as a matter of urgency I shall want you to change your surname to a more acceptable native one. I think Musa will be just fine. It's more native than Mensah and would be more acceptable in the long term."

The talk with Mr. Rosenburg was the longest speech Bulus had ever heard the white man make. And from that day onward, a mysterious link seemed to bind them together. Strengthened in his ambition to overcome the local discrimination, Bulus resigned himself to his fate at the college. He took to athletics at the school and performed superbly. In his final year, he became the captain of the school's football team. His success as the school captain earned him full acceptance and fueled his secret ambition of becoming a legal practitioner. An ambition that consumed his every energy, driving him until the goal was attained.

A year before Bulus graduated from college, Rosenburg was suddenly killed in an accident that claimed the lives of fifteen of the local workforce in the mining town. Bitrus was among the ones that died. The tragic incident led to Mensah's resignation from the mining company. The mine had taken the lives of his beloved wife and son both at very young ages. It was the death of his benefactor and godfather that really shattered the aspiration of the young Bulus. For in death, Mr. Rosenburg would never be around to send the diligent scholar to a place of higher learning in England. So heartbroken was Bulus on this singular crisis of his youth that his academic performance in his Cambridge School Certificate examination was dismally below expectations.

It was as if the death of Mr. Rosenburg had robbed Bulus of his hope of survival in his hostile environment. Life became more unbearable when Kofi Mensah was ejected from his comfortable boy's quarters in the late man's estate. Not finding an alternative employment, Mensah gradually took to the bottle and in a short time became a chronic alcoholic.

Mensah's drinking problem made Bulus abandon his aspiration for further education. He started working as a junior clerk in the local government authority office to cater for his father's economic needs. Lady luck was on Bulus side, for he worked hard and developed subtle defense mechanism in surviving the offensive insults of the discriminating neighbors.

By this time, of course, he had already changed his name to Musa, resisting the temptation of taking up Kofi as his middle name. The middle name Musa had since stuck and his father's name was completely erased from his life and memory. His alcoholic father had cursed his ambitious son for discarding his family heritage. But Bulus was far too gone in his dream to become a socially acceptable lawyer, that he could not care a hoot. Instead, he hoped for the quick death of his miserable alcoholic father.

When Mensah finally gave up the ghost, Bulus had taken his

Cambridge Certificate Examinations again. This time he passed effortlessly. Armed with his certificate, he had migrated to Kaduna to seek greener pastures. In Kaduna, his luck had held. His contact at the British Protectorate office in Kaduna had recommended him to the local Irish lawyer, Mr. Paddy Daley. Under Paddy Daley, Bulus worked as a clerk and studied on his own for the University of London, external degree in Law. He passed five years later to qualify for a bachelor of law degree. So impressed was Mr. Daley at Bulus' achievements that, he personally sponsored Bulus' bar examination in London's Lincoln Inn. Thus, at the age of thirty-four in the year one thousand nine hundred and fifty-nine, Bulus returned to Kaduna. He started the long climb that had enabled him at his present age of fifty-six to become one of the most prominent Lagos lawyers from the north. He became a highly successful wheeler-dealer and respected by all his colleagues in the Nigerian Bar Association.

Bulus' success had not been easy. Rather it was an uphill task. The mercy of God and intervention made it possible. Married with four children, Bulus had quite a lot to be grateful for. His sympathy at the moment was for the other members of the "Man Pass Man" club whom he was sure would not count themselves as lucky as himself.

Again his thoughts returned to the business ruin of Dr. Richard who would be visiting him shortly, to perhaps start a feuding relationship as a climax to his social demise. But the most frightening was the fate of Alhaji Abba Abdulmalik. Bulus' rich client in Kaduna and Port Harcourt, notably the Italian, Don Cattorini and Chief I,K. Madu, had both put out a search for Abba. He had reportedly received a large sum of money totaling half a million from the Italian, Don Catto, to clear import consignments in Port Harcourt through the Chief. He had refused to pay the chief for clearing the consignment. Abba had also taken the consignment of spare parts and sold them at very low price temporarily flooding the market with cheap machinery spare parts. Later, he informed Don Catto that the goods had been lost in transit. Why a man of Abba's reputation and caliber would involve himself in such a childish crime was beyond Bulus' understanding.

When Bulus heard the news, he had sworn he didn't hear the correct name because he could never believe Abba was capable of such vice. A man like Dumba could ruthlessly execute such ploy, but not the meek and elegant Abba. Thus, he did not believe the story until he had checked out the facts. He tried to get in touch with Abba but was told that he was incommunicado. All efforts to contact him was to no avail. In fact, Bulus had implored his Police friends to locate Abba, but none had been lucky enough to see him.

Still Bulus reckoned he was fortunate to have heard the news on time. He had been at the brink of another deal to raise over fifty thousand naira from his Lebanese and Indian clients. The money was to be given to Abba as a payoff to the government officials to enable his associates obtain the needed import licenses for their manufacturing activities. Had the shocking news from Chief Madu reached him a day later, Bulus would have regretted putting the huge sum into the untrustworthy hands of Abba. As always the gods were on his side. Silently he said a prayer to his guiding angels for saving him from the evil, which the austerity had forced on men of noble character. He remained in this prayerful stance when a loud cracking knock on his outer office door brought him sharply to his feet. It was the arrival of his long awaited, frustrated ex-client, Dr. Richard, lately, chairman of Kemidare Lines Limited, now gone burst.

"What may I offer you to cool your troubled soul my dear friend? You are looking like the mortician," beamed Barrister Bulus in his fawning voice. "Cut -out your lawyer talk and let's get down to basics." returned the garrulous ex-businessman. "I should have known you were bent on screwing my neck. I should not have trusted your friendship, for in my blind trust I assumed you would look after my interests. But how wrong can one be? Thanks to Bulus, my so called friend, I am to vomit what was already mine."

"Don't be so melodramatic," snapped Bulus, his anger rising. "Stop crying like a child. You do not impress me by crying wolf. The deal was all explained to you with exact instructions. I remember taking all the pains to explain your contractual commitments. But you were so much in a hurry to get rid of the rotten ships. If you had paid the exact taxes demanded by the customs officials, you would not have had to sell so much in a hurry. Your greedy nature led you to believe that you could eat your cake and have it too. But hard luck, you learned too late in life the rigid laws of natural balance. You do not have anybody to blame but your greedy self. And don't give me the cranky talk about trusting me, for all I know, you do not even trust your own shadow. Why must you trust me? If you assumed too much from our friendship, then, tough luck, for you're a shrewder business man than any person I know. But, do not let us argue, for what is done is done. And I must advise you that it's no use crying over spilt milk"

"Okay, maybe there is some truth in what you are saying. My wife insists that I go to London for a serious medical checkup. But how is she to know that I have already sold my property in Mayfair to service some outstanding bank debts. Bulus, my friend, my whole life is in shambles. If someone had shown me a mirror of my present self six months ago, I would have doubted if such ill fate was ever possible. At least not to such an educated person as myself. I should have anticipated the economic doom. But no, it all happened so suddenly as if in a grand climax. Like a huge dam gone burst and letting loose all hell without any means of control, ruining us all in the process," Dr. Richard concluded.

"That rather sums up the relative effect of the austerity. By the way doctor, I think you should still thank God. For despite all your woes you can still maintain your good name, Did you hear the latest about our globe - trotting world famous, Abba?" Bulus intoned.

"Why, sure, you mean Alhaji Abba Abdulmalik? The fabulous, fantastic and most dazzling to European blondes. Well, I heard that Binta Lilah was helping him to fix the minister for imports, Alhaji Mamman Taofik. I doubt if even Binta can convince the holy Mallam with her charm.

"Oh! Binta acts and behaves like a walking whore house. Not that I didn't chase her once, but she abandoned me for Abba Abdulmalik. I could not show my bitterness since I equally did business with Abba. Now I suppose it serves them both right. And the latest scandal concerning our beloved Abba Abdulmalik is that he duped our friend Chief I.K. Madu and my Italian client of various sums totaling over a million naira. I also heard he is equally up to his neck in debts in London, and all the other cities where he maintains expensive hotel suites in Europe. Talking about the beautiful, Binta Lilah, she will in time, characteristically ditch the fun loving Abba Abdulmalik for the powerful Mamman Taofik. That much I can bet some real money on."

"Is that so? I will not say I blame her, for the extent of the austerity makes it practicable for one to think and act strange. On a sober note, I am sure I'd do the same if I was faced with the alternative she had to choose from. And to be frank, I'll say I respect her instincts for survival."

"I had expected you will say that," laughed the barrister. He was glad at the way the conversation had progressed. It would have pained him to lose the doctor as a client. Especially now, Dr. Richard had convinced himself he could be elected to serve his people. Wishing to gain further information, Bulus brought the conversation around to politics.

"Do tell me what your duties would be as a politician," Bulus asked in a voice full of respect.

Right on target, Dr. Richard took the cue as though he had been waiting to steer the topic to his recently assumed profession.

"Aha, I will bring into politics all my business experience," he became enchanted like a man possessed. The trouble with Nigerian policy makers is that they have never run business in their lives, but rather concentrated all their time in the furtherance of their political careers. There is therefore, no balanced view in all the government policy decisions. My experience in the field of business of course, will be used in balancing this shortcoming."

"I think you presume too much. You are assuming that you can solve the bureaucratic maladministration. Is that your utopia or is there a more pragmatic approach?" Bulus questioned.

"Without boring you with political rhetoric, I shall say here and now that I strongly believe that our problems are both not so huge if we can be less pessimistic in our problem solving methods. Every nation has its special headache. We in Nigeria have ours, but we only need to bring our heads together; working together as a team we can find suitable solutions. We can singularly resolve to carry through our adopted resolutions with all hands on deck. I mean the three major tribes working in conjunction with and trust of all the minorities. Given such credibility and dedicated platform, Nigeria can effectively combat all her shortcomings. Thus composed and in the long term, the government of Nigeria will brace up to some of its chronic problems. We shall try to let our people have a paradigm shift in their mindset.

"Maybe you are being over hopeful. But what will you say to the fact that the electorate today is sufficiently jaded and cynical.

We recognize that government policy is not likely to change anything much in our present complex world? That is irrespective of all good intentions. Take the case of Great Britain under the leadership of Mrs. Thatcher."

"Honestly, I have no answer to the placid truth, but I have my desire to become part of the next government. I'll try, by all means, to ensure that. And I'll also do my best to become a member of the political system, either as a Senator or a Federal Legislator. When I become a Senator, I shall use all my power to ensure that our government performs better than the present one. For I know as a businessman, one can only do well if the country does well. By that, I mean better management of the economy. If we can ensure superior management of our resources, no matter what the complex world economic scene, our people will never have to suffer the tragic consequences of another austerity measure of this magnitude. Now, a depressed business cycle is acceptable but austerity will be banished forever. That I promise you. I believe this so much that I am using my last available funds to fight and will hopefully win a seat in the next election. Once elected, I will devote my time to accomplishing my vowed objective. So help me God."

"You do certainly need more help from the unseen powers of the universe in order to achieve you lofty ambitions. For my part, I wish you all the best and God's speed. Do remember me when you become the almighty elected politician. Meanwhile, I shall continue in my not-too-honorable trade of providing undeserved justice to the society's rich at reasonable cost. My fate will, of course, be decided in hell. But for the present I'm glad to enjoy the good fortune, which my naira power can purchase. So help me God.' Bulus concluded.

And so with their mind at peace, the businessman and lawyer sat down and mutually trashed out their negotiations.

CHAPTER TWENTY-THREE

The days had turned into weeks, the weeks into months, and everything was nearing a year. In fact, seven months had passed since Abba Abdulmalik landed at the Ikeja Airport to be met on arrival by Dogon Talata. Since then, the pendulum of his living standard had gradually swung from bad to the present worst.

Financial problems were mounting from all fronts. The accountant Chibuko had demanded an extra sum of fifty thousand naira to pay for extra work at the project site. He had given the money with the assurance from his Kano friends that the government fund would soon become available. But it had all been a hoax. The debt ridden ministry of works was in no position to even guarantee interest repayment of outstanding loans from the local banks. Had he known this, the money given to Mr. Chibuko would have been used for payment of his hotel bills. It was when the funds at his command dwindled to almost the last thousand, that he became desperate to the extent of stealing Don Cattorini's consignment of machinery spare parts.

Dumba had been the first to suggest that Abba dispose of the spare parts belonging to Don Cattorini. Not that Abba needed any encouragement to enact the crime, but it was with Dumba's backing that the unscrupulous buyers readily came up with the cash up front. They paid even before seeing the goods in question.

Dumba had introduced the two Indian pot-bellied spare parts traders based in Lagos Island. They had visited Abba's hotel suite with the agreed sum. It was only half of the market value Don Cattorini had paid for them. Acting as the middle man, Dumba received the bill of lading, which had arrived from Abba's Kaduna office for onward transmission to Port Harcourt. The first bill of lading having been reported missing by Abba. Dumba had taken the document to con artist associates who had the papers transferred in his own name. After the traders had paid the agreed sum, Abba had given Dumba his own fifteen percent share. He therefore flew to Port Harcourt to collect the goods from the port, for delivery to the buyers.

When it came to how to settle the pirate chief, for his handling expenses on the first batch of the consignment, Dumba had falsely promised to pay for the services, but it had not worked out. Little did Abba know of the feud between the two men. To spite the pirate chief, Dumba had refused to pay the high fees demanded of him and returned to Lagos leaving Chief LK Madu threatening vendetta.

The chief declared war at Dumba's refusal to even settle the amount quoted to have been spent as standard payoff to the government officials. He promptly visited Kaduna and reported what had transpired to the Italian, Don Cattorini. Chief Madu had also contacted Barrister Bulus Musa to find a way of making Abba pay him back his dues. He also detailed hired killers, with whom he would use to settle the score.

At first, Abba greatly regretted his public involvement in duping his friends. But Dumba had pushed him on, stating with street smartness. "Either you sunk or swam. The trick," he had argued, "was to find a way to survive no matter how disgraceful. Try and push for the government to settle your bills. That way everything shall be okay" Dumba nonchalantly advised.

The real facts of it all was that Abba had masterminded the rip-off. He cunningly used Dumba to carry out the actual operations. He was tormented with guilty conscience for only two days after the incident. He had resigned his mind to life as a desperado. He had used the small fortune from disposing Don Catto's spare parts to pay for his outstanding bills. The urgent necessity of paying the hotel bill made him ruthless. It was either the bills were paid up at the fixed date or he had no fixed address in Lagos. Besides, Abba reasoned, Don Catto had the legal deed to his living homes in Kano and Kaduna, as well as having his dream car the Silver Spirit Rolls Royce. Should he prove to be too much of a nuisance, Abba resolved to use his influence to have the Ministry of Internal Affairs deport Don Catto to Italy. It was a decision he prayed he did not have to make. Rumour had it that Don Catto had underworld connections in almost every part of the world. Probably the Italian will use the house and the Roll Royce as sufficient compensation. Abba reckoned on Don Catto's ability to use his native intelligence to appreciate Abba's desperate action. If cornered, the Italian would have reacted in similar manner.

Desperate men commit desperate crimes.

Since the weekend with Binta Lilah, Abba had only seen her twice. The first had been before her first interview with Mamman Taofik. The second time was immediately after she heard news of the spare parts scandal. She had called at the suite to find out the truth. She had fumed and raved at his indiscretion. When she realized his ruthless mindset, she chilled her emotion. She then impressed on him how hard she was trying to get Mamman Taofik to comply with issuing the licenses. To show his appreciation, he had foolishly given her the sum of ten thousand naira. The amount was enough to cover one month's bill for his basic necessities. He promised her more money when she succeeded. Even at that point, Abba still hoped on Binta brining him salvation. And in his frenzied enthusiasm, Abba barely noticed the cooling effect in Binta's passion when compared with the previous occasion. When he demanded she spend the night, she had politely refused. Her reason was that she had usual women sickness. That her periodic pain gave her extreme stomach aches. It would be improper for him to see her in physical torment. And like a fool he had believed her.

Deep inside, he was beginning to feel the need for a strong woman to relate to. Someone to look forward to and in his dreams Binta was crystallizing as his new wonder woman. Little did Abba know what disappointment he would endure on account of the business-minded Binta.

The next time, Abba ran into Binta, it was at the rooftop restaurant of the Ikoyi club. Abba was having dinner in the company of Alhaji Dogon Talata with some junior members of the cabinet. The conversation for the evening had centered on ways to pressurize the Ministry of Works to pay at least half of the debt owed to Abba's company. The amount was barely enough to keep the AAA company afloat.

The four members had all agreed to do the best they could. But their best did not impress him as much as it used to. He had therefore, expressed aloud his hope on the successful outcome of Binta's visit to Mamman Taofik. The other members of the group had heard him but none chose to comment. Sensing their quietness, Abba had frankly asked if anything was amiss, but was greeted with more silence.

"Do take the courage and be a man," he shouted across the table at Dogon Talata." Tell me the reason why you must take me for a fool." Bracing himself, Talata had let the cat out of the bag. "Rumor going around the top circles has it that Binta and Mamman Taofik are both deeply in love."

"Okay, if that is what you are hiding, then it is no secret for I engineered that. That is the only way Binta can help me get the import license to reopen my new industry and get my corporate finances re-organized, "replied Abba, his confidence returning.

"But you don't exactly understand. The truth is that Binta has abandoned you for Mamman Taofik. I've personally asked you to this place tonight so you can confirm that. In precisely fifteen minutes from now, Binta and Mamman Taofik will walk through that door. I shall want you to present yourself to her and see what will happen, "replied Talata.

"So let us not argue. You are very, very wrong. Anyway, let us wait and see," snapped Abba. His thoughts racing back to analyze the validity of Talata's statement. The Talata he knew was not given to making up stories just to hurt friends. But who can say, life was becoming hostile on all fronts and people change from what they used to be. Abba prepared himself, therefore, not to be surprised at whatever happened. Deep down he could feel the tremor in his blood vessel. Binta was gradually coming to mean more to him than any other woman he had ever known. Her image would always remain in his memory as a fun appreciating woman. He had manipulated her into tackling his foe for him. He deeply wondered how he got himself entangled in the emotions of love for the simple-hearted girl. Abba could rightly guess the child-like sensitivity, which existed in the tough exterior that Binta exhibited. It was that child-like simplicity, which Abba knew and imagined Binta possessed that had drawn him completely into loving her. In his demented mind, his love for Binta had grown daily but he had not the discipline to keep himself in check. His weak mind had waited in the hope that she would come back as the child he had imagined her. Only then would he pick the courage to inform her of his burning love for her. Childish as such a display of emotions might become, Abba was realistic enough to know that he had crossed the Rubicon. That, to Abba was the truth. Either that or the chemical effect of the cocaine, which he had continued to consume was responsible for his sentimentalism.

No woman had ever meant so much as his present thoughts of Binta revealed to him. But then he reasoned, maybe it was too late. With Talata's news that Binta had fallen for another, more endowed than himself, there was no reason to hope. It was in this resolute frame of mind that Abba remained. Ten minutes later, he was sharply tapped on the shoulder by his nearest neighbor, Idi Usman.

"Look straight to the club door. Watch exactly the look on their eyes. See how much they seem to love each other," Idi Usman whispered, conspiratorially. He watched intently to see Abba's reaction.

Abba stared ahead and beheld his cherished Binta and deadly foe Mamman Taofik. They displayed deep intimate nearness as they sat on the west side of the dining hall. The light bulb revealed eyes that lusted to devour the squat little man, reputed to be one of the most powerful men in the nation.

For about two minutes, Abba sat mesmerized in his seat. He froze unable to say a word. His eyes transfixed on the grim picture staring directly in front of him. Noticing Abba's melancholy his colleagues remained equally speechless waiting for him to restart the conversation. One could notice the rapid transformation in Abba's countenance. Acute pain bottled up inside him. He momentarily seemed to age ten years with lines of anguish printed on his face. Never in his entire life had he been so humiliated. How was he to cope with such utter disloyalty of an opposite sex he had come to love? He wondered and thought of love - a word that had never been present in Abba's dictionary of life. All his worldwide playboy escapades had been consummated without any real feeling or deep lasting relationship. It was as though he had received a terrible punch when he least expected and from such quarter as never imagined. While he stared at Binta, his hate for Mamman Taofik grew. So mad was his reasoning that he prayed he had a gun. Two clear shots at very close range and his revenge would be final and smooth.   The truth was guns were not legal nor easily bought in Lagos. That could have been the best way to stifle Taofik's masochistic competition, which had now extended to his female territory.

Abba's further silence for the next twenty minutes prompted his colleagues at the table to rise and swiftly make their exit. Not responding to their gesture, Abba waved them good-bye in silence. He nodded to the worried Talata, but refused to utter any word.

After they had gone, Abba returned to his chemically impaired thoughts and let his imagination loose on the best way to seek revenge. This indignation continued for almost thirty minutes, when Abba's logical sense seemed to return to take command of his unbalanced reasoning. Gradually, and with a determined willpower, Abba fell back to his philosophical inclination. He labored mentally to see things in better perspective. As he relaxed in his thought sequence, he objectively reviewed Binta's case.

He recollected the story she had told him of her life with Jacob and her desire for a man for permanent relationship. Her desire was for a strong man to personally own her. In fact, Abba recollected that during the early hours of the Monday morning before she left his suite, she had extended her arms as if pleading for him to own her. But he had bluntly refused to play her childish game for love.

Allah had blessed her, with the half-witted Mamman Taofik, stupid enough to be manipulated by Binta. In fairness, the fault was not Binta's. She had offered herself, body and soul, but Abba had not responded positively. Mamman Taofik with his successful destiny in life had seen the opportunity and seized it.

It was, therefore, to Binta's good fortune that Taofik came up to satisfy her aspirations. Allah must work in mysterious ways. Not begrudging Binta her good fortune, Abba resolved to think no evil thoughts towards her. He concentrated on how to make his exit without Binta seeing him. If only she or Taofik would excuse themselves to go to the rest room, Abba could use the chance to leave without being seen. So making up his mind, Abba waited to make his exit at the right moment.

Shortly before the closure of the night club, the honorable Alhaji Mamman Taofik excused himself to go to the toilet. Abba therefore, briskly walked up to Binta's table.

"Relax,' he advised, on noticing the terror in her face. "It is alright. I can understand, and have forgiven you." He assured her.

Before she could reply, he raised his hand signaling her to say no more and continued. "When I saw you I was dumbfounded. It was quite a shock. But I'm man enough to withstand life's inconsistencies. I want only to reassure you that you do not owe me anything. Rather I'm thankful for the much you tried to do for me. I shall hope to remain your friend."

After completing his speech, he continued his stroll towards the door. He gave her no chance to further comment or reply to his self-righteous magnanimity.

When he reached his hotel suite, he could not sleep and consumed the last drop of the cocaine left in the vial Dumba had given him. The realization that his hope had been badly shattered left him restless. When he finally drifted to sleep, in the nightmare that followed, he could see himself on the verge of suicide. The thought gave him the consolation with which he got through the bad night.

In his dream, he saw a number of men in chains, all condemned to die. At sunrise, some were lined up and butchered publicly in the full view of the others. Those who remained saw their own condition like that of their mutilated fellows. They looked at each other painfully and without hope as each awaited his turn.

When the time came for Abba's turn, he could vividly see his spiritual guru, the venerable Imam Fulani. He accompanied by ten other imams. Though their voices were muffled, it seemed as though they were pleading for Abba's soul. Possibly their prayers in the holy land of Mecca would help to resolve the immediate death confronting their master and benefactor. Abba waited, hopeful that the lobbying of the pious imams would in the end buy him more time to spend on earth. But alas, this was not to be. Death, the master of the realm of darkness was bent on claiming his soul. And just as the vision of the pleading imams faded from his sight, he felt lightness and chilled. He felt cold sweat pouring from all over his body. Terror eclipsed his whole body. Painfully, he gasped for what would become of his dead body. He regretted his body would not be laid in state to be respected by friends and foes alike. This was against his religion.

Even in death, Abba had wanted most of all an exit in style and grandeur. Rather than be buried in the colorless manner, which his Islamic faith required, Abba wished he had the pomp and pageantry usually reserved for members of the Christian faith. He groaned to be laid in state for days. He wished he could be laid in the most expensive casket, ornamented in gold and imported from abroad. He imagined to ride the long distance in a colorful hearse to the cemetery for his last journey on earth.

But all these wishful desires were not to be. The dream continued. He saw the butcher hack off his head and as he breathed his last breath, the Imams moved in with dispatch to dispose of his carcass. Within an hour after the formal incantations, his once handsome remains was wrapped to be deposited into mother earth. His naked body wrapped in the local Hausa mats, they dropped his corpse into the less than six feet hole without much ado. The sharp pain as a corpse hit the dirty earth made him cry out at the top of his voice and almost immediately, he woke up from the nightmare. He sat up in bed and checked his wristwatch to learn it was almost three-thirty in the morning.

Cursing, he got up to shower and to prepare for the hard day ahead. At breakfast, he silently reviewed the activities that had degenerated into the anguished nightmare. Was fate trying to tell him his time on earth was up? But who could tell? The ultimate solution at this point in Abba's life was to find sources of income to save his reputation and corporate survival. He would either work out favorable alternatives to generate income or woe betide him. Time, he surmised, was fast running out. Some money would have to come through before the next week, or he would have to vacate his suite.

It was a great shame what Binta had done. But he could not blame the lovesick woman. Abba was not bitter at the betrayal due to his over developed sense for fair play. This made him understand that perfection in human relationship was a kind of utopia. Yet, he cursed Binta for her wrong sense of timing. Thus, it was not easy for him to fully forgive Binta for her treachery. Abba's knowledge of love made him understand that it is selfless and being able to forgive. The desire for instant selfish gratification was ever so tempting to couples not exactly sold on mature relationship. Betrayal was therefore the rule, except, there be an overriding commitment on the part of the concerned couples. Abba in his sane mind, reckoned he had only been infatuated with Binta. He therefore, resolved that Binta or no Binta, he would fight his own wars. He decided then that of the two ways to fight the corrupt system, he will use the crooked method since his hook strategy had failed woefully.

An alliance with Dumba was most desirable for the moment. Together they could plan ways and means to overcome the present difficulties. They could even possibly plan cocaine trip to New York and London. Thus making up his mind, he finished his meal and picked up the phone to call Dumba. He had uncanny and vulgar ways of making money.

Dumba had told Abba that he made his first money illegally importing marijuana into London. That his secret holdings included a bank in Bahamas. This and many more unconfirmed information described the criminal activities of Dumba.

CHAPTER TWENTY-FOUR

Dumba reported as requested, shortly after ten o'clock in Abba's suite and together they sat down to plan their next strategy.

Dumba could be heard saying, "Affluence is one of the hardest things that man can cope with. The history of man proves that the man who struggles survives. Thus, poverty should be looked upon as a nuisance, an uncomfortable situation but not an embarrassment. With time and industrious effort one can always overcome poverty, not so affluence. Look at Britain it has lost the will to be competitive in the international business scene. The English have lost the will to struggle, due to the welfare state; free education, free medical service, subsidized housing, etc. Like the athlete who becomes complacent from lack of challenges.' He continued 'The Roman Empire stagnated due to affluence when it brought slaves to do everything for it. All this goes to prove that if you have to earn your own bread, you must be prepared to work for it. Look at the Jews and Pakistanis in London, they are becoming so well off on account of their productive labour." He slowed his speech and glanced towards Abba.

Abba sat silently waiting for his friend to finish his long speech. Dumba, it seemed, was in a happy mood for usually he was not a man of many words. Abba was therefore glad Dumba was not in his usual reticent composure.

Sensing that Abba was not ready to interrupt him, Dumba continued his trite. "I know most of the politicians in power have become complacent on account of individually amassing vast fortunes in foreign banks. Thus, they cannot care less what happens to the likes of us. But I'm sure they will sooner or later meet their nemesis."

"You may be right," replied Abba, carefully choosing his words. "Not many people have lives marked with high achievement or notable adventure. Personally, I'll not say I blame these men for what they stole. It was their only chance in life and they did not let it slip. I blame myself for lack of wisdom in being prudent with the vast reserves when the going was good."

"There is a proverb, which states that with every great fortune comes an equally devious crime lurking around," commented Dumba. "Come to think of it, let me tell you how I became a member of the "Man Pass Man" club. I was born into a family of thirteen. My father was a local fisherman in our village. My mother traded in cassava tubers. The local cassava market shifted every four days to the main trading town of Abor. And as was mandatory I accompanied my mother on this very important day to market. It was a distance of about forty miles from my village, on the side of the Delta River.

It was there that I learnt the need for a man to be ambitious in life so as to live a happy life. On one market day, I had left my mother's stall to buy my lunch for the day. A pickpocket had followed me with the intent of stealing my pocket money. At a lonely corner, the thug jumped on me forcefully impounding my wallet. The thug then stole the money given to me by my mother, and threatened to break every bone in my body should I complain or cry out loud. I tried to get my money back but he beat the hell out me. Midway through this ordeal, a much bigger member of the group had approached and seeing the little me being beaten up, was moved by compassion and ordered the thug to stop beating me. But for this big brute, I do not know what would have become of little me. Later when I came to study at the Delta Grammar School, I developed a rapid friendship with the big thug popularly called "Oluchukwu," meaning the work of God.

"He taught me how to be street smart, what I can call the rudiments of survival mechanism. I remember him once stating that ambition is what makes a man a real man. His illegal preoccupation not only gave him respect and dignity among his fellow men. It also afforded him an enviable lifestyle. When asked why he must resort to crime to survive? He arrogantly replied that either he was personally the thief or someone else more ruthless would have taken his position. Oluchukwu saw himself as a compassionate thief. A local Robin Hood. An avenger for the poor, who would not hesitate to steal from the needy if the situation warranted his doing so.

"And what became of Oluchukwu?" Asked Abba, his interest aroused.

"Well! What do you think? He got himself killed by the Police. The law finally caught up with him at the height of his success. Such is the fate of greedy unsophisticated rogues. Anyway, let me continue my boring life story. After my secondary education, I came over to Lagos and got employed as a ship crew on the Elder Dempster Shipping Line. That was how I went overseas the first time. In my second year as a ship crew, I jumped ship at Liverpool. I took on all sorts of odd jobs. Later, I moved over to Brixton in the South West area of London. There I carried on with all types of odd jobs. The most degrading was cleaning the corpse in the mortuary. It was a sordid job and on my first day at it, I was so sick I thought I would die. But I had gone back the following day because it paid the highest hourly rate. While I worked, I lived in a Brixton bed-sit accommodation and saved most of my money. It was as if I was awaiting an opportunity to use the growing sum to start something big. This chance eventually came and I did not delay in grasping it. Late in 1962, some Nigerian co-workers at the Brixton Hospital took me to a party in the Finsbury Park residence of a business woman from Lagos. At the party, I was told the woman was a successful trader in "Nigerian National Grass" that is, Indian hemp, or Marijuana. So lucrative was the drug trade that she had bought two residential properties in the North London borough. She made two shipments from Lagos to Liverpool each month." Dumba smiled and grinned. He continued "Anxious, I had inquired about the risk element in the illegal trade and learned that it was minimal. The police authorities at that time lacked sophisticated equipment for detecting marijuana. The British legislation restricting the drug was not really enforced, but still it was considered a risky business. Further investigation into the drug trade had assured me it was a profitable business to be in. Two months after, I resigned from my job at the Brixton Hospital and took a trip to Nigeria. While in Nigeria, I made contact with farmers in the deep forest of the Midwestern region where huge plantations of marijuana existed. Through these farmers, adequate supplies were made ready for me on a monthly basis. I duly shipped to Liverpool. From Liverpool I contacted Jamaican pushers in Bradford and Birmingham to dispose of the wares.

From there, I built a base in Brixton. Gradually I built up my capital base before setting up a property company in the East End London. I suppose, I had been lucky. By the year 1974, I had made my first million in pounds sterling. By mortgaging each property with two different finances, I got enough credit to buy other houses. Mostly I bought derelict properties in rundown neighborhoods. I used poor Nigerian students as laborers to renovate and upscale the building after which, I sold these properties at three times the price I bought them. It was really hard work and I had been lucky using cheap and labour, without police investigations."

"Does that mean your investments in the properties are still intact" threw in Abba.

"No! At least not anymore, "replied Dumba. Business is never static. To remain fixated and be stationary in business is to lose all one's accumulated holdings. My trouble started when I listened to the rhetoric of the Lagos military administrators. I was enticed by their policy about encouraging foreign investments in the country. In 1975, I thought I could exploit the relative political and economic stability in Nigeria to enhance my success in Lagos. Thus, I went into various partnership deals to establish manufacturing concerns in the country. I used much of my hard earned money. You can call it bad luck that none of these enterprises became profitable. The be-devilled government regulation was one reason. The other being that I am was never liked by the power brokers. The effect is that my cash flow is currently restricted."

"But what about your bank in the Bahamas? asked Abba. I've heard so many rumors. There must be some truth in them."

"Those banks belong to my British associates. I'm, as the saying goes, only the middleman, without any equity holding. In fact, it's my hope that my associates can raise the funds to sponsor me into the Senate in the next election. That is the only way I can see myself getting my money and prestige back. As a Senator, I'll have influence in the country's oil trade. My friends want this badly."

"I don't know about politics. At least I am not capable of functioning as a politician. Rather, l am hopeful you will help me find a way to raise some money either in London or New York for the short term."

"Ah! That can be a major problem. The credibility of Nigerians in the international finance market is not very encouraging at the moment. There is also the world debt crisis. Bankers are all jittery regarding third world borrowers. They would demand collaterals, which I'm sure you cannot provide. "

"Yes, that is rather an oversight on my part. All my years of living overseas, I had never wanted to pay the exorbitant annual municipal occupancy rates demanded by the local authorities. I had preferred to lease annually giving me the chances of moving when I so wished. Also as a matter of rule, I had always stayed in five-star hotels, going back to my leased apartment only when utterly necessary."

"If you cannot get easy credit the legitimate way, how about taking some marijuana or cocaine abroad? I still use it to earn income now and then. Only I employ the services of some diplomatic associates to transport it into London. It is, no doubt, terribly risky, but I only do it when I'm in great need and desperate for cash."

"Allah forbid, my reputation will be too much at stake for me to be so reckless. I reckon I don't have the physical courage for it. I will be easily found out. Except if you will undertake the contract for me."

"Not on my life. Times are becoming too dangerous. I can ask a man I know. His name is Sunday Shaka, a post-graduate student at one of the universities in New York. His conditions would be rather expensive because he will have to take the rap himself if caught. I can ask him if you want. He will do anything for ten thousand bucks."

"No, I'd rather not. The complications might be too much. Besides I've never been the ruthless type and it would not be too good to start this late in life. On further thought, I think I will leave for New York to have a chat with my bankers in Wall Street. I think my problems can only be solved either in New York or London. Should I fail to find suitable solution in either place, then, I might as well give up the good life. In fact, this morning I dreamt of my own funeral. It seemed so real." "You mean you had a dream of death? I suppose almost all Lagos business men at this time have death dreams in the night. It's the only way one can escape the harsh realities after each tough day. In my native proverb, when one sees death in a dream, it means the opposite in real life. You may yet live to be a hundred. The important thing is not to give up hope--at least not before death strikes you down." Dumba advised.

"Speak for yourself, Sam. I cannot stand life on the poverty side. Not after all the grand styles I've helped to inject into the Lagos society. I'd rather take the easy way out."

CHAPTER TWENTY-FIVE

Following Abba's conversation with Dumba, the Chairman of AAA Limited prepared for an unscheduled trip to New York the next day.

Chibuko was invited to Lagos for instructions on how to manage the corporate purse while Abba was away. When asked how long he intended to be away, Abba was non-committal.

Dogon Talata was introduced to Mr. Chibuko as the person to approach in the event of any problem. Imam Fulani also was hosted for two days before his holy pilgrimage to Mecca accompanied by ten younger Imams. Outstanding bills were paid-especially those owed to the hotel management. Abba was pleased that his credit at the hotel was still good.

Abba also made time to contact Barrister Bulus Musa requesting him to advise Don Cattorini that every effort was underway to redeem the missing spare parts. That was, of course, not true, but Abba was not willing to anger the Italian who was renowned for his worldwide Mafia connections. At least Abba was not looking forward to any Mafia shock treatment as he planned his trip to New York.

The remaining cash left after paying off accumulated debts was barely enough to cover the extra expenses his visit abroad would incur. Not wishing to take chances, he had called up Dogon Talata and borrowed an extra fifty thousand naira from the minister. The minister reluctantly parted with the money when Abba gave him a promissory note indicating that a total sum of sixty thousand naira would be repaid immediately after the government paid for AAA's completed projects. Dogon Talata's argument that the fund to pay the outstanding debt was yet to be found helped to convince Abba that the sooner he got out of the country the better.

Shortly before leaving for the airport, Abba visited the local foreign exchange market situated at the neighborhood, popularly called the Bristol Black Market. This place is the mold of such foreign currency markets found in strategic places around the major cities of Saudi Arabia. The Bristol market traded in the major foreign currencies and at very high rates of exchange. It provides the basic service for currency exchange transactions, which the local banks could not adequately handle.

The total sum in dollars and pounds sterling Abba bought was much lower than what he previously obtained. The exchange rate of the dollar had significantly increased because of the austerity measures. Exchange rates had shot up to take into account the increasing risk, which the black market traders incurred especially from the hands of security officials. The cost of buying protection and payoffs to law enforcement officers meant further mark-up in the traders selling price to ensure profitability.

The Nigerian Airways Flight No. WT 850 from Lagos to John F. Kennedy Airport in New York duly left the Murtala Mohammed Airport on schedule during the early hours of Tuesday.

The first class cabin was virtually empty, which was a change since the austerity. The only occupant apart from Abba Abdulmalik were four American businessmen and two Nigerian captains of industries. The two extended friendly gestures to Abba who profoundly ignored them. He preferred instead to abide by his own thoughts. He used the free flowing French wine as a stimulant to induce sleep for half of the journey.

The long sleep helped to relax his mind in preparation for the tough time he knew he would have in New York. Tim Gallaway would certainly make things difficult as a reminder of the previous insult he had received.

The landing at J.F.K. had been smooth and Abba could not help but be amazed at the wonderful city of New York. The city is so amazing in its own unique ways. The dominating Manhattan: a narrow rock island 12 miles long with twenty bridges and tunnels that connect New Jersey and four other boroughs. The most important of these bridges the Brooklyn Bridge with its imposing presence like a cathedral.

About two million people work on the little island with only half a million living there. Being the capital of the world finance market, it is no surprise that the city is crowded with luxury apartments costing two thousand five hundred dollars a month for a two bedroom apartment.

Abba maintained an apartment situated opposite Central Park for a renewable four-year lease, a contract his banker Gallaway took care of.

Life in the Big Apple was worthwhile only if one had a comfortable apartment in Manhattan and especially close to the famous Wall Street.

Money doesn't go so far in New York, but it doesn't come as far either. The numbers for all the money in America are handled in Wall Street on lower Manhattan. The banks, the businessmen and even the government do most of their money shuffling and dealing there.

New York has the most intemperate weather in the world. It is too hot in the summer and too cold in winter. During all its season, the wind has a way of whipping the weather at you and the rain is always coming from an angle that umbrella manufacturers never considered.

The funny thing about New York is its innate ability not only to survive, but to thrive in the face of natural obstacles. The inhabitants, being accustomed to inconveniences of every kind, learn early to proceed against all odds. The will to survive life's imposed limitations is always uppermost in the minds of New Yorkers. They do not pretend sad resignation to defeat. All New Yorkers have the belief that they will always win. They are capable to do whatever it took to achieve impossible odds.

But strangers only see New York in transit. They leave with the impression that the city is one great mindless rush to nowhere. To the casual visitor, all New Yorkers are loudmouths and full of ill-will towards one another. Everybody and everything gets too pre-occupied with their own motivation. They do not really care for others and are thus comparable with Lagos.

New York is the city of extremes. It had more of everything and with an average of seventeen hundred murders each year. The crime statistics of New York always alarmed Abba. He thought of the good times he would have enjoyed in New York had a criminal incident not influenced him to change his base to London.

Back in 1974, when AAA had been involved in the supply of strategic weapons for the army. Abba had met with Gallaway who had advised him that the AAA corporate headquarters be based in lower Manhattan. Abba had agreed and had given Gallaway the go ahead to lease the AAA office accommodation. Abba had also taken up the Central Park two bedroom apartment. The office and the apartment were fully paid, with the lease being renewable every four years. Abba had decided to stay in New York for a period of three months every year. But he had not reckoned with the rate of mugging in New York.

As fate would have it, he had the experience of his life one summer night in 1975. A group of five leather jacketed black youths had stopped him on the Penn Central underground train station. They robbed Abba of all in his possessions.

When he told Gallaway of the incident, the banker had laughed. He asked Abba to thank Allah he had not been viciously beaten. Since then, the AAA International corporate headquarters had moved out of New York. He relocated at the White House Hotel, near Regents Park in London. One's chances of being mugged in London stood at one to a hundred.

After alighting from the plane at J.F.K, Abba hired a cab to take him to his Central Park apartment.

At the apartment, Stacy Williams, the live-in hostess waited, having been informed the previous night of his arrival. She had been excited and had wanted to order the limousine and be present with the chauffeur at J.F.K to welcome him but he had declined the extravagance. He humbly requested instead that she should wait for his arrival at the Manhattan apartment.

"Hi De Alhaji" She saluted, kissing and hugging him. The emotion all swelled up in her desire for the energetic play she had dreamt about all night. One thing about her African boyfriend is his sure ability to perform.

"Hello sweetie! how have you been?" asked Abba, elated and curiously glancing round the expensively furnished den. "Come up here and let me feel of your warmth. Hmm! You taste as good as the last time. Do help me get out of these clothes."

Afterward, Stacy got dressed to prepare lunch as the wall clock chimed two o'clock in the afternoon.

"Now tell me lover boy, why didn't you want me to meet you at the J.F.K? Is it because I might be jealous seeing you with another woman?" Stacy asked in a matter of fact tone.

"Not so dear. It ain't nothing like that. I was only intending to keep a low profile." Abba replied.

"By low profile, you mean the current world-wide recession has some effect on your business?"

"Yes, I didn't know your beauty is graced with first-class brains. Yes, my business activities in Nigeria is at present so starved of funds that I've a vague feeling it might herald my corporate demise." He answered.

"Oh my darling, I'm so sorry to hear of it. In fact, the account I'm allowed to draw from is very much in the red. Already I got an overdraft from the downtown bank for ten thousand dollars. Before that, I got about five thousand from Gallaway. He promised me more but he had the apartment lease to settle. The last time I met him he was about to renew the four year lease on the apartment. I'm sure he must have done that as it was due two months ago," recounted Stacy innocently.

"To renew the lease for the apartment for another four years is exactly one hundred and twenty thousand dollars. That could well be, the exact total sum I've in my stockholding. I will visit Gallaway at the bank tomorrow to find out my account position. But don't worry your head about my financial problem. I will sort things out with time. Now hurry up with the food and relax." He commanded.

"Thank you, master. Your wish is my command. I've waited and can't wait no longer."

Abandoning the cooking for the time being, Stacy snuggled over to Abba. Only very much later, did she opt to tend to the meal cooking in the 10- foot marble and parquet kitchen.

Stacy spent the entire day making him happy. She was glad to be living in the elegant Manhattan 60th floor Truman Towers.

CHAPTER TWENTY-SIX

The anger on Tim Gallaway's face seemed to choke the speech that came tumbling out of his mouth. There was no gain-saying the fact that the banker was in a terrible mood. His physical exterior revealed the red blood cells in his veins. It seemed like they were waiting to burst open.

The angry response had been prompted by the nonchalant way Abba had accused Gallaway. He had used all the cash in the AAA's account to renew the lease on the Central Park apartment.

Responding in anger, Gallaway bursted out, "You damned well have the guts to come here and throw words at me as though I am your house boy. For over three months, we sent letters and reminders for your urgent advice to your London and Kano addresses. Had you bothered to reply any of our letters we would not have taken the position we took. In fact, we were only acting according to your standing order. It was categorically stated in the two previous renewal agreements that we, as your bankers, can act on your behalf. The bank does not owe you any apology. We acted in good faith based on your instructions. It was your duty to advise us to the contrary when you found your financial situation had changed. Another important factor is your blonde woman, I think she calls herself Stacy, who is resident in the apartment. There was no way we could have moved her out of the place without your instructions."

"Okay, so I'm wrong and you're right as always. Kindly accept my apology for my outburst. But you must understand this is the first time I'm in the red in your bank. And the feeling does not do much for my moods."

"Well, we do understand your position has been adversely affected by the international economic recession. We hoped you would have contacted us since the past five months," replied the banker, gradually regaining his composure.

"I know I should have, but I was up to my neck trying to save my investments in Lagos. I was so occupied with finding the solution there and then that I completely forgot my other commitments abroad." "Maybe you will blame yourself for such thoughtlessness, but I will advise you that Stacy, your blonde mistress had insisted on using up your bank reserves. Not that it is my business but I've heard stories of your dozen blondes. If they all burn money the way Stacy does, then, I am sure you are in a hell of a mess."

"That sir, is my business "blurted Abba. "When I want you to run my life as well as my money, then I'll tell you."
"Ah! You're right, it is none of my business. But still I'll give you one shrewd business advice. If I were you I'll dispose of those greedy whores. With the current economic recession, you will need to husband not only your reserves but your physical strength."

"I'll let that pass. Like I've said, that is my own responsibility," thundered Abba, his temper beginning to rise.

"Yes, it used to be, but not anymore. You're owing my bank fifty thousand dollars. I also gave some loan to your Stacy woman. I'm not so sure you're in any position to repay that. Or am I in the wrong?"
"I suppose I can raise the money to pay you back. Can we move out of the Central Park apartment into a smaller place. Can you help me organize the switch? On second thought, I think I will like to move permanently to London and give up having a home in New York, the expense is too much."

"Alright, but it will take some time. The market is rather depressed at the moment. Are you willing to lose as much as thirty percent on the deal?"
"I suppose I don't have any choice. Only I want the left over after your fifty thousand plus interest had been deducted and

others forwarded to my private account at the Barclays Bank, Oxford Street branch in London. I will be leaving for London tomorrow afternoon since I believe standard of living is considerably cheaper there."

"All will be attended to. Just sign these slips. And by the way, there had been a lot of talk about the Nigerian Enterprises Promotion Act in the Manhattan Chamber of Commerce. Our American clients wanting to do business in Nigeria are complaining about the protectionist bias of the Act. It over regulates the manufacturing sector where most Nigerians are afraid to venture into. These businessmen are looking for any influential Nigerian who can be paid to lobby for a favorable review or repeal of the Act. The long term benefits would mean more foreign investment funds flowing into the country. It would also allow American trained technicians into manufacturing processes in the difficult aspect of the industry where Nigerians lack technical expertise. What do you say to that?"

"I don't know. How serious are these businessmen? If they are serious enough you can get them to visit my London office. I can be contacted through the London White House Hotel where AAA International Limited still maintains an office."

"Okay I'll see what can be done and 1 will also have the money sent to your bank. Good bye for now and good luck, you will need it."

Leaving the lower Manhattan premises of the bank, Abba strolled over to the nearby MacDonald's eating house. He needed a place to sit and think. He bought two big Mac hamburgers and a drink of coke. He ate and reviewed the meeting with Gallaway. One major information from the banker was that the present economic hardship would continue for quite some time. Thus, it would be best to do away with all his interests in Stacy. Before the meeting with Gallaway, Abba had the previous night vaguely promised to bring Stacy along with him to London. This was not feasible as Maggie Lee was currently residing at his Knightsbridge apartment. That would have posed a problem, for unlike the other members of the dozen, Stacy and Maggie never got along. Apart from emotional heartaches which bringing the two together might promote, Abba thought of the extra expenses involved. The truth was that the cash on Abba was fast running out. Common sense also told him that Maggie Lee must have used up all the money in his Lloyd's Bank account. She had managed to grab his signed blank check booklet before he left her at the Brussels Sheraton Hotel. She would fill her wardrobe two times over. All thoughts narrowed down to the fact that if he must ditch Stacy, then, the best time to do it would be now.

Picking up his briefcase, Abba checked through to examine if his travelling documents were in order. He noted that all was in order including the funds he had left Lagos with. He impulsively decided to take a yellow cab to the J.F.K Airport. At the airport, he would call Stacy and explain why he must leave immediately for London. He hoped she would cope with his deserting her.

She would be mad at him but would calm down when informed she could dispose of all the furniture and antiques in the apartment. The furniture was worth over fifty thousand dollars. That would cushion her, until another lover boy cum bread winner came along. No doubt, he would miss the pleasure-giving Stacy. She was more compassionate than Maggie Lee. Maggie was rather more efficient like her German forebears and male opposites. What compensated for Maggie's mental efficiency was her ravishing beauty. She stood radiant like the goddess Venus. At the J.F.K Airport, Abba had placed a call to Stacy telling her he had to be in London for an urgent business. She had sounded very angry and called him all sorts of names. The news that she could dispose of the apartment furnishing could not get her to reduce her verbal attack. Abba out of annoyance, had slammed the phone on her. He reasoned that he would call her up when he got to London.

Next, he placed a call to his Knightsbridge flat. The phone answering machine requested him to leave information.
Abba was filled with anger and all sorts of imagination as he listened to the recording again. He quietly replaced the receiver of the telephone without leaving any message on the recorder. Was she in England at all?

Lastly Abba dialed the cab agency of his part-time driver Mr. Harry Baker. The receptionist picked the phone and promised that Baker would be at Heathrow to welcome Abba, when the British Airways, Flight BA 654 from New York touched down at the airport the following morning.

CHAPTER TWENTY-SEVEN

Abba had no illusion that London would herald better news than that which he had received in New York. London was not a city where one could hope to obtain easy credit. With his messed-up credit rating, Abba knew he could expect no better news in London.

On board the British Airways flight from J.F.K. to Heathrow, Abba wondered what exactly it was that was pushing him to go to London. Subconsciously, he remembered the dream of death. He had expressed his wish for a glamorous funeral. Maybe that was exactly why he was anxious to get to London.

Since the beginning of the austerity measure, there had been no doubt in Abba's mind that AAA Corporate mortality must mean also the end of the founder's own life. The knowledge of this had been the reason for his relentless drive to maintain his wealth via getting his importation license renewed.

Abba recalled that on the night he saw Marnman Taofik together with Binta Lilah, he had eagerly envisaged his death. On realization of the real facts of his dream, it dawned on him but he didn't complain. It became therefore, his wish to die in a stylish surrounding. He did not want to be disposed of in the colorless manner as dictated by Islamic rites.

The logic of these reasoning made him to overlook the careless way in which Stacy had incurred huge debts. On the whole, he had lamely paid the outstanding debts incurred by Stacy. That was apart from those owed to Gallaway's bank.

Abba also had the expectation that more debt settling would be demanded when he got into London. For one thing, Maggie Lee was more extravagant than Stacy. Also she had been devious enough to have mesmerized Abba into giving her signed blank check book. All these expenses would not have bothered Abba had the austerity not cut off his huge source of income. Easy import license had bank rolled his corporate survival. With the avenue closed, there seemed no other way for AAA to survive.

The reality now meant that AAA's corporate survival was only a question of time. Also, the social connections that wealth had given Abba had evaporated since the austerity began. All things considered,

He saw no way of saving himself. His reputation was messed up in Lagos. His ego and perhaps most important of all, his glamorous jet-set style of living was finished.

Gone also was the dream of building his group of companies into an economic force to be reckoned with in the Nigerian business community. The one deal, which would have enabled AAA international to keep its foreign exchange earning capacity abroad was with the German brewery firm.

The deal, if it had gone ahead would also have made Abba a consultant to the German brewery company's hotel chains around Europe. By introducing Nigerian businessmen to the hotels, Abba would have been earning a steady annual income of over fifty thousand pounds sterling. This sum will be payable for life. But the austerity had disrupted the continuation of the deal. Right now, there was no further source of income either coming to Abba or into the corporate purse. In fact, until the new city project contract funds were paid, there would be no way of receiving income. The expected money from this source was not expected to be paid before six months.

AAA International was indebted to the local banks up to the tune of two and half a million naira. The money had been used to start up various manufacturing factories for consumer goods. These projects had been stopped due to lack of import license for bringing in the necessary production equipment. Until the country's foreign exchange earnings improve, these projects must be abandoned. Furthermore, the lucrative money Abba made getting import licenses for needy entrepreneurs had ceased since the beginning of the austerity. Everything was hopeless. All seemed lost.

At the airport, Harry Baker was waiting to pick up his passenger. He was dressed in black suit. It was shiny like the flashy Mercedes limousine he drove. "Oga Alhaji! Welcome to London," Baker cheerfully saluted.

"And how is life with you," Abba asked. "Rough as usual?"

"Yes! It has been much worse lately. But I hear it has been the same in your country. My Uncle Sidney recently died of heart attack when his business burst. You remember him, he used to attend your parties at the White House Hotel in Regent's Park."

"Yes, I'm sorry to hear about your uncle. I know it has been rather difficult to do business with Nigerians lately," consoled Abba.

Baker drove Abba in his black Mercedes Limo to his Knightsbridge apartment.

Not having the keys to his home, he knocked at the basement door of the caretaker and was given a spare set of keys. Abba wondered what had become of Maggie as he took the elevator up to his sixth floor apartment. Had she gone to her folks in Dusseldorf? Had she gone for the weekend? He paused to remember that Maggie usually left a note in her manly handwriting stating where she could be contacted. Inside the four bedroom apartment, Abba was shocked to notice the disorderly manner of the whole place. The living room seemed like it had been ransacked by amateur staff of the K.G.B.

"What a mess?" Abba spoke out loud.

Hurriedly, he moved into the bedroom and was shocked to notice that all his clothes and Maggie's were gone. On the table was a note with a short message.

"GOOD-BYE FOREVER."

IT CERTAINLY HAD BEEN GOOD WHILE IT LASTED." Maggie Lee.

No doubt it had been fun. A rage began to build up in him. First there was Binta. Now Maggie and what next.

Looking further into the drawer of the desk, he found pile of letters. All in bold red lettering indicating the final notification of unpaid bills. The utility bills all amounted to about ten thousand five hundred pounds. Two letters from the auto repair garage confirmed that the Jaguar sports car had been repaired and seven hundred pounds was yet to be paid. The insurance company had also written demanding renewal for the car's policy. The letter was dated six months ago.

The Savoy Hotel's solicitor had written, threatening to take Abba to Court for unpaid hotel bills totaling twenty thousand pounds.

But the most shocking of all was the Lloyd's bank statement, which registered a sum total of twenty-five thousand pounds in the red.

There was a letter from the property agency for the Knightsbridge apartment demanding the renewal of the lease. This had expired a week ago. The threat of eviction was eminent if payment was not received before the end of the month. This was precisely five days from that date. Payment for the new lease would amount to a further twelve thousand pounds.

Also the AAA's office premises in the White House hotel was indebted to the management to a sum of seven thousand pounds. Either the money was paid at the month's end or court action would be taken. Abba again checked the calendar on the wall and confirmed only five days was left in the month.

A letter from the London Merchant Bankers demanded repayment of the sum of fifteen thousand pounds sterling, which Abba had borrowed sometime in the past to finance exports to Lagos. Checking further into the desk, Abba could see many more pile of red marked bills but could not summon the courage to continue reading them. A Swiss stamped letter registered in his name caught his attention from the heap of letters. Remembering it was from his doctor in Zurich, Abba hurriedly opened the envelope his heart skipping a beat. Abba's heart sank further as he read the doctor's sad tiding.

In his wild flamboyant days as an international fun lover, Abba had employed Dr. Kathy Hoffman one of the best Swiss doctors on sexually transmitted diseases. Twice each year, Abba submitted himself to Dr. Hoffman's thorough medical examinations. The most deadly disease Abba contracted had been cured rapidly by powerful antibiotics, which the office of the specialist doctor provided. Abba knew of the risk of his flirtations. He lived in fear of some sinister infectious disease. Even before his mind could fully assimilate the content of the letter, Abba knew he'd had it. The information stated with authority that Abba's last blood test showed signs of degenerative Chlamydia trachomatis. A disease that caused pelvic inflammation and was a major cause of sterility. Blindness could develop in old age if not properly cured. The doctor advised Abba to send urgently the sum of five thousand pounds sterling for necessary drugs. Abba should plan to come to a Paris private specialist hospital for a month intensive care treatment. It was imperative that the treatment began soonest. No time must be wasted in fighting this scourge of the sexual revolution, Dr. Hoffman had emphasized. Abba finished reading the letter and wondered if he had not contacted the incurable acquired immune deficiency syndrome. The thought of AIDS made his mind race back to the week's shocking scandal in New York Greenwich Village. On the day he arrived at New York's J.F.K. Airport, the radio news was centered on the two men with the dreaded disease. The news had it that in a room decorated with fresh-cut flowers, two men shared a final bottle of wine. They tied themselves together at the waist and then plugged from their 35th floor luxury apartment. They evidently chose instant death over the slow ravages of the incurable disease. As Abba re-read Dr. Hoffman's letter, thoughts of the double suicide sent cold shivers up his spine. His legs shook so much he almost fainted.

Sitting down on the unmade and sheet less bed, he tried to mentally erase and forget thoughts of sexual related disease from his depressed mind. Pretend Dr. Hoffman didn't exist. He forced his mind to obey him but the thought kept troubling him.

Thus mentally tormented, Abba weighed his helpless and hopeless situation. He lamented his inability to pay the various outstanding debts, but the loss of Maggie's intimate companionship hurt him the most. The realization that Maggie Lee whom he had hoped so much would be around to comfort him having deserted him grieved him deeply. The two ladies Abba trusted, it seemed, had conspired to desert him at the most ill-opportune time.

First, there was Binta, the survivor ultimate survivor who ditched Abba for Mamman Taofik. Then Maggie Lee had taken her turn, departing at the very juncture she could have helped to sustain Abba with her affections. Once Imam Fulani had told Abba to beware of the betrayal of the blondes, but he had ignored his advice.

The guru's prediction it seemed had come to pass. The devastating effect of these betrayals devastated him. The Lagos austerity propelled Abba in his abject powerlessness to contemplate death as his only way of escape.

He figured rightly that when one loses everything including hope, life becomes a disgrace and death a duty.

In his death wish, Abba imagined what the Swiss match magnate Ivar Kreugger must have felt before blowing his brains out with a shot gun. What special courage is required before honorably making one's exit from this wicked world?

Abba wondered if he had a gun, whether he would have the guts to pull the trigger, thereby sending himself into oblivion. This was London, he reminded himself, had he been in New York, it would have been easy to obtain fire arms. There being no gun, Abba reasoned blowing one's brain was out of the question. He decided to think more. Be creative, he cautioned his sick mind. Suddenly as if by flash light, an idea caught his attention.

The London Heathrow bag contained the jumbo size Remy Martins brandy he purchased from the duty-free airport shop gave him a chance to escape from his dilemma.

Glancing past the bag, his eyes focused on the bathroom door, inside, which he knew contained the first aid box. He wondered if Maggie's extra powerful stimulant drugs were still available.

A massive dosage of fifteen tablets of the lethal drug supplied Maggie by Bonn's drugstore washed down with a glassful of the superior brandy would, Abba concluded, solve his problem. The combination of the drug and the alcohol consumed should be enough to induce an everlasting sleep.

Standing up, after his brief meditation, Abba walked up to the liquor cabinet. He retrieved a super- sized champagne glass, he hurriedly opened up the bottle of Remy Martins brandy. He moved smartly as if in a trance to the bathroom, opened up the first aid box and brought out the drug bottle containing amphetamines and barbiturates. The German brand was twice as powerful and the label stated in red bold capital letters that an overdose was most fatal.

As he shook the pills out of the bottle, he momentarily looked into the cabinet mirror and was terrified to notice a face shriveled. He snapped his face away from the mirror, noticing as he did so, that his eyes seemed to have retreated into their sockets. His insane mind saw correlation between the face on the mirror and the Time magazine picture shots of a famous Hollywood actor days before his tragic death from AIDS. His was a personification of the gloom

203

and doom of the dreaded sexual disease.

A dejected hopelessness painted on the death-like face, a face that belonged to the wild flamboyant heart-throb of Lagos. He recalled his younger days when he as prince charming roamed the globe making the opposite sex wild with pent up desires. In his fury and intensity at the strange figure portrayed in mirror, Abba suffered a rupture of a tiny blood vessel in his brain. The rupture was responsible for sending instantaneously a surge of electric current to the brain.

Seconds later, Abba began to feel an eclipse coming over his reasoning faculties. With considerable will power, he slowly walked over to the bed, poured a handful of the tranquillizers from the container and hurriedly swallowed all. From the Heathrow Airport duty- free bag, he took out the Remy Martins and fitted the opened bottle into his mouth gulping down many mouthfuls. Repeatedly he took more tablets from the drug container chewing as he swallowed more mouthful from the brandy bottle. He seemed like a child excited at the task of chewing and drinking at the same time. The strong liquor gave his body instant heat and Abba sprang up from the bed. He labored feverishly at opening all the apartment's massive windows. Almost immediately the temperature in the room was reduced to freezing point. With that done, he came into the bed and laid down in subconscious anticipation. His face lit up a smile as he wishfully embraced the darkness that gradually enveloped him far beyond the unknown.

The continuous cold blast sweeping in from the open windows; legacy of London's worst winter in decades helped to preserve Abba's body until the Scotland Yard Officer came to the scene.

'The dead sleep comfortably in this earth
It warms them and dries up their misery--
They had melted into a thick absence.
The red clay had drunk the white substance.
And the gift of life has passed into the flowers;
Where are their familiar phrases;
The personal style, the unique soul?
Maggots crawl where tears formed!'
– Valery.

CHAPTER TWENTY-EIGHT

Abba Abdulmalik's funeral was finally held in Kano six weeks after his death. The lapse in time was spent by Scotland Yard on investigations.

Dumba and Dogon Talata spent this miserable period of London's tough winter helping the police. The corpse released from the Hammersmith Mortuary was flown from Heathrow Airport in a special chartered plane to Kano International Airport.

The entire employees of AAA International Company, influential members of the Naira Club and most of the inhabitants of the Goron Dutse district of Kano were present when the plane touched down. Such was the overflowing capacity of the crowd, many were tearful in their sorrow. The local politician mourned the asset the city would have utilized had death not struck the swashbuckling playboy.

The gold bedecked coffin fashioned by a Westminster craftsman was borne down the aircraft by six pallbearers. Three members of the Federal Government administration and three junior Ministers from Kano were present. His friends were represented by, Sam Dumba, Dr. Richard Kemidare, and Barrister Bulus Musa.

In London, Dumba had a tough argument with Dogon Talata on the best way to proceed so as not incur the wrath of the spiritual Imams. Common sense had helped to convince Dumba that the floral bouquets and giant-sized colorful wreaths, which the Westminster funeral home provided should be left on the plane on arrival in Kano. If Dumba had his way, Abba would have received a fashionable funeral.

The pallbearers marched up to the platform and gently deposited the coffin on the raft. The next fifteen minutes was for Dumba's eulogy. It was part of the compromise agreed upon with Dogon Talata after which, Imam Fulani would take over his late master's body for the final Moslem rites.

Dumba spoke with a voice choking with emotions. His deep sorrow and sense of loss moved the crowd equally to renewed outburst of wailings. He spoke of Abba Abdulmalik's love for the people of Kano. How Abba spent millions providing employment for AAA's staff. His struggles geared towards the betterment of the common folks. His great drive in politics and how he helped put the present civilian administration in power. He highlighted Abba's remarkable international business connections. It would have brought future economic benefit to Kano had he lived. Finally, Dumba swore he was going into politics, and would seek to avenge Abba's death in the long term by helping to bring financial stability into the nation's economic system. His voice cranked on, taking on the showmanship of a future politician.

"I know our system is such that you cannot prosecute people for bad management and stupidity. However, I can assure you that this administration has witnessed grand style extortion, fraud and gross misrepresentation. The austerity directly contributed to the death of Abba Abdulmalik. This austerity has killed and continues to kill off many prominent businessmen. What we need are leaders with realistic visions. We must vote for people with the financial skill to develop long-range plans. That our country may continue to move forward away from austerity programs. Present day problems have become more economic and financial than ever. It follows, therefore, that we elect leaders who know how national and international economies operate. Leaders who can tackle the financing of our public programs like schools, social services, and other basic infrastructures. We need leaders to make complex decisions in today's global village, which is an increasingly complex society. We need leaders to get us out of this present austerity. Without this austerity, I can assure you Abba will be alive today, hale and hearty like you and I."

After the energetic eulogy, the impressed masses chanted up the native song on austerity-the unforgiving man-made evil, which had taken away Abba in its deadly blitz. The chant continued as the imams led by Fulani promptly moved up to the platform and took possession of the coffin. From there, Abba will be removed and wrapped in a native mat to be deposited into mother earth for his eternal rest,

Dumba, stood enthralled, and in deep thought contemplated the significance of the burial ritual. The promptness of it all baffled him. A final thrust of the naked body to the soil and the ceremony would be over. The process was neat and economical. Why waste money on expensive wreaths and unappreciated bouquets?

"That was a powerful speech,"rang out Bulus' baritone voice as he walked up to Dumba. "I must say you were blunt. I mean very blunt in your attacks."

Dumba nodded and replied in a quiet voice, "Perhaps not blunt enough."

You could be locked up in jail for such slanderous statements. Our political friends may yet make a case against you."

"I suppose they may. Even Plato made note of the small and unrighteous soul of power brokers. Of course, most of our leaders are lawyers. Our leaders are people trained in law. Lawyers are definitely not trained in economics. They lack the financial skill to lead the nation out of austerity program."

"Very well, I can see your point. You're right, we need leaders with strategic vision. Maybe we can get this with time. But who can tell? Do you seriously think you've the rare practical qualities for leadership?"

"Honestly, I don't know. That is why I'm going into politics. I'll have the opportunity to find out."

"I admire your ruthless honesty. It may also interest you to know that Abba was a victim of personal successes, too intoxicating to last- A miniature King Khashoggi without the financial assets. "

A serene smile creased Dumba's face, his eyes sparkling in amusement. The picture of a manipulator with keen understanding of public political speech radiated in his mind's eye.

"Frame is the spur of all political speeches. The immediate benefit is all that matters. Expediency is the name of the game. I recently decided that I shall be running for the Senate in the next elections. This administration has lost touch with the people. A leader who surrounds himself with yes men is like a pilot flying blind with instrument that doesn't tell him accurate reading but only what he wants to hear. The austerity measure is causing havoc. But the powerful men in office lack the compassion to bring relief to the masses. A classic example of Tsar Nicholas and the Charlatan Rasputin reporting of outdated economic statistics. They give misleading encouragement before the Russian revolution. The resultant calamity brought death to the population in various stages. A leader like the legendary Old Fox would have ruled the nation with experienced wisdom. Of course, our political system will not allow men of such caliber."

"Yes, but there is another side to this legend. I hope someday it will be told" Bulus replied in strong, vibrant tone. "Time, they say, brings everything. May it bring you the experience and the platform to intelligently market your dream for political rulership."

"Thank you and I wish myself God's speed" Dumba said in a low melancholic voice. He wondered how trustworthy Bulus was.

The next nine months sped by while the nation prepared for a general election. Dumba prepared for the election with a formidable war chest. His City of London and Wall Street associates had generously supported him. Dumba, if elected, would in no time pay back the kind gesture. His intention was to become the Chairman of the Senate Committee on Petroleum The position would provide Dumba with the authority to exploit the nation for personal ambitions. Ambitions that his international associates were ready to finance with hope of greater gains when he got elected to higher office.

The dream propelled Dumba with a sense of energy. It animated his every move but which exhausted those around him.

Everywhere he campaigned, he vehemently accused the administration of gross mismanagement and lamented the austerity measures. He promised structural changes when elected to the Senate. As a Senator, he promised to use his Wall Street experience and City of London connections to make the nation become integrated with industrialized economies. Thus, the nation would make more efficient use of its resources, bringing a change in the government macro-economic policies.

He shed crocodile tears when he traveled the devastated roads that needed rebuilding. He held champagne parties for the staff of the local press, lecturing them on the mystic climes of the financial world and his contacts whom he would employ to work economic miracles for the nation. At these sessions, he undermined his opponents by ludicrous leaks to the press. Dumba the manipulator used every uncanny means at his disposal to intimate the undiscerning public of his selfless motive in seeking office.

The nation's educational system, he stressed, was not ready to turn out skilled workers, but given four years in the Senate, Dumba hoped to make the nation become black Africa's Silicon Valley.

To drum up support for his political party, his London friends gave Dumba a Gulf Stream jet. With this, he flew his party supporters to political rallies. On the day of the party's presentation ceremony for political nominees, Dumba promised to use his position as Senator to set up an anti-corrupt system in the nation. This would in time eradicate the combination of colonial ideologies, corrupt, inefficient state apparatus, and the crippling bureaucracy. The anti-enterprise culture of the civil servants would all be removed.

Dumba, the tycoon, promised to raise one hundred million dollar venture fund with which to promote small businesses. He promised to solve the problem of graduate unemployment. His bold program would evolve a renaissance of the nation's enterprises and shape up the economy to become more competitive.

Dumba's campaign headquarters comprised of technologically superior devices. His office had Hewlett Packard Computers, with laser Jet printers, audio system, video recording equipments. He dazzled the natives with what an office of tomorrow should be. He stated that the nation needed effective resource managers so as not to be caught in future crisis of austerity measures. He addressed his audience with a grin so full of deviousness and amoral undertones. He knew that raw power won the race and he had ample money to buy off difficult competitors. And so, full of personal conviction, he campaigned ruthlessly for his dream for the Senate. His political aides spent fortunes gathering statistical information with which to dazzle opponents and the public alike. But unknown to all, the austerity was gathering a dangerous momentum of its own that would shatter the nation's second republic.

Africa's politicking at the top is always most damaging and nasty. This is because of the profound insecurity of publicly elected leaders. This insecurity drove the African leaders to forcefully fight for life-long tenure ship at the top positions. Elections may come and go but the leadership position would only be changed by the barrel of machine guns and the blood of poor natives. This trend of politics played in the language of war seemed to forever repeat itself. Such is the Achilles heel of the African political structure.

There will forever be shortage in the political courage to change this trend. Perhaps, only time will teach African leaders that power offers little protection from the perils of politics. This is a necessary lesson that must be learned in order to move African societies from the tribal value system to that of a corporate state system.

The predictable storm signal started after the Senate elections where reports, of massive rigging promoted tribal tensions in Dr. Richard's local constituency.

It was commonly known that regional rivalry had always been very strong in this part of the nation. A fact made worse by Dr. Richard's gross insensitivity to the local politics. His high-mindedness made him unacceptable to the rural populace. The people resented Dr. Richard's flaunting of his huge Mercedes car. The natives hated the money he carried around bribing the local clergy and the powerless chieftains in the community. The ruling party had marginalized the region and spent massive funds to ensure its candidates were elected. Nothing was to be left to chance. And so it came to pass that Dr. Richard was announced as winner after the first counting of the ballot papers. Dr. Richard's political party did not, however, reckon with the people's reaction towards the shocking news.

The resultant political riot that followed the night after his victory claimed the lives of Dr. Richard Kemidare, his wife, two sons and six members of his household.

Dr. Richard's lavish home and estate was burnt down with all his earthly possessions. A worse fate was to befall the dead when the local chief decided it would be an abomination for Dr. Richard and his family to be buried in the village with full traditional rites. Such was the wrath of the voters that the result of the election was reversed.

It counted to Dr. Richard's great loss that he failed to understand the politics of a situation before propping up himself as a messiah of valueless substance.

Dumba on the other hand, won his Senate seat. And prompted by his London associates he started campaigning for the executive position of head of the Senate. So much distance existed between Lagos and London that the associates were imbued with optimism for their investment schemes. They calculated that Senator Dumba now in the mainstream of Lagos power house would start to open doors. Dumba, however reckoned he had used his friends to angle for visibility. The goal achieved, he set his mind to function as a pragmatic politician. He understood that the structural changes he had promised his constituency would never materialize. As a clever tactician he learned of the unstable state of the economy and that the austerity daily gained more suicidal momentum. The economic depression had a lethal effect that threatened to shatter the life of the second republic.

"Our challenge" he told the press on his first television interview as a Senator, "is to rebuild the country. We must work as a team to pull her out of the shackles of world debt crisis."

Senator Dumba shocked his colleagues by suggesting that Nigeria needed a similar concept as the 'British-U.S. Live Aid Program' to raise   money for the poor in Africa. This would help the country out of its financial pitfalls. "It will take tenacity and patience. We'll need a decade of dedication before the austerity blows over. Either that or we must seek help from our established sons in foreign nations. We know many of them are derrick of strength in multinational corporations. Many of them are individuals of integrity with enviable financial power. Let us move gradually towards seeking their trust. Their aid would be to us, like the Krugerrand is to South Africa. We all, of course, can imagine what economic ruins the South African government will become without its Krugerrands - gold coins traded in the international markets."

Such powerful comments from Senator Dumba gave him certain credits in the public media. And like the parables predict, having all the credit may boost one's viability but it also ensures many enemies.

A real friend who thought along these lines was Barrister Bulus Musa. Bulus knew that the restless civilian administration needed someone of integrity for guidance. A moral leader to lead the people in a time of turbulent changes and of capitalist values in conflict. He saw correctly that Pedro da Souza had the intellectual position and moral authority. He could fulfill the effects of combined Ralph Waldo Emerson and Henry David Thoreau on America. The Waldo who had a moral vision for America, spent his life realizing this vision. Thoreau achieved authority as a rebel against vested authority. It was manifest that da Souza's authority on the people reached far beyond his ethnic constituencies. The Lagos legend on the international scene had transparent integrity and humane courage.

Bulus argued and impressed it upon Senator Dumba that da Souza had a vision for Lagos. The lawyer then went on to vividly describe the secret mission he had undertaken for certain clients to da Souza's home in Geneva.

Bulus reckoned his mission had started a spark in da Souza and knew that the old man would show his hands with time. He summed his narration by pleading with Senator Dumba to form a Senate lobby to visit da Souza in Switzerland. Once such a lobby of powerful people was formed in the Senate, Bulus promised to act as intermediary to San Marino. He completed his argument by advising that such a bold move on investment holdings be effected in Lagos. It will be a neat way of battling the austerity in Lagos.

Senator Dumba had taken the da Souza issue seriously. He used every opportunity he had to positively stress the impact da Souza's huge resources would have on the nation's life. The main opposition to the da Souza's lobby became the Lagos fat-cats and oligarchic group. The Mafia-type power brokers whose activities had helped in sending da Souza to exile. The thug of war that followed Senator Dumba's stance on the issue went on to threaten his very life. He became a man marked down to be assassinated. This feud continued until the military arrived on the scene to take over power. Three months into his four year term as a Senator of the realm, the army took over the Lagos government in a bloodless coup. Several politicians and top ministers were clamped into jail.

Dumba remained in his Lagos residence and was later arrested, taken to the Kirikiri Maximum Security Prison where he was detained for many months. He was not a victim of economic sabotage but a fool for his lack of foresight. An intelligence report had come from Dumba's associates in London informing him of the very day the government was to be toppled.

The London associates had strongly requested that Dumba make good his escape to England. But he would not accept to run like a coward. Stoically he decided to stay in Lagos and accept whatever treatment the military conquerors had in store for him. Lagos. He had begun to understand, that Lagos was the only place on earth he could really call home.

And so Dumba spent close to fifteen months in the Kirikiri Maximum Security Prison. He was a victim of the arrogance of conquerors. Conquerors who had taken power with high hopes and expectations of what utopia Lagos would become in their reign. In their propaganda they envisaged a blueprint for utopia, such as Lenin had before he was to gain the political levers of power to put his dreams into effect.

Dumba underwent several shock treatments in his prison cell and gradually began to appreciate the swindle of African political revolution.

African military coup plotters arrive promising abundance for all, but bringing only misery and deprivation to many. They make rich men poor overnight and the poor much poorer. The only exception to this massive stage of abject poverty are the very few men in high military ranks and their relatives. Such is a typical demonstration of the social vandalism as practiced in the high places of African nation states.

Da Souza received the news of the change of the Lagos government with mixed feelings. He had followed the follies of the civilian administration with an open mind.

In fact, da Souza had gathered more detailed intelligence from Lagos. He was aware of the motives of Barrister Bulus mission to San Marino. He had found out that the Lagos attorney had been fronting for a group of patriotic politicians who foolishly believe da Souza would provide them with the foreign exchange in Switzerland with which to topple the civilian government.

Their ill-conceived plan had not materialized when da Souza bluntly refused any overt action to help them out. Furthermore, da Souza had gained insight through Ted Hunter that the rare matrix of economic circumstances of the Lagos austerity would in time bring in the military. Hunter's prediction had thus come to pass.

Experience however informed da Souza that a position of military power offered no immunity from political peril. Power generally offered little protection from the perils of politics. For politics at the top of military regimes can be the nastiest and most damaging to the head of state. It was always only a matter of time before a group of disgruntled junior officers hatch subversive plots to undermine their bothersome superiors.

On the positive side, da Souza was happy to acknowledge that the military junta would bring more discipline into Lagos public life. A disciplined regime would also help da Souza in his investment plans for Lagos. da Souza's private dossier on Lagos stressed the leverage , which the unannounced platinum mines had on its successful outcome. da Souza smiled with contentment when he thought of the hidden platinum mines scattered on the remote side of Lagos Island.

The year was 1961 when he had acted as the temporary minister of Lagos Ministry of Mines and Power. A study group had been setup with the help of African Missionary Society based in Lagos. Reverend Father Thomas Waddel, head of the team and a renowned geologist, had noticed a group of very rare metals on the island north of Lagos. A hidden site where the Lagos Archbishop had decided to erect a church. Father Thomas had taken the metal to Cork in Ireland to be analyzed. On his return to Lagos, Father Thomas got in touch with da Souza who privately commissioned further field examination. The research was to be top secret with only one report to be made to da Souza.

Six months into the clandestine exploration Father Thomas reported that the metals had been confirmed to be platinum. Feasibility reports on the metal's financial potential proved very negative as world supply exceeded demand. The 1961 price of the platinum metal was considerably low on the New York commodity market. There being no real demand for the metal, da Souza decided therefore, that the knowledge of the platinum find be kept secret from his colleagues. When he left for exile in Switzerland, he took all the evidence of the platinum mine with him. Father Thomas Waddell had by this time died. Thus, nobody but da Souza had the knowledge of the platinum. A weapon he would use strategically as his Lagos plans thus unfolded. With his thoughts on the precious metal, he checked through the pages of the Wall Street Journal to confirm that the price of platinum was eclipsing that of gold.

The editorial page also made mention of the chances that

platinum metals would be on catalytic device to lower emission from automobiles throughout Western Europe and the United States of America.

Tactfully, the effective business mogul calculated that the timing of his Lagos plans will coincide with the surge in the world's demand for the platinum metal. He knew without doubt, that the demand for the metal will exceed supply before the end of the decade. Timing, da Souza knew, was everything.

CHAPTER TWENTY-NINE

"The sale of Zeus Chemical plants in Salt Lake city will irreparably damage a pending grand jury investigation. This case has been on for

the past three years and it involves criminal tax violations and illegal currency transactions," said Craig Masterson. He lit a thin Cuban cigar, and stretched out his legs as he peered down on the three pages of Hunter's report on the table.

Hunter sat transfixed on the visitor's chair as the New York attorney studied the detailed list of the Zeus Group subsidiaries marked for immediate sale.

Andy Lincoln smiled. "Swiss laws are such that business transactions are conducted with considerable secrecy but such investigations will not be big problem. What other alternatives do we have?"

Craig Masterson put down his cigar and regarded Lincoln with feigned graciousness. His lips parted a trifle and he clasped his hands together.

"Of course, there are loopholes, but with predetermined risks. The key word will be outside buyers speculating for higher profits but equally ready to assume unlimited risks. Find such a buyer and I will use persuasion to delay the investigations. It will be no mean task since they have a cacophony of complaints. Your next major problem could have been the Security and Exchange Commission."

"Yeah, thank God, Zeus Industries are all privately owned. So we've freedom from the prying eyes of the security analysts and financial press. The worst burden of being a public company is the eternal pressure for short term result that distorts decision making. "Hunter spoke gravely. He paused, "Zeus is in big hurry to build a huge equity pool. The sooner the better. "

"I've known the old man for the past twenty years. I've acted in various legal capacities for the Zeus Group. I wonder why he's selling all his investments in the U.S." Craig questioned.

"Craig, I know you're worried but da Souza is still sane and alright. The glut in the oil market and the rapidly changing nature of Rotterdam spot market has a lot to do with Zeus's future long-range plans. Ted knows more about the oil market and he agrees with da Souza." Andy Lincoln spoke with authority.

A faint look of loyalty came upon Hunter's face and he spoke in a clear high voice. "Capital is the oil that makes the investment machine work. There is an endless need for capital today. A corporation can never have enough. Zeus conglomerate needs to break into new grounds."

Craig Masterson stared at both Andy Lincoln and Hunter with open derision and dislike. How should he lie so randomly? What schemes were the two spinning for Pedro da Souza? Was the old man getting senile, Craig wondered.

"The U.S. we both know is the center for the world wide information revolution. Any established business here will increase its investment holdings annually for the next decade. Such opportunities should not be dismissed entirely. Are you sure da Souza knows exactly what he is doing? I know it is not my business to ask. I'm however very curious."

"We'll pass on your concern to da Souza." Hunter informed Craig. "Meanwhile there is a Japanese group of unnamed investors headed by a Hong Kong attorney scheduled to be at the San Marino, Geneva next week. Then, you will have your curiosity amply satisfied."

Craig Masterson caught his breath, not-expecting the outburst from Hunter. In the silence that followed, and to the lawyer's astonishment, both men rose and excused themselves from the lawyer's office. Hurrying to catch the Swiss Air Flight departing the John F. Kennedy Airport in New York to Geneva Switzerland.

Danny McGovern sat in da Souza's favorite chair, hat in hand, his eyes stern. "You should have informed me you were selling. You owe me that much, Pedro," Danny murmured.

da Souza turned to him with passionate gesture. He did not expect much from this cool and selfish man. Danny was different from Sean. He always protected himself, at all costs, from the anxieties and tribulations of others. A ruthless businessman reputed to have destroyed many in his path for powers. Danny, operated like the real life J.R. Ewing of Dallas fame. da Souza tolerated Danny because he had helped to launch the Zeus Group as advised by his brother Monsignor Sean. In the first years of Zeus' existence, da Souza had relied on Danny for every major financial decision. It was in this spirit that da Souza had in the year 1969 approached Danny with Zeus' bid for dormant oil refinery plant in Houston, Texas. da Souza had been negotiating this deal, which was to give huge leverage to Zeus Holdings. Danny had been intrigued at the dramatic deal. Everything had been top secret. Danny had taken immediate interest in the refinery. An overriding interest moved his shrewd mind to seek to acquire the plant for the Greenspoint Oil Company. And so he opted to act as the intermediary. da Souza accepted Danny to be his middle man in the final contract sale.

Danny had reported back after a week that the company was no longer willing to sell to Zeus Group. A rival oil company in Pasadena had overnight acquired the refinery in a most dramatic manner. da Souza had accepted Danny's verdict on the face value and the following day visited New York where he employed the services of Craig Masterson, a top Wall Street oil attorney.

Masterson then carried out a thorough investigation that revealed the true ownership of the Pasadena Oil Company. It had been a subsidiary of Greenspoint Oil Company. Such was the typical scheming in the oil industry and a typical style of Danny McGovern. da Souza had received the news with equanimity and decided in the future to trust Danny no more.

"I should have told you," da Souza spoke looking angry and withdrawn all at the same time." All this wild talk of me owing you is very silly indeed. You know I've repaid your kindness a thousand fold. I trusted you once but Danny, the manipulator could never respect that trust. You did what you had to do to acquire the benefits of fame in the year 1969. Remember?"

"Had you been in my shoes, I'm sure you'd have done the same" Danny said softly. His eyes distended and he looked like a terrified creature that was captured by a vicious pit-bull dog.

"Yeah! only the fittest will survive. Your very words Danny," da Souza said in a quiet voice. "That was the famous words I learned from you at the start of my business career. It certainly had helped to keep me on guard. Over the years, I've accepted the principles. In fact, they were drummed into me when I took a series of strategic management courses at the New York office of the Dale Carnegie Institute. In retrospect, I should thank you."

Danny's courage seemed to have returned. He appeared a formidable package of a man. His skin was pale, almost transparent, his eyes were grey and motionless. His mouth with its intense persuasive voice seemed fixed and settled in its refined cruelty. Sean McGovern had been the family member of honor while Danny was immoral and without human feelings. There was a lot to be said of breeding-where the same mother could give birth to one good son and one devilish brat.

Tan and distinguished looking with grey hair, Danny wore a black double breasted pin stripe suit. His exquisite sight seemed like that of a New York banker.

Danny McGovern represented the old-type of financiers and oil barons. His ability to combine large scale speculations with careful scientific analysis had helped him to amass considerable fortune at a young age. Danny's Greenspoint Investment Group was like a modern day House of Morgan. Danny McGovern had set out from his native Ireland, penniless and had arrived in New York, a lanky dialectic young man of twenty. In the stock exchange crash of 1929, he worked as an investment clerk at Wall Street. From his vantage point, he learned the financial mathematics to become a crack mathematician, a celebrated human computer and financial analyst. The stock exchange panic and the huge business bankruptcies provided him the chance to begin speculating for himself.

Six years into this and Danny had stashed away some considerable fund to launch Greenspoint Oil Company. Over the years, Danny made and lost several fortunes. However, Greenspoint grew into a huge success, becoming in the process one of America's largest privately owned oil companies.

"My late brother Sean always said you were a born and bred gentleman."

"Sean was a great man. But for him we would never have met. And on his account we have been like blood brothers. But tell me what brings you to San Marino."

"I've come to bid for Zeus ultra-modern research and development laboratories in Ponaca City, Oklahoma. The plant would give Greenpoint comparative advantage against DuPont and Conoco."

"All right. I'll only accept cash. No leveraged buyout and no junk bond issues. Give me cash payment of $150 million and it's all yours.

"The plant has a debt of $130 million. In the second quarter, it had a $7.5 million operation profit, but a $6.7 million net loss after a $3.3 million charge from expenses for environmental pollution control devices. Profit in the next quarter will be better. I reckon $140 million will be fine, considering its potentials."

"The great mathematician in you should tell you it's a steal. I know your competitors can offer slightly more than I've asked."

"Maybe they would, but I want the plant and I'll pay half cash and half by zero-coupon notes.

"Okay, I'll accept $100 million cash. The rest can be in zero-coupon notes."

"You drive a tough bargain. A severe cash squeeze of that magnitude can cripple even Adnan Khashoggi's larger than life business plans. Greenspoint happens to be having a liquidity crunch at the moment. Give me two months and I'll meet your requests."

"Sounds good to me. Say, how's Danny junior and his mother?"

"Mary is alright. Getting on in age, same as you and me. Danny left law practice and has gone back to Harvard for his M.B.A. He is yet to decide on joining me at Greenspoint. I wish he will decide favorably. Without him, Greenspoint will disintegrate after I'm gone.

"I know the feeling. All my hope for Zeus Group got evaporated the day I lost my wife and David."

"Sony, I wish I had visited to console you."

"Thanks, I understand and appreciate your sympathy. The Lord giveth. The Lord taketh. I've borne it well considering the mental traumas. The sale of my company makes m happy knowing Zeus Group assets will serve a purpose. A grand purpose."

"Just what are you talking about? Is this a sort of venture with synergistic possibilities?"

"No, I'm pulling all my assets to build equity for the Souza Foundation Trust. I aim for it to channel over the next five years ten billion dollars to help set up Industrial enterprises in Lagos. It's basically an investment for those who can afford to lose money. You can say it is out of the category of ventures you would be interested in. It is a holy adventure without profit motives. If it succeeds, great. If not, I'll enjoy the action as it unfolds."

"Are you aware of what you're doing? You can lose everything." Danny cautioned.

"Yeah, so I can. I suddenly realized I came into this world with nothing. It will be no great shame if I depart with nothing."

"That sounds more like the socialist reasoning of the late Monsignor McGovern. May his soul rest in perfect peace."
"Amen!"

CHAPTER THIRTY-ONE

"Craig Masterson thinks we may have some problems with the chemical plants in Salt Lake City," Andy Lincoln said. Pedro da Souza sat across the room on the Victorian couch. He was absorbed in the Souza Foundation Trust dossier. At the sound of Lincoln's voice, da Souza looked up at Hunter who was starring absent mindedly.

"If it has to do with Federal investigations and other related matters then we must withdraw the plants from the sales agenda. I cannot risk any legal repressions. At least not before I'm ready for adverse publicity from the press."

"We don't have to worry about the financial press. I've used every professional trick I know to cover any press leakages."

"Thanks Ted. I knew I could count on your integrity. Tell me about your contingency plans for renewed world-wide banking crisis. Remember we must be ready before the next smoke signal." da Souza demanded.

"There does not seem to be any comprehensive or all-embracing contingency plan. New international debt crisis erupt from different countries points of view. With regard to O.P .E.C., my predictions are that oil may drop another $10 per barrel before next year runs out. Saudi Arabia, the derrick of OPEC will soon reach a point where she would abandon the cartel. This is solely my own assumption. It may never happen. Most Latin American borrowers are moving up the point where each may refuse further re-payment of loans and interests. The fear factor might almost immediately drive the price of gold up." Hunter summarized.

"What specific aids could Zeus offer Lagos at this moment." da Souza asked.

"That would entirely depend on you. I've read the Souza Foundation Trust Manifesto. I like very much the intention of Lagos Investment Guarantee Agency to be based in Geneva Switzerland. Subject to the ratification of the Lagos government, the foundation shall operate as a bank subsidiary with authorized capital of $10 billion. The foundation will then insure investors against various commercial risks especially uncompensated expropriation. The agency would greatly improve foreign investments in Lagos. The big question is, would the Lagos government agree to the non-political element in the contract?"

Hunter asked.

"I would hope so. They don't have a choice but to agree to make ethnicity an economic asset. Either that or the investment insurance will end up in double jeopardy. The Lagos fat cats would then still continue to wield immense powers, which would not be acceptable to me. Entrenched as the Lagos fat cats are, I subscribe to the wisdom that even the greatest monuments crumble with time." Da Souza enthused.

"Yes, you're right. Give the young bloods better chance with increased investments and in time a new order will emerge in Lagos." Hunter complemented.

"That is the dream. The realization of Which Will not be easy. Progress and success, no ever said it would come easy." da Souza joyfully completed.

Even as the old man spoke, Ted Hunter and Andy Lincoln began to understand the brilliance of his scheme. They had used the past ten months gathering statistical and financial data necessary to dispose of the vast Zeus Holdings. The massive data that both men went through convinced them that Zeus Industries was worth approximately $15 billion. As the assets were to be disposed for cash sales only, Hunter further calculated that the net sum of $10 billion would be on hand when the sale was completed in ten days.

$10 billion in cash was a vast sum of money for a man to control. With no debt owed to anybody, Swiss taxes already taken care of, da Souza could buy two of African's poorest nations if he wanted. The old man however had better strategy. He would use his cash to liquidate any member of the wolf pack that refused to go along with his plans. If all the members of the wolf pack play along with da Souza, then a unique cartel would be created, such as never have been imagined before.

A sum total of $10 billion would be set aside to fund the Lagos investments program guaranteed by Souza Foundation Trust. A self-supporting agency, which in time will have callable capital to build giant industrial estates in Lagos. It will improve the Lagos investment environment leading to more positive flow of funds from the world's international organizations. But more important of all, it will be da Souza's investment strategy that will detribalize Lagos.

Lagos would then gradually move from an African tribal society into a corporate state where it would not matter what geographic part or ethnic group .It would authentic integrity in the nation. Where no bright boy's future will be blighted because he did not belong to a certain tribe.

Hunter's journalist's mind raced on seeing all the noble possibilities of da Souza's scheme. He began to develop a genuine respect for the genius of the old man. So engrossed was he in his thoughts that he loudly repeated the old man's favorite quotation.

'Fame is the spur.' Hunter beamed spiritedly.

Hunter knew however, it took considerable foresight and hindsight for da Souza to set about his plans for Lagos. "It took tough love on the part of the suitor to be still caring and in love with a betrayed lover."

CHAPTER THIRTY-ONE

Five weeks after the sale of the Zeus Group of companies at a secret bidding ceremony in the Doler Grand Hotel in Zurich, Pedro da Souza set about planning for the meeting with the wolf pack. He was pleased that the Zeus sales pitch had provided him the sum of $10 billion after payment of U.S. and Swiss corporate taxes. da Souza happy that his present financial resources gave him the bargaining power to accomplish his mission. He zealously digested for the second time, Hunter's massive report on Lagos. He read long into the night pausing occasionally to leisurely stretch his massive body. He took proper care not to scatter the papers lying all around him.

His tired eyes for the umpteenth time sighted the detailed list of the wolf pack bringing his mind to full alert.

Mentally he pictured each member of the wolf pack as he read out aloud each name. With each name, he mentally filled the historic gap Hunter had left out in his research.

Lord Hardcastle, Britain, - Oil

Sir Edward Melfort, Smith, Britain - Chemicals

Gregory Ashford, Britain - Textiles

Francois Seramu, France - Ocean Liners

Rudolf Schwartzman, Germany - Civil Construction

Donald Samuel Herman, USA. - Financial services

Albert M. Meyer, USA - Oil

Thomas Lambert, USA - Banker

Amin Patel Singh, India - Import, Exports

Levi Zarpass, Greek-Nigeria - Import, Export

Jerry Wang Lee - Hong Kong, Import, Export

The list revealed the most powerful operators in the Lagos economy. The men had arrived Lagos penniless at the turn of the century and became rich through wheeling and dealing. These had been men with economic foresight, able to achieve trade monopoly in their respective areas before Lagos became independent of Britain. These business magnates towered even to date far above any other in trade with Lagos. Each trading holdings had beyond the imagination of the authorities. Men who brought the Western banks, oil companies, agro-based business, chemical, textile and shipping concerns into Lagos. Their various assets had continued to grow and most had turned into multi-national industries.

Though all of the men currently lived out of Lagos, they and their heir apparent still remained fond of the Lagos business environment. Lagos was the root of all their worldwide achievement. They had undergone the Lagos baptism of fire. Each had, like the Pedro da Souza used their bitter experience to diversify world-wide. Each had equally hated Lagos and was bent on destroying its economy.

The wolf pack gained their symbolic significance and historic link as the men who had backed Pedro da Souza. When as a young politician, he hungered for the throne of Lagos. The forces of the colonial masters and the oligarchy had helped to thwart the collective aspiration of the wolf pack to make their man king in Lagos. Now more than thirty years later, the group the Lagos fat cats, working together with elected politicians had literally ruined the Lagos economy, they made sure that the market forces in Lagos remained on a collision course. By giving the naira a false value, the Lagos currency had become the root of corruption and the main stay of the corrupt ruling elite.

da Souza reckoned that only with a good clean up would there be any new foreign investments for Lagos to be used in the platinum extraction and marketing. The key was to find the foreign investment capital to pour into Lagos. This would, in time, other things being equal, remove the falseness out of the naira. That done, the people of Lagos would worship the naira less and Lagos would, in time, become a little rich place whose economy will not be basically at the mercy of greedy fat cats.

And so da Souza dreamed on, hoping that the thread of history , which the men of the wolf pack represented would, if properly co-ordinate bring about an infusion of vitality for the his plan for Lagos. The plan if successful would serve to release the creative energies of the people so they could come up with new products and services to get their economy moving once again.

da Souza's knowledge of the business world convinced him that the wolf pack would back him up as they each would end up more profitable in the long run. The Lagos tale of woe was not extreme in the world debt crisis. Hunter's report emphasized the fact that there was nothing ominous about debt. Debt has ceased to be the burden it was at the time of the Great Depression. The older generations of Americans may have experienced the real meaning of what living in debt was, but the modern American on the other hand accepts debt as a means of maintaining today's standard of living.

Consumer debt has therefore, become like the billows of hot air from the balloonist's propane torch that keeps the economic balloon flying. Shut off the air and life blood and you set off a chain of events that would bring down the capitalist system for the communists to take over. This system, really took off with Henry Ford's mass-produced automobile. It revolutionized the means of making life more livable by creating mass credit to Americans. It also begot the creed of buy now and worry about paying later. This mind set with time, became the worldwide creed of the capitalist. Shut off this easy credit and even Washington would become a communist state.

According to Hunter, American's fiscal year 1985 owed a total of $664 billion in debts for consumer loans on cars, home improvement, college education, mobile homes, plus other domestic appliances.

American homes carry $1.4 trillion in debt funded by a proliferating variety of mortgage loans. American corporate merger and takeover boom has enabled many businesses to stack up huge debts. Add the above to America's Federal Government deficit spending, which has pushed the nation's total public debt from $930 billion to $1.8 trillion between 1980 to 1985; and one can understand that foreign debts will continue to grow. Either that or the socialists will come up overnight to take over the governments of the Western world.

This makes sense of the economist's argument that debts grow because there is more demand for them. Thus, Wall Street financiers play their world important role of supplying financial securities such as junk bonds.

Barrister Bulus Musa had informed da Souza that the situation of austerity in Lagos would soon reach the stage where a group of socialist militants would take over the government. The velocity of business in Lagos had outpaced the existent capital resources. The I.M.F.'s reluctance to grant further foreign loans to Lagos meant more austerity as the world oil glut continued.

With news of the Lagos ledger sheets being soaked in red amid the ungodly activities of the Lagos fat cats, da Souza swore to have the wolf pack help him with his plans to cut-off I.M.F's red tape and so bring healthy economic expansion to the nation.

As a master of psychological strategy da Souza knew that in the battle ground of need, help was the greatest weapon. He smiled in that knowledge. He knew that he would be killing two birds with the fund from the sale of the Zeus holdings and so fulfill the desire of Monsignor McGovern.

Again Barrister Bulus' vivid description of young educated Lagosians besieging the U.S embassy re-echoed in da Souza's mind.

The young adults duly lined up every working day from 5.00 a.m. to the close of the Embassy gates each pleading for a visa. Many got turned down leaving only a few who got lucky to migrate to America. In America they become illegal immigrants working on expired visitor's visas. As illegal aliens, they incur employer's victimization. They also lack social welfare benefits with the permanent threat of deportation and of being refused re-entry should they visit Lagos out of necessity. The Lagos authorities only lamely discouraged the massive brain drain; They appreciated the safety valve, which the emigration of the huge numbers of educated but frustrated youth provide. Youths with expectations and dreams turned sour by the empty nest syndrome. Helpless victims of the great debt crisis and the world oil glut.

Thinking about the recent shocks of the oil glut, da Souza smiled contentedly at the speed at which Zeus huge oil holdings had been disposed of. It seemed he had the perfect timing. For in the month that followed the sales pitch at the Dole Grand Hotel, owners of the world's oil reserves sustained capital losses in excess of the totaled assets valuation of the land and buildings in all Manhattan, and in all New York City for that matter. It was as if the sinking of the Titanic, the Chicago fire, the eruption of Vesuvius all happened in the space of four weeks evaporating almost $8 trillion in wealth. It was an event unprecedented in history. Never had the value of the world's assets experienced such sudden and vast devastation. Not even the stock exchange collapse in October of 1929.

The decline in oil prices once perceived to be a sensible goal in the 1970's had turned out in reality to become a dreadful portent-creating history of the biggest write-off of world's equity holdings. There was no doubt the ripples on the world's consumption were made poorer by $8 trillion and this was difficult to calculate and terrifying to imagine. It would in time set off an empty-nest syndrome in the world's 370 oil-belt banks. Such trend da Souza reckoned, would force President Bush's administration to go into the banking business in a big way so as to bring order into the resultant anarchy. A similar task was da Souza's objectives to avert social anarchy in Lagos, and bring about the rebirth of meritocracy, thereby destroying the Lagos fat cats.

CHAPTER THIRTY-TWO

As da Souza prepared for the meeting of the wolf pack, he wondered whether the group still had its cohesiveness to act as a team. Time had changed considerably and memory of the past may not be as enduring. These thoughts and more weighed heavily on his mind as he addressed his special aides, which had expanded to include Zeus New York attorney and Barrister Bulus Musa. Hunter and Andrew Lincoln watched with sharpened admiration as the Old Fox addressed the team before the start of the meeting.

"Gentlemen, we all know that the history of civilization is a story of continuous change and people's reaction to it. Those who adapted to a changing environment suffered temporarily but grew and prospered. Those who didn't adapt have all perished and forgotten. The business world is full of giants here one day, gone the next. Today, it is not change itself but the tremendous increase in the rate, volume and type of change. Rapid change is causing unforeseen revolutions in every sector of the business environment. We are gathered here today, to initiate change. We do this, knowing full well that in the long run, the race belongs not merely to the swift, but to the farseeing. To those who anticipate change and are ready to balance both their short and long range plans or promise to give irrevocable commitment to a change strategy. I want to thank especially Ted Hunter and Andrew Lincoln "And so da Souza spoke on, recreating the mystery of the Old Fox's magic. The phenomenon that made him a man of the people. A man of immense personality and a unique ability to communicate. Hunter listened with tangible emotion. As the Old Fox spoke, his imposing physical presence dwarfed ail in the room. His massive shoulder and body seemed remarkably preserved with the face that was etched into popular consciousness almost 40 years ago as the Lagos politician with dreams of higher accomplishments. The large head, chiseled features and massive black face. It all added up to give da Souza the appearance of strength and solidity. A born leader and patriarch - with widened eyes that gave nothing away.

Hunter thought of the months of intense hard labor spent on da Souza's project for his beloved Lagos. Nine months, which seemed to have taken its toll on both Andy Lincoln and Hunter but which made the Old Fox glow daily with renewed strength. Like Antaeus of the Greek mythology in his celebrated battle with Hercules who gathered more energy from the earth each time he landed flat on the ground. Hunter's admiration for the old man had grown as he gained awareness of this solidity. He gradually began to cherish da Souza's strong political instincts. Hunter valued his deep patriotic belief and the political emancipation plans he had for Lagos. It was certain from all available data that da Souza would force the wolf pack to endorse his investment strategy for Lagos. Hunter also knew that the Pedro da Souza Trust Fund the four associates were to administer would pour $5 billion into Lagos annually. This would add up with the wolf pack ground investments totaling up to $10 billion. Part of which would be set aside to extract the Lagos platinum mine. The platinum concession would in time generate further foreign exchange earning capacity for Lagos. da Souza's ambitious scheme would serve to give Lagos a financial clean slate. That done, it would be out of da Souza's power to remedy things should the Lagos economic vessel become leaky again. Hunter listened on as the great man's speech drew to an end. He wondered if the War against Indiscipline Act to be launched in Lagos would survive long enough to become socially acceptable to the masses. The War against Indiscipline Act would become Lagos watch-word to make the society that of meritocracy.

da Souza paused in his long speech by stating: "I'm fully aware of the fact that we live in an Aesopian universe where chickens counted before they are hatched never see the light of the barnyard day. Recognizing this universal truth as I must, I also know that our efforts would make certain difference if we will give it wholeheartedly loyality. Again I repeat life's race belong only to the farseeing, to those who anticipate change and can make the sacrifice to achieve same."

Pedro da Souza then continued sounding life the Prophet that he had transformed it

"Let us not forget this truth, that God watches our heart. Our motives matter. True faith works by Love. Love simply does what it can to help others. Period. Love does not require appreciation.

Love is the reason of the demonstration of God's sacrifice. JESUS is the Rock of our salvation. He is the unshakable Rock with which we win the conflict between the good and evil. Truth wins over lies. Love wins over selfishness. If we love truth in our heart – we shall do the right thing. Tough discipline is needed to do the right things for the right reasons. Motives matter. Only those who have Jesus as their most valuable treasure will see through the world's carnality. They will see through the superficial treasures valued by this world.

Only He can give us true wisdom. He impacts true joy and great peace. His coming is the world's only Hope. So we conclude by Hailing Maranatha. Even so, come Lord JESUS. Amen.

When He had stopped speaking the group sat in stillness. None spoke until Hunter stood up. He was glad that the capacity to solve Lagos's hardest problem and transformed it to global relevance had been addressed.

He briefly explained the Old Fox's power plans. The focus was to stimulate Lagos as an international hub. He listed the infrastructural projects. These will give the city its economic wings. With this economic development, multinational companies will be attracted.

"Gentlemen, when we do these things, it shall be well with us. It shall be well with the future generations' talent and merit will have its place in our city. We will welcome new ideas. Creation of products and processes depend on creative talents. As we support great ideas with money and electric power – we shall all prosper.

I conclude with the history of Air Conditioners. "If you bought a car with air conditioning in the early 1960's, everybody knew you had it. The huge monstrosity of an air conditioning unit hung from the bottom of your dashboard. Like a pimple on the end of your nose, you couldn't miss it. The dealer installed all the early air conditioning units because the manufacturers had yet to begin installing them at the factory. Because these cars were not designed with air conditioning in mind, there were some major sacrifices a person had to make to stay cool. For instance, if you turned the unit on while the car was idling, it would stall. If you were going up a mountain with the air on, the vehicle would overheat and if you decide for some silly reason that you needed to pass someone on a hot summer day, you had to turn the thing off so you would have the power to overtake.

Of course, none of this is true of air conditioning in the vehicles of today. Vehicles are now conceived and designed with air conditioning in mind. The mechanical engineer knows the car is going to have air conditioning, so he integrates all the ductwork into the interior of the vehicle in a way that makes it one with the décor. The electrical engineer designs the wiring harnesses with all the looms set up for the air conditioning system. The architect of the cooling system develops the entire system knowing there will be air conditioning in the vehicle, and the list goes on and on.

Everybody who designs these vehicles does so with air conditioning in mind. Now when the driver wants air conditioning, he simply pushes a button on the dash. The switch doesn't actually turn the air compressor on, but it sends a message to the computer informing it that the driver wants it cooler. Next, the computer sends a message to the cooling fans demanding they come on and that the engine management system produces more horsepower so the A/C compressor can be turned on. Finally, the alternator is instructed to raise the electrical output to meet the increased load on the system. This all leads to a cool driver who is completely unaware of the intricacies of air conditioning because it was all developed with the mind."

CHAPTER THIRTY-THREE

Many are driven by the memory of their childhood of deprivation. They are driven to overcome the stigma of having grown up on the "wrong side of the town." They are driven by their own feelings of inadequacy. Most are driven to prove themselves. They compete and fight for everything.

The measure of a man is gauged by what he does when he gains increasing power. Those who gain total power believe that those who stand in their way are expendable. They believe that other people owe them whatever demands or use they require from others.

They demand that others obey rules that they totally disobey. Therefore, the "leader" with this mindset is an accident waiting to happen. They never learn from history's tragedies. In fact, they repeat the falsehood of thinking themselves to be invisible. For such-history will always repeat itself. Except God intervenes to turn the situation.

Those who are wise know the transient values of power. Everything on earth is ephemeral. All is vanity vanity upon vanity.

To lead is defined as whatever-it-takes-success. And success verified by conquest. The vision quest for today's world leadership is to seek always to be in front of the crowd. Regardless of all.

To attain this desire either by hook or by crook. Therefore, the leader will do the followings to get ahead and stay on top. There is the crafty maneuvering to beat the traffic red light. Burning the night candle and cheating to be top of the class at Law School.

And since we all live in a competitive global village--lavish rewards of prestige and more powers is given to the "winner." This is the due reward. Therefore, today's human pursuit for leadership fosters the fierce chase and instinct to "kill them all and stand up alone."

Imagine yourself competing with those with the above mindset. Think of the athlete using performance-enhancing drugs, to win the gold medal. Imagine the businessman bribing government officials to win huge contracts, the accountant cooking the books, the attorney using backstabbing treachery to gain victory in the court, or the politician rigging to win national election. The list goes on, increasing into massive global corruption. No wonder the Bible says that the whole world, "lies in wickedness." Modern-day definition of leadership has outclassed such traits as: - trustworthiness, integrity, honesty and wining in the old fashion manner.

In its place we have these buzz worlds: - goal getter, consummate achiever, proactive promoter, and politically in-tune. These pragmatic word usage contribute to defining mans' ruthlessness to man. They become the very armor that the top dog must possess to win great laurels.

The Global Financial Meltdown is part of the New World Order game plan to provoke social cataclysm and to ignite economic disorderliness globally. The dominion effect of the chaos of global financial markets is yet to fully unfold.

Such global confusions will enable the New World leaders to set up own controlled world organizations to police global debts and world poverty. Of course the complex problem cannot be solved by individual nation.

Financial meltdown is not new to Nigeria. Between the years 1982-1998, Nigeria experienced economic disorders. The current economic woes are like the past repeating itself. This confirms, that history repeats itself unless God intervenes.

OGED OREKYEH

ABOUT THE AUTHOR

Oged Orekyeh is a U.K trained Global Management Consultant, a third generation technocrat and prolific writer. He mentors African gifted professionals and technocrats on global governance rules of engagement. He researches on the dynamics of the Digital Revolution and how it impacts national economies. His story line stems from this verse in Revelations 1:19. "Write down, therefore, what you have seen and what is happening, and what will happen afterwards"